Almost before the blond giant was landing on the floor, Dusty sprang to the left over him and into the room. No less aware of the situation and its ramifications, the sheriff followed in an identical fashion except that he leapt in the opposite direction. On alighting, each of them was slanting his weapon towards the bed. The way they had behaved was intended to confuse the occupant and, brought from sleep by the commotion, render him uncertain as to which of them posed the most immediate threat.

Laudable as the precaution had been, it proved needless. The room was in darkness, but some light came in from the passage. Sufficient, in fact, to illuminate the bed – and the motionless figured sprawled half in, half out of it!

'What the hell?' the sheriff growled and, despite considering there would be no need for caution, advanced without relaxing his vigilance.

'Are you all right, *amigo*?' Dusty inquired, also walking forward.

'Don't worry,' Mark answered to the small Texan's back, coming to his feet, 'I've only bust three ribs and both arms. But I should be able to keep anybody who we've woke up from interfering.'

'Good for you,' Dusty called back over his shoulder, keeping his attention upon the man on the bed. Then his gaze went to a glass which lay alongside the motionless figure's hand and he asked, 'Is it Sproxton, Uncle Tim?'

'Looks like him,' the sheriff replied, taking out a match and lighting the bedside lamp. Having done so, he knelt and raised the corpse's head. For a moment, he could barely recognize the agony-distorted and almost empurpled features. Lowering the head, he nodded grimly. 'It's Sproxton all right. But he sure didn't die peaceably or natural. Fact being, I'd say Beguinage's done it again.'

D1324287

List of J. T. Edson titles in chronological order.

Ole Devil Hardin series:

YOUNG OLE DEVIL
OLE DEVIL AND THE CAPLOCKS
OLE DEVIL AND THE MULE TRAIN
OLE DEVIL AT SAN JACINTO
GET URREA

Civil War series:

COMANCHE
YOU'RE IN COMMAND NOW, MR. FOG
THE BIG GUN
UNDER THE STARS AND BARS
THE FASTEST GUN IN TEXAS
KILL DUSTY FOG!
THE DEVIL GUN
THE COLT AND THE SABRE
THE REBEL SPY
THE BLOODY BORDER
BACK TO THE BLOODY BORDER

The Floating Outfit series:

THE YSABEL KID
.44 CALIBRE MAN
A HORSE CALLED MOGOLLON
GOODNIGHT'S DREAM
FROM HIDE AND HORN
SET TEXAS BACK ON HER FEET
THE HIDE AND TALLOW MEN
THE HOODED RIDERS
QUIET TOWN
TRAIL BOSS
TROUBLED RANGE
WAGONS TO BACKSIGHT
SIDEWINDER
RANGELAND HERCULES
MCGRAW'S INHERITANCE
THE HALF BREED
THE WILDCATS
THE BAD BUNCH
THE FAST GUN
CUCHILO
A TOWN CALLED YELLOWDOG
TRIGGER FAST
THE MAKING OF A LAWMAN
THE TROUBLE BUSTERS
SET-A-FOOT
THE LAW OF THE GUN
THE PEACEMAKERS
TO ARMS, TO ARMS, IN DIXIE
HELL IN THE PALO DURO
GO BACK TO HELL
THE SOUTH WILL RISE AGAIN
THE QUEST FOR BOWIE'S BLADE
BEGUINAGE
BEGUINAGE IS DEAD!
THE RUSHERS
THE FORTUNE HUNTERS
THE RIO HONDO KID
RIO GUNS
GUN WIZARD

THE TEXAN
WACO'S DEBT
THE HARD RIDERS
THE FLOATING OUTFIT
APACHE RAMPAGE
RIO HONDO WAR
THE MAN FROM TEXAS
GUNSMOKE THUNDER
THE SMALL TEXAN
THE TOWN TAMERS
RETURN TO BACKSIGHT
TERROR VALLEY
GUNS IN THE NIGHT

Waco series:

SAGEBRUSH SLEUTH
ARIZONA RANGER
WACO RIDES IN
THE DRIFTER
DOC LEROY, M.D.
HOUND DOG MAN

Calamity Jane series:

COLD DECK, HOT LEAD
THE BULL WHIP BREED
TROUBLE TRAIL
THE COW THIEVES
CALAMITY SPELLS TROUBLE
WHITE STALLION, RED MARE
THE REMITTANCE KID*
THE WHIP AND THE WAR LANCE*
THE BIG HUNT

Rockabye County series:

SIXTEEN DOLLAR SHOOTER
THE PROFESSIONAL KILLERS
THE ½ SECOND DRAW
THE DEPUTIES
POINT OF CONTACT
THE OWLHOOT
RUN FOR THE BORDER
BAD HOMBRE

Bunduki series:

BUNDUKI
BUNDUKI AND DAWN
SACRIFICE FOR THE QUAGGA GOD
FEARLESS MASTER OF THE JUNGLE*

Miscellaneous titles

SLAUGHTER'S WAY
TWO MILES TO THE BORDER
SLIP GUN
'CAP' FOG, TEXAS RANGER
MEET MR. J. G. REEDER
BLONDE GENIUS (written in
  collaboration with Peter Clawson)
J. T.'S HUNDREDTH†

*Awaiting publication
†In preparation; not yet with publishers.

Beguinage

by J. T. Edson

CORGI BOOKS
A DIVISION OF TRANSWORLD PUBLISHERS LTD

A CORGI BOOK 0 552 10769 7

First publication in Great Britain

PRINTING HISTORY

Corgi edition published 1978

This book is set in Intertype Times

Corgi Books are published by
Transworld Publishers Ltd.,
Century House, 61–63 Uxbridge Road,
Ealing, London W5 5SA
Made and printed in Great Britain by
Cox & Wyman Ltd., London, Reading and Fakenham

For Robert McCaig and Nelson C. Nye, two damned fine authors, although neither will concede that I'm young enough to have read his books when I was a boy.
I won't admit anything, either!

BEGUINAGE

Author's note: *I would like to apologise to those of my readers who are awaiting various 'In Preparation' titles on the chronological list for having introduced this volume ahead of them. However, Alvin Dustine 'Cap' Fog has gone to a great deal of trouble obtaining permission from the descendants of the Relphstein royal family to have the facts made public and we want to get them into print before there is a change of mind.*

As usual, to save my 'old hands' from repetition, for the benefit of the new readers I have given the relevant details of the floating outfit's backgrounds in the form of Appendices.

J. T. Edson.
Active Member
Western Writers of America,
Melton Mowbray, Leics, England.

CHAPTER ONE

IT'LL MAKE THE POT WORTH WINNING

Taking everything into consideration, as he was raking in the money that formed the pot, Thorley Acheson felt that his luck had definitely made a turn for the better. It had not been his intention to leave the passenger ship, *Island Queen*, at Brownsville, Texas, but the captain – a man of bitter tongue and forceful personality – had gone beyond merely intimating that he and his partner had better do so.

It was not, the grim-faced master mariner had said, that he could *prove* it was something other than an exceptionally fortunate run of the cards that was responsible for the partners' success at poker. However, he preferred his wealthy passengers to reach the West Indies without having suffered substantial losses and wondering if they might have been cheated. The aspersions against their honesty had not particularly worried the partners, being justified if unproven. What had come next was the bitter blow. In fact, the captain had continued, he felt certain that Mr. Windle and Mr. Midgley – the names they had adopted for the voyage – would prefer to return all their winnings as a gesture of good faith – and to avoid having to swim the two miles separating the vessel from the coastline of Texas.

For all their New Yorker city-bred toughness and skill in combat, the partners had been too wise to resist the captain's demand. They had known he was not bluffing and there was sufficient evidence – such as marked cards and loaded dice – in their baggage to establish their guilt beyond any question if he should institute a search. So they had disgorged their ill-gotten gains and agreed to leave the ship at its next port of call.

There had been even worse to come on the partners' arrival at Brownsville. Both had entertained lavishly on board, as a bait to draw in their intended victims, charging it to their accounts and keeping their respective bank rolls intact for use in the games. Before they were allowed to go ashore, they were presented with accounts which took most of their money.

Standing on the quay and watching the *Island Queen* depart, after mutually wishing that she sank with all hands, the partners had turned their thoughts to the future. Each had decided that the situation could be worse. By all accounts, the Sovereign State of Texas had made such good use of its vast herds of free ranging longhorn cattle that it was no longer suffering from the financial depression left in the wake of the War of Secession.[1] In fact, many of its citizens were reputed to be very wealthy.

While the partners did not doubt that they could extract a fair proportion of such wealth from its newly-rich yokel owners, there was a major snag to be faced and overcome. To gain access to the strata of society at which they had set their sights called for the expenditure of much more money than they had available. So they conceded that a certain retrenchment of their ambitions was inescapable. There was to be a reception in honour of Governor Stanton Howard in two nights time, but they had known it was unlikely, in their current financial straits, that they could make the necessary connections to obtain an invitation.

Yielding to the inevitable, the partners had set themselves to re-establishing their depleted fortunes. They had made the necessary changes to their appearance and sought for victims at a level suitable to their bank roll. Moderate success had crowned their first night's activities, but it was marred by the kind of incident that they least desired under the circumstances. Just as they were starting to win steadily, a young cowhand had objected to the way in which Acheson was dealing – which was far less competently than was usual for him – and received a bad beating for his temerity. Only the saloon owner's wish to avoid involvement with the local law enforcement officers prevented the affair from developing into an unpleasant situation. As it was they were ordered from the premises and told to stay away.

Having acquired a somewhat healthier stake, that was still grossly inadequate for their ultimate needs, the partners had found a more lucrative field for their second night's efforts.

Situated at the inland side of Brownsville, on the fringe of the 'better' section of the town, the Running Iron Saloon's

1. How this came about is told in: GOODNIGHT'S DREAM (American title, THE FLOATING OUTFIT) and FROM HIDE AND HORN. – *J.T.E.*

clientele denoted a rather higher social standing and wage-earning potential than the customers of the previous evening's establishment. In spite of the name, the men in the bar were a pretty fair cross-section of the population. Nor did it take long for the partners to become involved in a game of draw poker with four other players.

A skilled performer, Acheson looked, dressed and behaved exactly as was expected of a 'whiskey drummer', his identity for the evening. Big, burly, with thinning brown hair and sun-reddened, jovial features, he exuded a bonhomie that made him appear to be a good sport. This and his loud chest suit, white shirt, a multi-hued cravat upon which a massive 'diamond' stickpin glinted in the room's lights and a 'derby' hat perched on the back of his head effectively prevented anyone from suspecting that he and his partner were in cahoots.

Nobody looking at Josiah Meekly could doubt his claim that he was an undertaker. Not only did he wear the sombre black attire mandatory for such an occupation, he had a medium-sized, lean frame and a demeanour ideally suited to dealing with corpses. His thin, miserable face had taken on such a look of pained disapproval every time Acheson launched a jocular comment directed at his 'business' that it might have convinced even people who knew them that they were strangers with nothing in common.

Certainly the four local players seated around the table were showing no doubts. In fact, they all had clearly accepted the partners at face value and were unaware of any connection.

To Acheson's right sat a big, bluff seaman who had introduced himself as Jemmy Hawk of the cargo ship *Ben Travis*.

Next was one of the two players picked out by the partners as their main victims. Still not out of his teens, wearing clothing that marked him to range-wise eyes as a cowhand, he was a blond haired, handsome youngster around six foot in height with a powerful physique. A low crowned, wide brimmed black J.B. Stetson hat dangling by its fancy barbiquejo chinstrap on to the shoulders of a brown and white calfskin vest. Tight-rolled and knotted around his throat, a flaming red bandana trailed its long ends over a dark green shirt. His well worn Levi's pants hung outside a pair of tan coloured high-heeled, sharp toed boots with spurs attached to their heels. Around his waist, a well-made brown leather gunbelt supported a pair of stag-horn handled Colt 1860 Army revolvers in contoured hol-sters. However, before he had sat down, he had unfastened the pigging thongs by which the tips of the holsters had been held securely to his thighs. He had announced that the other players could call him 'Waco', but made no mention of what the rest of his name might be.

Meekly had taken the chair between the two main victims.

Matching 'Waco' in height, the second 'mark' clearly had connections with the cattle industry. However, there were indications to eyes which knew the signs that his work was not so extensively concerned with handling the ranch's stock. The flat heels of his boots implied he spent more time on his feet than a cowhand would while carrying out his various duties. Clad all in black, even to his gunbelt and footwear, the armament he was wearing was accorded ill with the almost babyish innocent cast of his handsome, Indian dark features. However, there was something in his red-hazel eyes that suggested the old walnut handled Colt 1848 Dragoon revolver riding butt forward in the low cav-alry twist holster on the right of his belt and the enormous ivory handled James Black bowie knife sheathed at the left might be more than affectations. He had been addressed by the other youngster – for he seemed to be little older – as 'Lon' and, again, that was clearly considered sufficient of an introduction.

If anybody had been asked to pick out Acheson's partner, the choice would almost certainly have fallen on the man to his left. Just as loudly dressed and jovial, Benny Benner was a genuine drummer and made no bones about declaring that he 'travelled in ladies' underwear', leading the jokes the comment aroused and promising the others a peek at his wares if they allowed him to win.

While making his preliminary survey, Acheson had fol-lowed his habit of learning all he could about the oppo-sition. According to the bartender he had questioned, Hawk served on a ship that specialized in transporting cattle to New Orleans. Having been paid off after having helped to deliver a herd of their ranch's cattle for shipment, the two cowhands were indulging in the kind of spending spree which characterized their kind when in the money. Deciding that they had the type of attitude best suited to his and Meekly's needs, Acheson had not bothered to seek further

12

details. Nor, being newly arrived in Texas, would it have helped if he had known more about them. In fact, he was so eager to descend upon his prospective victims that he left the counter before the bartender could impart further significant information.

The more Acheson saw, once he was involved in the game, the greater grew his conviction that he had found the 'marks' he desired. Each of the cowhands had been flashing more money than he had anticipated. And he did not envisage any especial difficulty in separating them from it. Of the two, he considered the younger would be the easiest to take.

From all appearances, the blond had drunk just enough to have given himself an over-inflated view of his own toughness and sagacity. Which, added to his loudly stated claim to be an expert player of draw poker, made him an even more likely candidate for trimming. Seeking to emphasize his knowledge, he had 'exposed' a couple of cheating tricks so ancient and well publicized that no card sharp dared use them any more. He had quoted epigrams on the order of, 'Cut 'em light, lose all night,' and, when hauling the first pot taken against his companion had chided, 'Hell's fire, Lon! Won't you-all *never* learn's when you hold a lil ole kicker,[2] you double the odds against improving your hand.'

In spite of discerning that the blond youngster did have a certain skill in the game, Acheson soon decided that it formed a case of a little knowledge being dangerous. While he obviously considered that he was being smart, the way he played soon showed off all his weaknesses. When he had a powerful hand, he was all too apparently eager to throw his money into the pot. Announcing a firm policy against drawing to inside straights[3] and four flushes[4] unless the pot was worth it, he had done so on at least three occasions. When he pulled off a bluff, he invariably displayed the cards to prove

2. 'Kicker': in the terminology of draw poker, to hold a third card – usually an ace or a king – with a pair as an aid to improving the value of the hand. The odds against the draw making up even two pairs are five to one and those of producing a greater improvement are proportionately higher. An explanation of the relative value of poker hands is given in: TWO MILES TO THE BORDER. – *J.T.E.*

3. 'Inside' straight': one which has a card missing from the sequence; i.e. 2.3.5.6. The odds against 'filling' the straight are eleven to one – *J.T.E.*

4. 'Four flush': self-explanatory; a hand containing only four cards of one suit. The odds against obtaining the fifth on the draw are 4·5 to 1. – *J.T.E.*

13

he had done so. Or, on taking a pot with a powerful hand, he would not allow its value to be seen and affected to have won by bluffing. Taking advantage of the rules, he made 'mouth' bets and did not cover them. Or, when called and announcing he held two pairs, he would show the lower value cards first to let an opponent who held a similar hand think he had lost, then turn up the others and win.

Taking everything into consideration, Acheson and, from various signs known only to them, his partner had no doubts about the result of their efforts.

There had only been one disturbing moment and neither of the partners was involved in it directly. Having heard 'Lon' address the blond as 'boy', Benner did the same soon after Acheson had started to draw his satisfactory conclusions.

'*Hombre!*' Waco growled, oozing cold and grim menace overlaid with a tinge of drunkenness that could prove dangerous. 'There's not but four – or at the most five – men's can call me *that*. Which you-all aren't none of them.'

Wanting to prevent anything that might disrupt and terminate the game, Acheson put aside his contented thoughts on how the situation was progressing.

'No harm done, I reckon,' the burly 'whiskey drummer' said, exuding amiability. 'Let me set up the drinks, shall I?'

'You can afford to, way you've been winning,' Waco grumbled, then glanced at his companion. 'Hey, "Lon", is it your white side's's doing the drinking?'

'It'd be illegal any other way,' the second cowhand replied, his voice, a pleasant tenor, showing just a trace of relief over the blond's anger having been diverted.

'How's that?' Acheson asked, wanting to keep the conversation turned from the clearly annoyed Benner.

'Don't know how it is up to New York, Thorley,' 'Lon' answered. 'But down here to Texas it's again' the law to sell hard liquor to an Injun.'

'Which Lon's grandpappy's Chief Long Walker of the good ole *Pehnane* Comanch' is,' Waco went on. 'Only nobody's best start making comment on it.'

'I can haul in my own rope, boy,' 'Lon' put in, sounding annoyed, as the blond glared truculently around the other occupants of the table. 'Which you'd best haul in your horns. You-all know's the boss allowed we was to stay out of trouble.'

'Dusty Fog's only the boss when we're riding for him,' Waco snapped back. 'He don't scare me none, nor tell me what to do.'

'You get into fuss and he'll do some telling,' warned 'Lon'.

'Huh!' Waco snorted. 'Worse he can do is fire me and jobs aren't so hard to come by's I need that one.'

'You get fired by him and he puts out the word,' 'Lon' stated, 'you'll not get any decent spread to take you on.'

'There's better paid 'n' easier work 'n' riding herd on a bunch of stinking cows like I've been saying all along,' the blond declared, then shook his head and grinned. 'Come on, I thought we was playing poker.'

Although the game of poker was taking place at one of the bar-room's centre tables, it was arousing little interest among the other customers. The stakes were not sufficiently high to warrant attention, nor had anything untoward occurred to make spectating worthwhile.

However, on the mention of a name which was very prominent in the affairs of Texas, the two men at the nearest table looked around.

Of all the room's occupants, the pair seemed to be the most out of place. The smaller might just have passed as one of the general run of customers. Of middle height, bespectacled, with pallid and commonplace features, apart from his brown suit being of the latest style from New York, his clothing suggested that he belonged to the higher levels of the income bracket which formed the majority of the Running Iron Saloon's clientele. Unlike the elegant Cattlemen's Hotel at one end of the scale and what had once been Francisco Castro's inelegant *cantina*[5] on the other, the establishment catered for the middle echelons of the population.

Much the same height, though more heavily built than his companion, the second man presented a similar clerkly appearance. However, his raiment showed clearly that he had a higher status. There was something foreign about his swarthy features which was accentuated by the way in which the tips of his large brown moustache were waxed to sharp points and by the small spike of beard on the tip of his chin. A black cloak with a red silk lining was dangling on his

5. Why Francisco Castro no longer ran his *cantina*, which was still a notorious den of thieves, is told in: THE BAD BUNCH. – *J.T.E.*

15

shoulders, exposing to view a black dinner suit and one of the new-fangled detachable stiff false shirt fronts known as a 'dickey'. While the clothing was of good quality, he appeared ill at ease in it. In a lesser establishment, his black opera hat – which he had collapsed and lay on the table before him – might have been the cause of uncouth comment, or even actual abuse, but the bouncers employed by the Running Iron Saloon were swift to quell such behaviour against paying patrons.

Having listened with some interest to the rest of the conversation between the cowhands, the men continued to watch as the game continued.

'Let's up the ante to twenty dollars,' 'Lon' suggested, watching as Acheson cut the cards for the seaman to deal.

'That's rather steep!' Meekly quavered, knowing that his partner was not in a position to take advantage of such an increase.

'I'd sooner play for something worthwhile,' 'Lon' replied. 'It makes the game more interesting 'n' go faster.'

'I'm for it,' Acheson declared, guessing that the Indian-dark cowhand was hoping the higher stakes would hold his companion's attention and avoid trouble. 'Who else wants in?'

'I'll give it a try, seeing's it's my deal,' Hawk replied.

'It'll make the pot worth winning, that's for sure,' Waco enthused, but the 'whiskey drummer' thought he looked more than a little uneasy at the prospect of having to chance so much of his money even before seeing the cards he would be dealt. 'I'm for it.'

'Well, I—!' Meekly began hesitantly, playing his role in a masterly manner.

'Scared your missus'll find out you've been gambling, grave-digging man?' the young blond sneered.

'N – No, it's not that at all!' Meekly replied, contriving to give the impression that the cowhand's comment had been correct. 'I – Oh, *very well.* I've come *this* far, so I might as well stay.'

Faced with such a unanimous acceptance, Benner shrugged and went along with the others. So, as each received his first card, he inserted the sum of twenty dollars into the pot. Watching Waco, Acheson observed a certain reluctance to ante up which confirmed that his earlier thought had been correct.

Still kept under observation by the 'whiskey drummer', on receiving his fifth card, the youngster picked them up and studied them with the same excessive care to keep their value a secret that he had exhibited all through the game. At the sight of them, he stiffened and, having taken a second peek, folded them one on top of another swiftly. Adopting a none too convincing air of nonchalance, he laid the pile before him and began to count his money.

'She's open for another lil ole twenty, gents!' Waco announced, his lazy drawl speeding up noticeably, shoving forward the stake while Acheson was still awaiting the last card's arrival.

'I'll see that,' Meekly countered, waiting until he received an almost imperceptible nod which told him his partner had a hand worth such behaviour.

'That sounds way too rich for lil ole me,' 'Lon' drawled, folding and tossing his cards into the centre of the table. 'So, seeing's how you palefaces don't let us Injuns play for glass trade beads, I'm quitting.'

'Huh!' Benner grunted disgustedly, also discarding his hand. 'I wouldn't stay in with them even for glass trade beads.'

'Your twenty and up the same,' Acheson declared, making the raise to gain information and on the strength of the three tens he was holding.

'I'm in!' Hawk stated.

'See that twenty,' Waco declared, still with badly concealed impatience. 'And thirty more.'

'That's enough for me!' Meekly almost bleated, again following a signal received from his partner and sharing the other's summation of the situation.

'I'll just see that,' Acheson declared, having drawn disturbing conclusions from the way the blond was playing.

'Cards?' Hawk inquired, as the primary round of betting was brought to its conclusion by the 'whiskey drummer'.

'Reckon these I've got're good enough for lil ole me,' Waco drawled, continuing his unavailing attempts to appear casual.

Only long experience at self control prevented Acheson from betraying his feelings of mixed emotions. His every instinct had warned that the youngster was holding a strong hand and the refusal to exchange cards seemed conclusive confirmation. What was more, the lowest hand which did

17

not require changing in any way was a straight and that was higher in rank than the three tens which had been dealt to Acheson. Unless he received assistance from the two cards he intended to draw, he was beaten.

Unless, of course, the blond was running a bluff by pretending to hold a pat hand!

Acheson could not believe such a thing was possible. It did not fit in with the pattern of the youngster's far from experienced play so far. Certainly Waco had never missed drawing if there was any way in which he might obtain a stronger hand than was dealt to him. If he had been successful in such a ploy, he would have been unable to resist the temptation of showing that he had done so.

Furthermore, according to the mathematical odds which Acheson knew to have an indirect bearing on what happened, in a six-handed game a pat hand could be expected about once in twenty-five rounds. He remembered that, as yet, none had occurred since they started playing. So, despite being aware that the figures covered only long term probabilities, he felt the odds were in favour of the blond holding a straight, a flush, a full house,[6] four of a kind – although he would probably have drawn one card in the hope of misleading the opposition into thinking he held a mere two pairs – or even a straight flush.

'Two cards!' Acheson requested, as the seaman glanced at him interrogatively.

'Hey, "Lon",' Waco drawled, while Hawk was dealing the replacements requested by the 'whiskey drummer'. 'Can you-all loan me thirty dollars?'

'Well now—!' the Indian-dark cowhand began, showing reluctance.

'Hell's fire, you'll have it back afore you know it's gone!' Waco protested. 'I'm turning her loose for forty lil ole iron men, Thorley-boy.'

Raising his eyes from a bitter study of the three of hearts and seven of clubs which he had received, neither of which did him the slightest good, Acheson watched the youngster eagerly thrusting the money forward. If he had wanted further proof, the brief interplay of comments between the two cowhands had supplied it.

6. 'Full house': three of a kind and a pair; i.e. 999–33. Beats everything from a flush down. The odds against receiving one on the deal are 693 to 1. – J.T.E.

18

'All right,' the 'whiskey drummer' said, with an assumed joviality he was far from feeling, as he folded and tossed his hand among the other discards. Confident that he would be able to recoup the losses in the subsequent hands, he went on, 'You win, young feller. I'm not fixing to call your bluff.'

'Now that's a *real* pity,' the blond replied and his whole demeanour had changed in a subtle, yet highly significant way. Turning over his cards and spreading them out, he continued, 'Because, *hombre*, a bluff is all it was.'

For a long moment, Acheson stared as if unwilling to believe the evidence of his eyes – at the jacks of diamonds and spades, the deuces of clubs and hearts and the queen of spades which had been exposed by the younger cowhand.

Two pairs!

Which did not beat the three of a kind discarded by the 'whiskey drummer'!

A sudden rage began to boil up inside Acheson. Nor was it solely caused by the realization that he had fallen for an ancient and basic form of bluff. Instead of trying to trade the worthless queen of spades on the eleven to one chance of catching either a jack or a deuce to complete a full house,[7] the youngster had refrained from drawing cards as if he had a genuine pat hand.

Even the remembrance that his partner had pulled off a similar coup aboard the *Island Queen* was only a minor contributory factor to Acheson's fury. Raising his gaze to the blond cowhand's face, he began to appreciate just how thoroughly he had been hoodwinked. It went far beyond merely having brought off a very smooth bluff. The declaration had not been made in the slightly slurred tones of semi-drunken truculence and triumph which had characterized all the youngster's earlier speech.

No matter how Waco had been behaving so far, he was cold sober!

---

7. Some authorities advocate discarding the smaller pair and drawing three cards. The odds against improvement are then the same as when taking three cards to a single pair: making a second two pair hand, 5·25 to 1; three of a kind, 8 to 1; full house, 97 to 1; four of a kind, 359 to 1. These odds only apply when no 'wild' cards, which can be used in place of whatever is needed, are being played. When wild cards are permitted, calculating the odds is practically impossible. – J.T.E.

19

CHAPTER TWO

THEY MEAN TO HAVE HIM KILLED!

'Captain Fog, sir. His Honour, the Governor, says will you-all be good enough to join him in Mr. von Farlenheim's study before going into the ballroom?'

The Negro butler of the von Farlenheim family's magnificent Colonial-style mansion took pride in carrying out his duties perfectly. It was also his boast that he was an exceptionally good judge of character. So he had no doubt that he was addressing the person for whom the message from Governor Stanton Howard was intended. Everything about the appearance of the taller of the two newly arrived guests was just as popular conception envisaged where somebody with the already legendary reputation of Captain Dustine Edward Marsden Fog, C.S.A., Rtd.,[1] was concerned.

Six foot three in height, the guest in question had faultlessly barbered golden blond hair. His almost classically handsome tanned face had strong lines and topped a magnificent physical development. Tremendously wide shoulders tapered to a slender waist above powerful legs. Although the hat he was handing to the butler was a white J.B. Stetson of Texas-style, with silver conchas decorating its brim, he was otherwise correctly dressed for such a formal and auspicious occasion.

Square cut, the blond giant's black jacket was sufficiently close-fitting to display his physique to the best advantage. Its narrow, low rolled collar joined the self-faced revers which stretched almost to the hem at the front and had five buttonholes. Clearly tailored to his build, the sleeves were tight enough to show off the bulk of his biceps and forearms, having turn-back cuffs sporting two buttons. The skirts

1. For the benefit of new readers, details of Captain Dustine Edward Marsden 'Dusty' Fog, C.S.A., Rtd.'s background and special qualifications are given in APPENDIX ONE. – J.T.E.

hung to knee level and, as fashion dictated, were fairly narrow. Fastened by three buttons, the single-breasted white waistcoat had a deep V-shaped front with a narrow turn-back and was almost horizontal at the bottom. The trousers were narrow, with a braid running down either side from the waist. Augmented by a small cambric bow-tie, the snowy white evening shirt had a high, closed collar and a stiff front. To complete the ensemble, he had on well-polished black dress boots and carried a pair of plain white gloves.

Lacking a good nine inches of his companion's height, the second of the new arrivals was dressed in a similar manner. However, while proportionately as equally well developed physically, he lacked the other's flair for wearing such excellently tailored and expensive clothes. While they did not exactly look as if they were somebody else's cast-offs, they detracted from rather than emphasized his far from puny build.

The smaller newcomer was also a blond, but of a dusty rather than golden hue, and equally well trimmed. While bronzed and good looking, his features were not of the eye-catching variety. However, if the butler had looked more closely than the cursory glance that had been taken, he would have seen there was a strength and intelligence beyond the average in the lines of his face. His grey eyes would meet another person's steadily, and, under the right circumstances, convey an impression of an inborn sense of leadership that family influence could never, and training only rarely, contrive to imbue.

It was the smaller guest who replied!

'Why sure,' agreed the dusty blond, handing his black Stetson and white gloves to the liveried Negro footman who was waiting to take them. 'Will you-all come along with me, Mark?'

'Happen you reckon I'll be needed, Dusty,' the blond giant conceded, also surrendering his headdress and gloves to a second identically attired coloured attendant.

For a moment, the butler came close to displaying the disapproval brought about by a suspicion that he was being made the victim of a misplaced sense of humour. Then he realized that, in spite of being *very* active in the working side of the cattle business, the nephew of General Jackson

21

Baines 'Ole Devil' Hardin[2] – late of the Confederate States' Army – and the *segundo* of the great OD Connected ranch would *never* resort to cowhand horseplay on such an auspicious occasion.

What was more, once his attention had been brought to the first speaker, the butler's flair for character analysis drew accurate conclusions. In spite of the lack of height, the dusty blond guest exuded an aura of commanding presence. Nor was it merely the self-important bombast of a small man in a position of authority by virtue of his family's connections alone.

'I'm sorry, gentlemen!' the butler apologized and, although it did not show, he felt himself blushing with mortification at having been so remiss.

'That's all right,' the blond giant said amiably. 'The only time I object to being mistaken for Dusty is when somebody sends me his bills, or one of his lady friends' daddy comes looking for *me* with a shotgun.'

Mark Counter had long since grown accustomed to people thinking he was Dusty Fog. Nor did he mind, considering it was a tribute to his good looks and appearance, and knowing that he had abilities, virtues and achievements in his own right.[3] In fact, he and the small Texan had turned the misconception to their advantage on occasion.[4]

'Any irate husbands are more likely to be looking for *you*, or those other two worthless varmints,' Dusty informed his big *amigo* sardonically, then looked at the butler. 'Will you show us where to go, please?'

'Yes, sir, Captain Fog,' the Negro assented. 'Will there be two more in your party, sir?'

'Not if the way they lit out as soon as they'd dropped off their gear at Sheriff Farron's is anything to go on,' Mark grinned, thinking of the reluctance expressed by two other members of the OD Connected's floating outfit when they had been invited to attend the function. 'I've never seen

2. Details of General Jackson Baines Hardin, C.S.A., Rtd.'s early career are given in the author's Ole Devil series. His exploits during the War Between The States and subsequently are described in the Civil War and Floating Outfit series. – *J.T.E.*

3. New readers can find details of Mark Counter's background and special qualifications in APPENDIX TWO. – *J.T.E.*

4. One occasion is described in: THE SOUTH WILL RISE AGAIN. – *J.T.E.*

them move so fast since the last time they was asked to do some work.'

'You're just riled up because they said I looked a heap prettier than you do, all dressed up like this,' Dusty objected, 'And you can stop ogling all the pretty lil gals in there until *after* we've seen the Governor.' He returned his attention to the butler, saying, 'No, we're the only guests from the OD Connected.'

'Very well, sir,' the Negro replied. 'Will you come this way, please, gentlemen.'

Casting a glance through the open doors of the ballroom, Mark accompanied Dusty and the butler towards the study. He saw enough in passing to convince him that, once the interview with the Governor was concluded, the evening offered possibilities for enjoyment. Already the cream of society from Brownsville and the surrounding district were presented. Elegantly attired men and women gathered in groups, helping themselves from the elaborate buffet or taking drinks offered by liveried Negro waiters and neatly uniformed coloured maids. A six-piece string orchestra of black musicians, clad in evening clothes were playing on a dais alongside the french windows which gave access to the well-tended and spacious gardens.

Studying the scene, the blond giant concluded that he was one of the best dressed and most presentable men attending the reception. What was more, there appeared to be sufficient attractive young women available to make having brought his formal clothes from the OD Connected worthwhile.

If Mark was finding the other guests interesting, the feeling was mutual where at least three of them were concerned.

Near to the buffet table stood Alex von Farlenheim. Tall, slender and in his early twenties, he was nephew to the host of the reception. Elegantly dressed in evening clothes, his close cropped blond hair and the little duelling scars on his cheeks emphasized the Germanic cast of his features. His bearing was suggestive of military training and something of his arrogant nature appeared in the way he elbowed the man by his side.

A sullen scowl came to Walter Scargill's far from prepossessing face as he received the nudge. It almost caused him to drop the sandwich he was about to stuff into his loose-lipped and over-sized mouth. His sallow features had a gaunt look which the deep-sunk and dull eyes did nothing to improve. Although his clothing was of good quality, it was far from tidy. That, taken with his long and unkempt brown hair, a drooping moustache and a scarlet silk cravat, had done little to endear him to his host and hostess.

Like most people with his kind of intellect, Scargill was an arrogant snob and had an over-inflated sense of his own importance. The knowledge that, despite being acclaimed as a great writer in some European circles, his presence was only tolerated at the reception because of his association with the host's nephew rankled bitterly. Finding out that nobody had heard of his work had not improved matters. Nor did he care for the way Alex von Farlenheim invariably treated him, which – by word and action – showed plainly that, while they might both be involved in a matter of importance, they were neither friends nor social equals.

'What is it, Alex?' asked the woman who was standing at the other side of von Farlenheim, before Scargill could raise a protest. Her tones were suggestive of French upbringing and a thinly concealed annoyance at her male companions' rivalry.

In any class of company, Charlene, *Comtesse* de Petain would be considered an exceptionally attractive member of her sex. Nor was she averse to displaying her obvious feminine charms. Slightly over five foot seven in height, her elegantly coiffured upswept brunette hair made her look even taller. Little of her statuesque 'hour glass' figure was the result of artificial aids. A flawless complexion enhanced the unlined beauty of her face. However, a discerning person might have noticed the coldly calculating glint in her eyes. Although she did not show it, she was some ten years older than either of her companions.

By far the most daringly dressed woman in the room, the extreme décolleté of Charlene's white satin ball gown bordered on the *outré*, but without going to the point where her hostess's susceptibilities would be offended. It might be arousing the envy of the other female guests, yet it was excused because she was a titled lady newly arrived from Paris, France, and had assured the plump, matronly Mrs. Frieda von Farlenheim that it was the latest fashion over there. Tasteful and not *too* much expensive jewellery graced her neck, wrists and fingers. While she too owed her invitation to the Germanic-looking young man, her welcome had been warmer than that accorded to Scargill.

24

'He's arrived,' von Farlenheim answered, nodding towards the hallway. He spoke excellent English, but with an intonation which implied it was a second language rather than that of his birth. 'The butler was told to take him straight into Uncle Ludwig's study as soon as he came.'

'Who's the small man with Fog?' Scargill asked and, although he spoke in the manner of one who had been educated at a famous university in Oxford, he carefully retained sufficient of his native Liverpudlian accent to emphasize his place of origin.

'Another of the Hardin, Fog and Blaze clan,' Charlene guessed, the question having been addressed to her rather than the other young man. Turning her predatory gaze reluctantly from the blond giant, she gave Dusty a brief, yet thorough glance which took in the first points she examined with every man. 'He is dressed well enough to be one of them.'

'But why is he here with Fog?' Scargill wanted to know.

'The Governor asked Hardin to send his floating outfit,[5] whatever *that* might be,' von Farlenheim replied. 'So he must be a part of it. And, as he is also a member of the family, Fog has brought him to the reception.'

'I can't say as I like that!' Scargill grumbled, his manner suggesting the additional visitor was an error on the other young man's part.

'Why not?' Charlene challenged. 'Even if Fog is killed, the rest of this floating outfit will still be available to help guard him. This way, we will be able to get rid of two of them instead of just one.'

'Dusty, Mark,' greeted Governor Stanton Howard, coming to his feet as the two young men entered Ludwig von Farlenheim's study. 'I'm pleased to see you both.'

Tall, good looking, of distinguished appearance, the Governor had the ability to appear impressive whether he was wearing evening clothes or – as on the last occasion he had met Dusty Fog and Mark Counter – dressed in well-worn garments suitable for hunting.[6] There was a genuine warmth in his voice and the welcoming smile as he shook

5. New readers will find an explanation of 'floating outfit's' function in Footnote 2, APPENDIX TWO. – *J.T.E.*
6. The previous occasion is described in: HELL IN THE PALO DURO. – *J.T.E.*

hands with the cowhands was far from the meaningless expression of a professional politician.

'Come and sit down, boys,' von Farlenheim offered, after he too had shaken hands with his guests. In spite of his thickset, crop-haired Teutonic appearance, he too spoke with the drawl of a well-educated Texan. 'There are cigars in the box. Help yourselves and see how you like this bourbon.'

'*Gracias*,' Dusty said, taking the seat indicated by his host.

'See we're not disturbed, Amos,' von Farlenheim ordered, after the butler had attended to the requirements of the newcomers.

'Yes, sir,' replied the Negro and left the room.

'I trust General Hardin was in the best of health when you last saw him?' the Governor asked and, again, the words were a genuine inquiry after a respected friend rather than a conventional opening remark.

'He was, sir,' Dusty confirmed, setting down his cigar on a glass ashtray. 'And he would want me to pay his respects to both of you. Was it just good luck that we were coming here with a herd when whatever it is came up that you-all need us for?'

'Not entirely, although I must admit it's fortunate that you're available,' Howard replied and some of the formality left him. 'Ole Devil sent word that you were coming here when I telegraphed to ask if he could spare the floating outfit for a few weeks' hunting.'

'I get a real sneaky feeling there's more to it than that,' Mark drawled, blowing out smoke appreciatively. 'Don't you-all, Dusty?'

'There was last time,' the small Texan replied. 'And, I'd be willing to bet it's the same this time.'

'Oh, you'll be going hunting all right,' Howard stated.

'But there's *still* more to it than just that,' Dusty insisted.

'There is,' the Governor conceded. 'Have you ever heard of Bosgravnia?'

'I can't say I have,' Dusty confessed and the blond giant also made a negative reply.

'It's a principality in Eastern Germany,' von Farlenheim explained, as Howard looked and nodded at him. 'And, although I've never been there, it's my home country. In fact, the *Grafs* von Farlenheim are second in rank only to the ruling house of Relphstein. Which is why I've such an

26

interest in this affair. In fact, it's mainly my fault that the situation has arisen. You know I'm a keen hunter?'

'Sure,' Dusty agreed. 'You've been out with pappy and Uncle Mannen a couple of times back to home.'

'Well, I've written to various members of the family in Bosgravnia,' von Farlenheim went on. 'Told them plenty about the kind of sport they could have over here. Two of my cousins were here last year and they took some better than fair trophies. When Crown Prince Rudolph saw what they'd fetched back, he decided that he'd like to see if he could do better. Now he's on his way over to try.'

'That's why we need you and the floating outfit, Dusty,' the Governor announced. 'To go along and act as his guides.'

'That's a mite out of our line,' the small Texan protested. 'There're plenty of men better qualified to handle the chore.'

'There aren't many with the Ysabel Kid's knowledge of wild animals, though,' von Farlenheim contradicted. 'If anybody can get Prince Rudolph some first grade trophies, he can.'

'Likely,' Dusty replied. 'But just doing it doesn't need all of us, Mark and—' He paused and took a sip of the glass of bourbon, then continued, 'So what else is *wrong*, sir?'

'According to information received by the U.S. Secret Service, a group of liberal-radicals intend to overthrow Prince Rudolph and set up a republic,' answered Howard, to whom the question had been directed. 'But he's a very popular ruler and they daren't make a move against him over there. So they mean to have him killed while he's out of the country.'

'Won't they make their move while he's on the journey to whichever port he's sailing from?' Dusty inquired.

'It's not likely,' the Governor replied. 'They want him as far away as possible before making their move.'

'On the ship that's bringing him over, then?' Mark suggested.

'That's even less likely,' Howard declared. 'He's travelling from Hamburg on a U.S. Navy steam-sloop. They'll have a hard time getting to him on that.'

'Belle Boyd nailed one of them out in the harbour here during the War,'[7] Mark reminded the Governor with a grin.

7. Told in: THE BLOODY BORDER. New readers can find details regarding Belle Boyd in Footnote 4, APPENDIX ONE. – *J.T.E.*

'Not that they're likely to have anybody as smart as her.'

'It's not likely,' Howard agreed, knowing the lady in question and of the incident to which the blond giant referred. 'So I'd say the Prince is safe until he's come ashore.'

'And, being as popular with the people as he is, they'd prefer to make his death look like an accident if they can,' von Farlenheim guessed. 'Which would be far easier to do while he's on a hunting trip.'

'And that's why we want *you* and the floating outfit to act as his guides, Dusty,' Howard went on. 'Congress doesn't want the assassination, or even apparently accidental death, of such an important person to happen on U.S. soil. If it does, there could be grave repercussions. It might even have a big effect upon this country's export trade. What's more, after the '*Alabama*' decision,[8] the British Government would make a lot of political capital out of it. They'd lay all the blame they could on the U.S.A. for helping to make it possible for a new republic to be established in Europe and the other monarchies wouldn't be slow in following their lead. So you boys can see, it's vitally important that you keep the Prince alive.'

8. In 1872, after long deliberations, an international committee sitting in judgement on what became known as the '*Alabama*' Arbitration Tribunal had ruled in favour of the United States of America. For allowing Confederate States' naval cruisers such as the *Alabama, Florida* and *Shenandoah* to be built in and operate from their ports, as well has having been involved in other activities which had been detrimental to the Union's cause, the Government of Great Britain had been ordered to pay compensation of $15,500,000 to the U.S.A. So, for many years after, the U.S. Congress trod very warily where Britain's interests were concerned. In fact, although as is told in THE QUEST FOR BOWIE'S BLADE, Belle Boyd, *q.v.*, had recently been in Texas, she was at that time engaged in another preventive measure, which is told in: THE REMITTANCE KID and THE WHIP AND THE WAR LANCE. – *J.T.E.*

CHAPTER THREE

WOULD YOU *KILL* FOR MONEY?

'God-damn it to hell!' Thorley Acheson bellowed, rage mingling with a sense of mortification at having been so thoroughly duped by somebody he had regarded as a far from bright young country hick. The emotions caused him to forget the advisability of avoiding trouble. 'Just what kind of a son-of-a-bitching game do you reckon you're trying to pull on me?'

'I'd say nowhere near's rusty as the one you-all pulled on our *amigo* down to Hannigan's place last night,' replied the blond haired cowhand called 'Waco', his handsome young face showing not the slightest trace of alarm over the burly New Yorker's obvious wrath. 'Or do you-all reckon's you're the only ones around who know how to play all slick 'n' tricky?'

For a moment, such was the churned-up condition of the 'whiskey drummer's' thoughts that the full import of what he had heard failed to impress itself upon his mind. Even when the understanding started to come, he still failed to comprehend the exact context of the cowhand's statement. In fact, he completely overlooked the significance of what should have been the most important and meaningful word, expressing the plural rather than the singular, of the second sentence. If he had noticed that Waco had said 'ones' and not 'one', he would have been less confident of his advantage in having an unsuspected partner in the game.

Instead of drawing the correct conclusion, satisfied that as always Josiah Meekly was ready to back his play, Acheson went into action. Having heard something of how swiftly some of the men west of the Mississippi River could draw and fire a revolver, although inclined to discount the stories as fabrications intended to impress the gullible, he decided against taking chances. So he caught hold of the edge of the table with both hands, meaning to tip it on to the youngster's lap.

Unfortunately for the 'whiskey drummer', he had failed to notice a precaution against such behaviour taken by the owner of the Running Iron Saloon. There had been no reason for him to experiment, nor had it even occurred to him to do so, but a test would have warned him that the legs of the table were bolted securely to the floor. He discovered the basic error in his tactics when, sending his chair skidding away behind him, he thrust himself erect and began to lift.

Finding that the table refused to move, Acheson let out a howl of bafflement and fury. However, instead of expending further effort upon what he sensed would be a futile attempt to carry out his original scheme, he took a long step to the rear and sent his right hand towards the sagging outside pocket of his check jacket wherein reposed a Remington Double Deringer. At which point, he discovered at least one man in the West who could produce a firearm with extreme rapidity.

In spite of being aware that there was nothing to fear from Acheson's attempt to overturn the table on him, Waco was too experienced to remain seated. Even as the man was trying to do so, he began to rise with alacrity. Excellent as the design and construction of his gunbelt undoubtedly was, its holsters could not be utilized to their full potential while he was seated. As his chair was being propelled from beneath him by his straightening knees, his right hand dipped down and rose in a flickering blur of motion. Steel rasped on leather as the off-side Colt 1860 Army revolver's seven and a half inch 'Civilian pattern' barrel[1] flowed from its contour fitting carrier. Swiftly as it was moving, its owner's forefinger stayed away from the trigger and his thumb did not began to draw back the single action hammer until the muzzle was directed away from his body.[2]

Before either the blond's overturned chair could land on the floor, or Acheson's hand as much as enter the jacket to close on the Remington's 'bird's head' handle, the 'whiskey drummer' found himself staring into the Colt's muzzle and trying to decide whether it had a calibre of two or merely one and a half inches. All he knew for sure was that behind

1. The length of the barrel of a Colt 1860 Army revolver designed for sale to the military was eight inches. – *J.T.E.*
2. An example of how dangerous a failure to take such a precaution when drawing a revolver can be is given in: THE FAST GUN. – *J.T.E.*

it loomed a young face as cold and implacable as fate. Nothing about the tanned and handsome features led him to assume that Waco was in other than deadly earnest, or would hesitate to shoot.

With one exception, the other players were rising almost as hurriedly as the main participants in the drama. Benny Benner had transported his ladies' underwear across the West for long enough to be aware of the danger of the situation. Nor had having spent much of his life at sea prevented Jemmy Hawk from appreciating the inadvisability of remaining in the close proximity of what could become a corpse-and-cartridge affair. Having had far more experience in such matters than either, the cowhand called 'Lon' responded with even greater rapidity; but he did not follow their example by springing away from the table.

From all outward appearances, Meekly either failed to comprehend the peril or was too terrified to move. He remained seated, but it was with a definite and deadly purpose. Knowing his partner's temper, he had sensed that there was almost certain to be trouble as soon as Waco's ploy was exposed. So he had taken the precaution of slipping his right hand into his jacket pocket and it was now enfolded about the butt of his Merwin & Hulbert Army Pocket revolver.

Just as the 'undertaker' was about to get up and draw the weapon, a larger, shiny metal object passed in front of his face. With a sensation of horror, his mind registered that it was the blade of an enormous knife and his instincts warned that it was razor sharp. What was more, in spite of it having gone below his range of vision, he could feel its edge resting lightly against the bare flesh of his throat.

'Now, *hombre*, for shame,' said an almost gentle voice. 'Did you-all reckon us half-smart lil ole country boys wouldn't conclude you pair're in cahoots? Why hell-to-damn-me, we've seen you-all wig-wagging back 'n' forth like two scared-white Osage scouts riding through *Nemenuh*[3] country and daren't talk out loud.'

Moving at much less than a snail's pace as he listened, Meekly turned his head to look at the speaker. What he saw chilled him to the marrow and brought the hand from his pocket at a much livelier rate than his neck had displayed in turning. Furthermore, he ensured that it emerged empty.

3. *Nemenuh:* 'The People', the Comanches' name for their nation. – J.T.E.

When the 'undertaker' had heard Waco's reference to 'Lon's' grandfather being a Comanche chief, he had regarded it as either a joke or an attempt to impress the other players. Now he had revised his opinion. Every vestige of innocence had left the black-dressed young Texan's face, being replaced by a chilling expression that would be well suited to those savage and blood-thirsty warriors about whom Meekly had frequently read in newspapers back East.

Startled by the sudden way in which the blond cowhand had drawn the Colt, Acheson froze as if he had been turned to stone. He realized that he could be in dire peril. There were many stories circulating in New York about the cold-blooded gun fighting killers of the West. In spite of his earlier scepticism, he now accepted that all he had heard and read was not a pack of exaggerations. He was sure that, young or not, his would-be victim belonged to that murderously efficient breed.

So, for all that he realized what the sight was likely to portend, the 'whiskey drummer' was not sorry to notice that three obvious bouncers and a man he guessed was either the owner or a floor supervisor of some kind were converging upon them.

'You just bring your hand up slow, easy 'n' empty, *hombre*,' the youngster ordered and, for all the lazy drawl with which they were uttered, the words were clearly a command and not a request. 'Or any other way you've a mind, comes to that.'

'All right,' called the best dressed of the four approaching members of the saloon's staff, as Acheson obeyed the first alternative. 'You-all can put up the gun and knife, gents. They won't be needed tonight.'

'Why sure,' Waco assented, twirling the Colt away so swiftly that it was back in the holster before he had finished his comment with, 'Seeing's you-all've asked so polite.'

'Aw, hot-damn!' grumbled 'Lon', and Meekly was only one of the audience who did not doubt that he was serious as he went on, 'Do you-all mean's I can't cut in just a *"leetle"* mite first?'

'Sorry, Kid,' the floor supervisor refused, straight-faced and soberly. 'The boss doesn't cotton to getting blood spilled on the floor.'

'Damned iffen you big city folks'll *ever* let us poor lil ole country boys have *any* funning!' 'Lon' protested, sounding disappointed, as he was returning the clip point blade[4] of the James Black bowie knife to its sheath.

Like the other occupants of the room, the two men at the nearest table were showing considerable interest in all that was taking place. They had come to their feet when the trouble started, but without following the basic precaution of removing themselves from the possible line of fire that had been adopted by such of the local customers who were in the immediate vicinity. Instead, they had merely stood and stared, drinking in all that was said and done.

'Did you see and hear *that*?' demanded the foreign-looking man, his guttural voice low and throbbing with excitement. It was apparent from the heavily accented way in which the words came out as ,'Dit you zee und hear *zat*?', he was not speaking in his native tongue.

'Yes,' confirmed his companion just as eagerly, sounding like a well-educated New Englander. 'They could be what is needed.'

'Then you will go and find Herr Sproxton,' the foreigner suggested, although the words came out more in the form of a command. 'I will keep them here until you return and sound them out on whether they will do it. From what they said earlier, the blond has no liking for Captain Fog and won't be averse to being paid to kill him.'

'You could be right,' the New Englander admitted, but he still looked dubious. 'Only it might be better if I stayed and talked to them.'

'You know the town better than I do,' the foreigner pointed out harshly, showing that he did not care for the objection. 'Go and bring them as quickly as you can.'

'Very well,' the New Englander acceded, giving a sullen shrug. He walked rapidly across the room to disappear into the night.

'So you're the two fancy-dan slickers we've been hearing about, are you?' the supervisor said, while the conversation between the two men at the adjacent table was taking place, turning a scathing gaze from Acheson to Meekly and back. Giving neither an opportunity to confirm or refute the accusation, he went on, 'Pick up any money you've got coming and get the hell out of here for keeps.'

4. New readers can find an explanation of a 'clip point' and further details regarding dimensions of the James Black bowie knife in Footnote 6, APPENDIX THREE. – *J.T.E.*

'That don't include what's in the pot,' Waco stated flatly.

'Leave the pot?' Acheson repeated indignantly, but he had sense enough to remain perfectly still.

'You lost it fair and square, me bucko,' Jemmy Hawk put in.

'Like hell I d—!' the 'whiskey drummer' began as, forgetting the way in which Waco had addressed him a short while earlier, Benner announced concurrence with the seaman's point of view.

'*Hombre!*' the supervisor interrupted, with grim and compelling intensity such as one might use when seeing another person approaching something exceptionally dangerous. 'You're lucky to still be alive and free to go. Which you-all won't be the first much longer happen you rile Waco here up a second time. Nor the second, should I have to send for the marshal to come and save you from getting shot. 'Him 'n' the county sheriff don't neither of them take kindly to big city tinhorns coming down here and taking business away from the local, tax-paying card sharps. So, was I you-all, I'd haul my butt out of Brownsville as fast as I could go. See them out, boys. Gently – unless they don't want it that way.'

'One thing, you pair!' Waco drawled, his voice hard and threatening, without apparently realizing that the foreign-looking man was listening with as great attention as the two card sharps. 'Don't you-all go getting any right smart big city notions about laying for us half-smart lil ole country boys after evens. It happened *once* afore.'

'Lordy lord, yes!' 'Lon' ejaculated, displaying a sadistic delight at the memory. 'Wasn't *that* a pistol, boy?'

'It surely was,' Waco enthused, never taking his menacing gaze from Acheson and Meekly. 'The feller's come at me sure looked peaceable and contented when they picked him up offen the ground. Don't know about t'other 'n' though. Wasn't only a neat lil forty-four calibre hole 'tween his eyes. Just an extra mouth – under his chin and bone deep – and his face was all covered with blood's hadn't come from it.'

'Where had it come from?' Benner asked.

Still without any sign to suggest he might be other than speaking and acting truthfully, the blond demonstrated. He made a gesture like drawing a knife with his right hand. Then, grasping a hank of his hair with the left, he drew it upwards and, with his extended right forefinger, made a sweeping gesture across his forehead.

'They wouldn't let me keep the blasted scalp, even though I told 'em it was for Grandpappy Long Walker's birthday,' 'Lon' complained, studying Meekly's head in a speculative fashion. 'Which it was close to a year ago and he'll be wanting a present for this 'n'.'

'I reckon's you pair'd better get going,' the supervisor advised and nodded to the waiting bouncers.

While being escorted across the room, neither Acheson nor Meekly doubted that the two young cowhands' comments were true. In fact, remembering the coldly savage face which had met his gaze as he felt the knife against his throat, Meekly was fully convinced that 'Lon' would have liked nothing better than to sink home the blade.

What was more, the pair knew that time had run out for them in Brownsville. Considering the speed with which news of their activities had already spread, there would be no chance of changing identities and gaining access to the more lucrative sections of the community. Nor any other kind, once word reached the local peace officers. Even the dishonest variety tended to favour their fellow citizens and nothing the two New Yorkers had heard led them to believe that either the town marshal or County Sheriff Tim Farron belonged to that category. So, much as the thought that they had been taken for suckers by their proposed dupes might rankle, neither of them was contemplating trying to take revenge against the deadly efficient young Texans.

In spite of the way in which he had dispatched his companion to find the local man he needed to fill his specialized needs, Franz Zapt soon found that achieving his purpose was less easy than he had anticipated. He appreciated that his proposal was not the kind that could be made in the presence of witnesses, so he wanted to speak as privately as possible with the two young Texans. He most certainly could not do so as long as the other men were gathered around them.

Fortune favoured Zapt.

While Acheson and Meekly were being shown off the premises by the bouncers, another matter arose to demand the floor supervisor's attention. Nor was the poker game resumed. Instead, telling the other two players to retrieve whatever money they had started with, 'Lon' and Waco divided the remainder between them. Having done so, followed by Zapt, the four men went to the bar. However, after only one drink, Hawk and Benner left in search of other entertainment.

'That was a very shrewd piece of play, if I may say so, gentlemen,' the foreigner praised, taking his chance before the Texans could be joined by anybody else. 'Would you do me the honour of letting me buy you a drink for your ability.'

'We'd be right pleased to, so long's it's only beer,' 'Lon' declared, looking at the speaker for a moment. Then he swung his gaze to the blond. 'Which *nobody's* ever come out and admitted we had any ability afore.'

'You just speak for yourself, *amigo*,' the youngster replied, but he was eyeing the well-dressed man in a faintly speculative manner. 'It's well known to 'most everybody's I've got ability to spare. But I'll be right honoured to go along. Beer'll do me just fine, too.'

'Excellent,' Zapt barked, then gave the order. Having done so, he turned his gaze back to the two young men. 'From what I heard you say earlier, perhaps your employer will not be pleased when he hears what has happened. Will he – how do you say – make the fussing for you?'

'Just let him so much's *try!*' Waco growled, much of his earlier truculence returning; but without the pretended drunkenness, which made it seem all the more deadly.

'But your friend, Mr.—?' Zapt commenced, pausing for an introduction. When none was offered, he resumed, 'But your friend said your employer would be angry if there was trouble and might discharge you.'

'He can try to do it, should he be so minded,' Waco replied and slapped the off-side Colt's staghorn grips with his right hand. 'Only, happen he does, he'll soon enough learn's he's not the only 'n's can do some of that there "discharging".'

'But I have heard that Captain Fog is a very dangerous man,' Zapt protested, darting a glance to the batwing doors of the main entrance, hoping that his companion would not return until he had reached some agreement with the Texans.

'He don't scare *me* one lil bit,' Waco declared. 'How about you-all "Lon"?'

'I sure's hell wouldn't back off from him none,' the Indian-dark young man answered. ' 'Cepting maybe on

36

the Fourth of July 'n' good ole Jeff Davis's[5] birthday.'

'But if he discharges you from his employment—' Zapt said, wondering why 'Lon' spoke in such a light-hearted fashion while also sounding so grim.

'Now that sounds real fancy, friend,' the blond interrupted. 'Only how about putting it into English, so's us half smart lil ole Texas boys can understand you.'

'But I am speaking English,' the foreigner objected, then realized what the comment had meant. '*Ach* so! If he says that he will no longer let you work for him, will anybody else allow you to work for them?'

'Sure they will,' Waco stated, but his voice lacked conviction.

'I dunno about that, boy,' objected 'Lon'. 'The last *hombre* Cap'n Fog set-down[6] had trouble getting anybody else to take him on, you mind.'

'I mind it all right,' Waco admitted, making a wry face, as he recollected the occasion to which his companion had referred.[7] Then he scowled menacingly and went on. 'Just let him try it on with me, is all!'

'What means this set down?' Zapt inquired and, after he had had the term explained, asked, 'And would Captain Fog do this to you?'

'He's done it afore when it suited his purpose,' Waco replied. 'But, by cracky, he'd best not try it on *me*!'

'Would you dare face him with a gun?' Zapt challenged, once again looking and, to his annoyance, seeing his companion and the local man at the door.

'I'll face *anybody* with a gun's I have to,' Waco stated, with an air of flat finality that was more convincing and impressive than any amount of loud boasting.

'Would you *kill* for money?' Zapt said quietly, noticing that the two men had not entered and were, in fact, withdrawing across the sidewalk. He decided to conclude the arrangements without delay.

5. Jefferson Davis (1808–89), U.S. statesman and President of the Confederate States of America from 1862 to 1865. – *J.T.E.*

6. Set down, also known as being set a-foot; the worst disgrace that could happen to a cowhand. Usually if one was fired and he did not own a horse, his erstwhile employer would loan him one so he could ride off in search of another job. If the circumstances of his dismissal were sufficiently bad, such a loan would be refused and other potential employers would fight shy of taking him on. – *J.T.E.*

7. Told in: SET A-FOOT. – *J.T.E.*

'Sure, happen there was enough of it,' Waco replied after a brief exchange of glances with his companion. 'Who'd you-all have in mind?'

'This is not a subject we can discuss here,' Zapt pointed out, elated by the ease in which he had accomplished his mission. 'Will you come outside with me?'

'Might's well,' Waco drawled, setting down his half empty beer schooner. 'Let's get going.'

'Shall I go first?' Zapt suggested. 'If you finish your beer, then follow, it will seem that we are not accompanying each other.'

'Smart thinking there,' Waco praised. 'We'll do just that.'

Setting down his glass and tossing the money for the drinks on the counter, Zapt said, 'Good night, gentlemen.'

After the foreigner had turned, but before he had taken more than half a dozen steps, the Texans finished their drinks and started to follow him. Unaware that his prospective employees had apparently misunderstood his instructions and were close behind, he reached the front doors. At first as he looked out, he could see no sign of his two companions. Then, emerging, he located them. They were standing in the shadows of an alley across the street. Approving of their cautious behaviour, he decided to let them know that all was well. Starting to raise his right hand to beckon them forward, he became conscious that the taller of them had adopted a strange posture.

To the accompaniment of the sound of detonating black powder, even as a realization of what the stance implied was striking Zapt, flame lanced from just below the level of the taller figure's eyes. Struck in the left breast by a ·44 calibre bullet from the Colt held double handed and sighted by the man he knew as 'Sproxton', the foreigner was sent spinning back through the batwing doors to fall at the feet of the two young Texans.

'What the—?' 'Lon' growled, but did not allow surprise to delay his reaction.

Twisting the old Dragoon Colt from its holster with his right hand, the Indian-dark Texan sprang past the dying man and flattened himself against the wall at the left side of the door. Although he was far from slow, his younger companion moved fractionally faster. Arming himself with a similar speed to that he had displayed earlier, Waco took up his position on the right of the main entrance.

'No sign of them,' the blond declared, after peering cautiously around the side of the door.

'Or me,' 'Lon' admitted, having duplicated the youngster's actions. 'Looks like we're going to have to find them the hard way.'

'Looks like,' Waco agreed. 'On five?'

'Five it is!' 'Lon' confirmed, with so little emotion that he might not have known what was entailed. 'One!'

'Two!' Waco went on.

'Three!' 'Lon' continued, taking no more notice than his friend of the interest their doings were arousing among the other patrons of the saloon.

'Four!' Waco counted, still scanning the street in the hope of locating the man who had fired the shot.

'Five!'

Saying the word in almost the same breath, the two young Texans plunged through the door practically simultaneously. However, instead of going straight across the sidewalk, they went at angles which took them past each other and allowed them to arrive on the street in shadows instead of exposed by the light from the saloon's main entrance. Although they were both ready to start shooting, there was no need for either to do so. The alley from which the fatal bullet had been fired was deserted. Nor could they hear anything to suggest in which direction the foreigner's killer and his companion had departed.

'Come on!' Waco snapped, holstering his Army Colt.

'You got any notion where to start looking for 'em, boy?' challenged 'Lon', also leathering his weapon.

'To hell with looking for them!' Waco replied, with vehemence. 'We're going to see Dusty. It was *him* as we was going to get paid to kill.'

CHAPTER FOUR

SHALL WE GO OUTSIDE, DUSTY?

'They're taking long enough with it,' grumbled Walter Scargill, through a mouthful of food, scowling bitterly at the ballroom's open connecting doors to the entrance hall. Spitting out a few morsels, he went on, 'They've been in there almost an hour.'

'I hope that talking to us won't stop you *eating*,' Alex von Farlenheim remarked, an expression of disdain coming to his handsome face as he flicked a small piece of bread from the sleeve of his jacket.

'Damn it!' Scargill snarled, his voice rising. He only revelled in having his bad manners commented upon by people who shared his views on defying the rules of conventional behaviour, and the Borgravnian did *not* belong to that category. 'If *you'd* gone as hungry as I have had to before—'

'You became a *famous* author,' von Farlenheim completed the sentence, his words also growing progressively louder. 'We *all* know how you've *suffered* at the hands of the tyrannical upper classes, you've told us often en—!'

'Why don't you both go and mingle with the other guests?' Charlene, *Comtesse* de Petain cut in and the timbre of her voice, for all that it was held to a low pitch brought the two young men's eyes to her.

'What—?' von Farlenheim began.

'Why sh—?' Scargill commenced at almost the same moment.

'First, because we've been standing here together at the buffet table almost ever since we arrived and ignoring everybody else,' Charlene explained, the smile on her lips and the appearance of making no more than polite conversation belied by the savage anger with which she was spitting out the *sotto voce* words. 'Which I don't think is considered good manners even in *this* barbaric country. Secondly – and *more* important – before your everlasting bickering becomes

40

noticeable and the other guests start wondering why you, Alex, invited you, Walter, to come here.'

'I assure you, Charl—!' von Farlenheim protested, but at least had the good sense to lower his voice.

'It wasn't my fault—!' Scargill complained, but also lowered his tone as the woman's cold eyes swung to him.

'Don't waste time apologizing!' Charlene interrupted, contriving to hiss the words out furiously while still maintaining the smile and look of someone making an innocuous comment. 'Go and mingle with the other guests— Now!'

'Who shall I *mingle* with?' Scargill asked sullenly, hating to even think that somebody else was displaying a better judgement than his own.

'The publisher of the local newspaper and his wife are over there,' Charlene answered, finding it increasingly difficult to keep her temper under control. 'Perhaps *they* would be suitable for a start?'

'You might even persuade him to publish one of—!' von Farlenheim sneered, but the words died away as the woman's furiously prohibitive gaze was turned upon him. However, as – receiving an equally angry scowl from her – the other young man turned and stalked away, he went on, 'The damned uncouth Englander bore. Why do we need him?'

'That's funny,' Charlene replied, but nothing in her demeanour implied that she was finding the situation in the least amusing. '*He's* asked me the same thing about *you* and just as many times.'

'If—!' von Farlenheim barked, reverting to his native German tongue and stiffening in righteous indignation.

'Don't become the officer with me, *please*!' Charlene snapped, only retaining her genteel posture with an ever-growing difficulty. Then her gaze flickered towards the ballroom's internal doors and what she saw was a source of relief in that it would allow her to change the subject. 'Ah, good! Now perhaps we can do something useful.'

'What do you mean?' the young Bosgravnian said coldly, having no liking for any reminder of how he had been compelled to hand in his resignation to the commandant of his country's military academy.

Noticing where Charlene was looking as he asked the question, von Farlenheim turned his attention in the same direction. He found that the meeting between his uncle, the

Governor of Texas and the two young men from the OD Connected had ended. Although there was no sign of the smaller man, the blond giant was strolling from the study towards the ballroom.

'Introduce us,' the woman ordered, for her words were nothing less in spite of the way in which they were uttered. 'Then leave the rest to me.'

Although indignant at being accorded such curt treatment from a member of the 'weaker' sex, something in her attitude prevented von Farlenheim from stating his objections. Since meeting her, much of his previous inborn belief in male supremacy had been shaken by an appreciation of her full potential. He was not sure of her exact status in the movement to which he was giving his support, but he had been made aware that it was superior to his own. In fact, much as the knowledge rankled, he had been given to understand that it was to be she who commanded their operations in the United States.

'Excuse me, Captain Fog,' the Bosgravnian said, having accompanied the woman across the room and accosting Mark Counter as he entered. 'May I present the *Comtesse* de Petain. Charlene, this is the famous Captain Fog, of whom we have all heard so much even before coming to this country.'

'Enchanted, Captain,' the *Comtesse* said, offering her right hand and, to her surprise, having it taken and kissed with an aplomb which she had not expected in spite of the blond giant's excellently cut dress clothes. 'Alex, isn't your aunt trying to catch your attention?'

'Y – Yes,' the young man answered reluctantly, glancing to where his aunt was chatting with some of the other guests and not even looking in his direction. Clicking his heels and bowing at the waist in the stiff Germanic way, he went on, 'Perhaps you will excuse me?'

'But of course,' Charlene replied. 'Unless, of course, Captain Fog will find my company inadequate?'

For a moment, Mark was on the point of correcting the misapprehension of the introduction. However, having drawn the conclusion – if not entirely correct, reasonably so – from the by-play between the woman and von Farlenheim that she wanted to make his closer acquaintance, he decided against doing so at that moment. Not only did he think the disclosure of the error might embarrass her, but also his sense of fun and remembrance of the conversation with the butler when he had arrived with his *amigo* made him change his mind. Although a previous encounter with an equally voluptuous member of the European aristocracy had been far from pleasant or enjoyable,[1] he considered that it would be amusing to let Dusty find out that mistaken identity had allowed him to meet with the most attractive woman in the room.

'*Comtesse*,' the blond giant declared, giving a gallant bow. 'Any man who found *your* company inadequate wouldn't need to be shot. He'd have to be *dead* already.'

'Bravo, sir,' Charlene applauded, deciding that not all 'Yankees' were as uncouth and lacking in the social graces as she had imagined. Throwing a commanding glance at the young Bosgravnian, she almost purred, 'It seems you are leaving me in *very* good hands, Alex.'

'So it seems,' von Farlenheim admitted, so annoyed that his accent slipped and the words came as, 'Zo it zeemses.' Giving another sharp heel click, but a shorter inclination of his torso, he barked, 'Excuse me, please!'

'Oh dear!' Charlene said, as she and the big Texan watched the young man depart with rapid and angry steps. 'I appear to have annoyed poor, dear Alex. One has to be *so* careful when dealing with military men—' Letting the words end in almost a gasp, she raised a hand hurriedly to her cheek and, looking coquettishly at her new companion, she gasped, 'Oh heavens! I forgot. You're a military man yourself, Captain.'

'Not exactly, ma'am, the outfit I served in were only volunteers who enlisted to fight the Yankees,' Mark replied, which was true enough. Like the Texas Light Cavalry, the regiment in which he had enlisted and been commissioned as a lieutenant were privately recruited. 'So I don't have any real right to the title "Captain".'

' "Captain" sounds so formal and stuffy anyway,' Charlene replied, turning on the kind of girlish and innocent charm which was her greatest asset. 'And almost all of the *captains* I have known, apart from *you*, were old, formal and stuffy. But how do you mean when you say that you fought against the Yankees. Surely you are a Yankee yourself?'

1. Mark Counter's meeting with Beatrice, *Vicomtesse de Brioude*, is told in: A HORSE CALLED MOGOLLON. – *J.T.E.*

'Not me, ma'am, I rode with – for the South in the War,' Mark corrected, exuding mock severity and remembering just in time not to mention the outfit in which he had served as it differed from that associated with Dusty Fog's name. 'So did 'most everybody else who's here tonight, including our host. Fact being, I wouldn't go calling *anybody* you meet down here in Texas a *Yankee* unless they're wearing a suit of Union Army blue and waving the Stars and Stripes.'

'Good heavens!' Charlene gasped, sensing there was an underlying seriousness to the lightly spoken words. 'Have I committed a bad *faux pas*?'

'Shucks, no,' Mark drawled. 'It's just that the War hasn't been completely forgotten down here and some folks get sort of touchy happen you-all put them on the wrong side of it.'

'I must remember that,' the *Comtesse* remarked, half to herself, as it was something she considered might be turned to her advantage in the future. It was her first visit to the United States and she appreciated that there was much about the customs she did not know. Then she put on her most winning smile and addressed the blond giant unreservedly. 'Are you *sure* that I haven't hurt your feelings with my little mistake?'

'Not even a little mite,' Mark assured.

'Then as we are friends and we've agreed that "Captain" sounds so stuffy and formal,' Charlene went on. 'Unless you think it too forward of me, might I call you Dusty?'

'If that's what you-all want, ma'am,' Mark answered, with a bow. 'Who am I to refuse you?'

'There must be a reward for such gallantry,' the *Comtesse* declared, throwing all of her winning charm into the smile with which the words were accompanied. 'And, besides, if I'm to call you "Dusty", it is only proper that you shall call me "Charlene".'

'Why, Charlene, I'd be honoured for the privilege,' the blond giant stated. 'And I've never been one to avoid doing anything that was "proper".' Then, recollecting what had brought him into the ballroom instead of joining Dusty, his host and the Governor who had been challenged to a game of billiards by Sheriff Timothy Farron and the local justice of the peace, his gaze flickered to the buffet table. 'Man, Mr. and Mrs. von Farlenheim lay on a right good spread. Can I serve you with anything, Charlene?'

'Good heavens, no, I've eaten far too much already,' the *Comtesse* replied, glancing at the clock in the corner of the room and wondering if the assassins would be waiting in the garden. Deciding that it was too early for them to have arrived, she continued. 'But please don't let me stop you.'

'Well now,' Mark drawled, throwing a glance pregnant with meaning to where von Farlenheim was standing and glowering their way despite being the centre of attention for several local girls. 'My daddy always used to tell me that, happen you leave a bird unattended, you're right likely to come back and find a cuckoo in the nest.'

'I'm not quite sure I like to be compared with a bird,' Charlene protested, putting on a pout, although she had no intention of allowing herself to be separated from the blond giant.

'Now me, I've seen some right pretty birds, beautiful even,' Mark countered. 'But even the prettiest wouldn't come close to you.'

'Hum!' Charlene answered, brightening up. 'Again such gallantry. And it must be rewarded. May I come with you while you eat? Just in case there are cuckoos about.'

'Why sure,' Mark consented, not averse to keeping the woman with him. 'They don't call me the cuckoo-killer for nothing. You'll be safe with me.'

Escorting Charlene to the buffet table, Mark helped himself to an assorted plateful of the various delicacies. Refusing the offer by a coloured waiter of a drink, he started to eat. As he did so, he decided that he had made the right decision in coming to the ballroom. While he enjoyed playing billiards and was good at the game, he felt that his present occupation offered better – if different – possibilities.

'Do you own a ranch, Dusty?' the *Comtesse* inquired, after the blond giant had eaten his fill.

'Nope,' Mark replied and continued truthfully, if not succinctly. 'But my folk have a pretty fair spread.'

'Then you are a – cowboy – do you call them?' Charlene asked, wanting to gain a piece of what might prove important information.

'I've worked cattle some,' Mark admitted, with considerable understatement considering his ability in that line of endeavour.

'But I thought that all you cowboys walked around

'bristling with revolvers,' the *Comtesse* protested, looking pointedly at her escort's hips and powerful legs.

'We do sometimes,' Mark conceded. 'Only it's like wearing an open-necked shirt and a bandana. A buscadero gunbelt doesn't seem to look right with these clothes.'

'I should think not,' Charlene smiled, relieved to find out that the blond giant was not armed. 'Anyway, you won't need any weapons here, I'm not dangerous.'

'Now I'm right relieved to hear that,' Mark drawled.

'My, it's hot,' Charlene breathed, another quick look at the clock telling her that the men she was expecting ought to be in position. She turned her gaze coyly to the big Texan, thinking what a waste it was going to be leading him to be killed and continuing, 'I know that this is going to sound terribly forward of me— Can we go outside, Dusty?'

'Well now,' Mark said. 'Would the *Comte* de Petain object if we do?'

'As he was killed while riding to hounds over a year ago,' Charlene answered, trying to strike the right kind of attitude to such a question. 'It is most unlikely that he will.'

'I'm sorry,' Mark said, in a flat tone. 'But I didn't know—'

'You couldn't have,' Charlene replied. 'My mourning is over now and I have come to America to forget.' She raised a hand and put on a fair simulation of a brave smile. 'It's all right, Dusty. I'm not hurt by your question. And you don't need to feel sorry for me. It was a marriage of convenience, arranged between our families and there was neither love, nor children. Besides, one can't live in the past, can one?'

All of which was true – as far as it went.

While Charlene's marriage had been manipulated, the end was achieved by her own rather than family efforts. The lack of love had been all on her side, as had the avoidance of such encumbrances as children. What was more, her husband's death while riding to hounds was far from accidental. Nothing had ever been suspected, much less proved, but she had arranged for his horse to fall in such a way and place that he could not have hoped to avoid breaking his neck.

'Nope, one can't,' Mark agreed, seeming to be impressed by the *Comtesse's* apparent sincerity. 'And, happen my question didn't hurt or offend you-all, I'd admire to walk with you in the garden, ma'am.'

46

For all his offer, the blond giant was anything but a naïve country boy who had been tricked.

Due to the way in which his exceptional good looks and physique attracted them, Mark had had considerable experience with women of many classes. Charlene would not have been pleased to know that he had made an accurate estimation of her age and was far from deceived by her behaviour. Having observed the way in which she had dismissed young von Farlenheim had only been the first clue to suggest that her later aura of girlish innocence was no more than a well-executed pose.

However, for all his summations, the blond giant had at first been unable to decide what the beautiful brunette's motives might be. He had wondered if she was a confidence trickstress who had scraped up an acquaintance with their host's cousin so as to gain entrance to the reception. Her clothing and jewellery were of excellent quality, but that proved nothing. Such a person attending a function of that magnitude would realize the only hope of success was to be correctly attired.

Having noticed the wedding ring as soon as they were introduced, Mark had asked his question the moment Charlene suggested leaving the ballroom for the seclusion of the garden. It was a precaution, especially after she had taken the trouble to find out whether he was armed, that he had considered was justified in view of his misgivings. Watching how it was answered, he had felt sure that she was speaking the truth.

The acceptance of the *Comtesse's* explanation had opened up another avenue of conjecture for the blond giant. A widow of over a year who was travelling might well be looking for another husband. In which case, particularly if the previous marriage had not ended in a financially fruitful fashion, she might consider the United States a good hunting ground and a well-connected young Texan could strike her as a better than fair prospect. More than one member of the European aristocracy had already married into wealthy American families, who regarded the acquisition of a title as highly desirable even if it did not come backed with money in its own right.

'And if she *is* after a husband,' Mark mused, taking the *Comtesse's* arm and escorting her towards the open french windows. 'I wouldn't be a good *amigo,* nor a loyal employee, happen I didn't do all I could to keep good ole Dusty out of the trap.'

Having established a suitable excuse, even though fully aware that the small Texan was well able to take care of himself, Mark went out into the garden with no other thought than satisfying his curiosity.

Normally, finding himself the centre of attraction for several pretty and attentive girls, Alex von Farlenheim would have been highly delighted. It had been his penchant for philandering which had brought about the demand for his resignation from the Bosgravnian Army's Military Academy and led to his joining the plotters against his country's ruling family.

So, being cognizant with what was to happen after the *Comtesse* had lured 'Captain Fog' outside, the young man found the eager questioning and frank admiration of the girls more distracting than flattering. It had not been too bad while Charlene was in the room. In fact, he had derived some satisfaction and amusement from noticing that Scargill was in far less agreeable company and not having as good a time. However, all that changed as she and the blond giant disappeared through the french windows. Looking into the darkness and straining his ears for the first sound of a disturbance, von Farlenheim wished he could think up an excuse to follow them.

'But, Aline, that *can't* be Dusty Fog. He's too small.'

'Small or not, Vivian Smethers, it's him all right. I was introduced to him at the Farrons' house. The sheriff's his uncle.'

The two comments, made in feminine tones from the party around von Farlenheim broke through his thought train with sudden clarity. They served to slam him back into an awareness of his surroundings. He found that all the girls were looking to where the small man who had arrived with the blond giant was entering with his uncle, the Governor, Sheriff Farron, and the town's justice of the peace.

Even as von Farlenheim realized that he and Charlene might have made a serious mistake, something was shouted in masculine tones from the garden. It was followed in rapid succession by a feminine scream, the splash of something falling into water and the crashing of gunfire.

CHAPTER FIVE

IT'S MARK THEY'RE AFTER

'Howdy there, Kid, Waco,' greeted the elder deputy on guard duty at the main entrance to the von Farlenheim family's property, recognizing the two young men who had ridden up and halted. 'Cap'n Fog allowed you pair'd threatened to ride off and start herding sheep rather than come to these fancy doings. Don't tell me you've changed your minds?'

'Not 'specially,' the Ysabel Kid replied, swinging from the saddle of a big, magnificently developed white stallion that looked as savage and untamed as any *manadero*[1] running free on the open range. 'If we had, we'd've put our fancy, go-to-town do-dads on.'

'Which Lon 'n' me surely look elegant in,' Waco supplemented, dismounting from a powerful and fine looking paint stallion. 'Fact being, we was fixing to come; but Dusty 'n' Mark wouldn't let us for fear we'd put 'em to shame.'

Far from being malcontents disenchanted by their employment, the Ysabel Kid[2] and the youngster whose only name was Waco[3] were more than just loyal hands of the OD Connected ranch. They were part of Ole Devil Hardin's floating outfit and, in fact, the Kid was one of its founder members.[4]

However, having an aversion to donning the required raiment for attending such a stiffly formal occasion and preferring to avoid affairs of that nature, the pair had found an excuse to stay away. Having been sent into Brownsville by Dusty to deliver a message to the man for whom the OD

1. *Manadero:* the Spanish-Mexican term for the master stallion in a herd of wild horses. – *J.T.E.*
2. Details of the Ysabel Kid's background, history and special qualifications are given in APPENDIX THREE.– *J.T.E.*
3. Details of Waco's background, history and special qualifications are given in APPENDIX FOUR. – *J.T.E.*
4. How this came about is told in: THE YSABEL KID – *J.T.E.*

Connected trail herd was intended, the horse wrangler had stayed overnight and fallen victim to Thorley Acheson and Josiah Meekly.

Hearing that card-sharps were in town and learning that – because no evidence of cheating was forthcoming – the local law enforcement officers could take no action against the miscreants, Waco had suggested that he and the Kid should attend to the matter. Knowing that he had acquired considerable knowledge of how card sharps operated,[5] Sheriff Timothy Farron and the town marshal had accepted the offer. Locating the two men at the Running Iron Saloon, a masterful performance had avenged the wrangler and recouped his losses.

After having completed their assignment, the Kid and Waco had been ready to spend a pleasant evening in what to them was far more congenial company than they had felt they would find at the von Farlenheims' reception. Their response to Franz Zapt's questions had started out as a similar kind of harmless fun to that of Mark Counter when he allowed the misconception regarding his identity to continue. However, they had soon realized that there were far more serious and sinister overtones to the foreigner's interest in them than mere idle curiosity.

On receiving the first intimation that Zapt wished to hire them to kill somebody, the two Texans had known that the sheriff would want to discover the identity of the intended victim. So they had played along with the same skill which had deceived Acheson and Meekly. The foreigner's murder had prevented them from obtaining the information, but Waco's deductive reasoning powers had suggested the answer. Although he had not explained why he suspected Dusty Fog might be the victim, the Kid had had sufficient faith in his judgement to carry out his instructions. Collecting their horses, which – as no cowhand would ever walk if he could ride – were standing at the saloon's hitching-rail, they had set off for the von Farlenheim's residence without waiting for the local peace officers to arrive.

'Whooee!' the youngster said, studying the high wall – with its top encrusted by closely spaced pieces of jagged-edged broken glass – on either side of the open wrought iron gates. 'Happen that goes all the way 'round his spread, I

5. How this knowledge was acquired is told in: THE MAKING OF A LAWMAN and THE TROUBLE BUSTERS. – J.T.E.

50

don't reckon Mr. von Farlenheim'll get many good borrowing neighbours sneaking in on him.'

'It goes all the way 'round,' the younger peace officer replied. ' 'Course, there's another gate at the back for the poor folks who come calling to use.'

'Maybe we should go in that way, boy,' the Kid suggested, realizing what had prompted his companion's comment and helping him to acquire the necessary information.

'Wouldn't do you-all no good to tonight,' the elderly deputy warned. 'Nor any other, comes to that. It's kept locked and bolted tight from sundown until morning. Only way in, less you-all try to jump that spikey-topped wall, is through the gates here. Which Larry 'n' me've got orders to make sure only them's have proper invitations go in.'

'We didn't bring ours, but we've got a message for Dusty,' the Kid drawled. 'So does that include us?'

'I reckon it'd be all right to let you-all pass,' the elder deputy decided, showing not the slightest hesitation. 'Only I surely hopes's you OD Connected yahoos know your place 'n' go to the back door most humble.'

'We'll do that, for shame,' the Kid promised. 'Keep your eye on our hosses, will you-all, Stub?'

'Sure,' assented the senior deputy. 'I wouldn't want 'em, being low critters like their owners, to go dropping their smelling ole dung on that fancy driveway. Hey though, is that damned white goat still's ornery as ever?'

'*Worse*,' Waco stated cheerfully, but he was still scanning the grounds with considerable interest.

'He *couldn't* be,' Stub objected, knowing that the big white stallion did not take kindly to strangers and was apt to display its antipathy with some violence if there should be an intrusion of its privacy.[6]

'Don't you-all get into a tizz,' drawled the Kid. 'I've taught him some real good manners since we was here last. He doesn't *hardly* never chew off both arms up to the shoulders no more. He *almost* always leaves one only shy as far's the elbow.'

'Now *that's* what I call a real good mannered hoss,' the elder deputy said dryly. 'Why don't you pair go deliver your message, 'stead of wasting our valuable time.'

'You-all might just drop a teensy bit of a hint that there's a couple of real deserving defenders of law 'n' order down

6. This trait is illustrated in: THE RIO HONDO KID. – *J.T.E.*

here at the gate's could use something to eat and drink,' the younger peace officer suggested, as the cowhands walked by. 'Which's Stub 'n' me, afore I'm asked.'

'We'll do that,' the Kid replied.

'This here's one hell of a size of a spread,' Waco remarked, looking around the spacious grounds as he and his *amigo* went along the wide driveway. From what he could see, the lawns extended around the sides as well as in front of the mansion. What was more, they appeared to be just as well supplied with clumps of decorative bushes and stone statues. 'He must have him a floating outfit to ride his back ranges in here.'

'Why sure,' the Kid agreed, making just as keen and detailed a survey of their surroundings. 'I don't want to sound nosey, mind, but why'd you-all reckon that jasper was after Dusty's hide?'

'I'll tell you 'n' him both at once,' the young blond answered. 'When I show off what a right smart *hombre* I am, I want the important folks's well as the nobodies to know it. Top of which, that way I'll only have to tell it the once.' Then the air of levity left him and he went on, 'Tell you, though, Lon. I did wonder if that jasper's *amigos* 've already sent somebody to handle the chore. They'd likely know that Dusty'd be asked up here, even if they're not trying to stop him finding out what the Governor wants. And they'd know's he couldn't come dressed to such a fancy shindig, which'd make taking him a whole heap safer than when he's wearing them old bone-handled Peacemakers. Only, after what Stub said, I don't know's they could get anybody in here unless they'd got a way of opening that back gate.'

'They mightn't need to do *that*,' the Kid warned. 'I mind Dusty telling me one time that Belle Boyd showed him how to go over a wall with glass on its top.[7] So they could've known how and done it.'

'I'd heard about it,' Waco admitted, glancing to his rear and discovering that neither of the deputies was watching them. 'So how's about you-all and me sort of sneaking around the back and seeing that nobody's done it?'

'Be best,' the Kid declared. 'Top of which, *I* know *my* place 'n' wouldn't think of going right straight up to the front doors there like we was real high-toned quality invited guests.'

7. Told in: THE REBEL SPY. – *J.T.E.*

'Let's split up and take a side each,' Waco suggested. 'It'd ruin me socially was I to be seen in the company of a low, ornery retired border smuggler like you-all.'

'I was thinking's how I wouldn't want nobody to think I'd come with a mean cuss like you-all,' the Kid countered, realizing that his young companion's idea had merit. 'And, seeing's I know you're scared of the dark, I'll go around to the right.'

'Mind you don't fall over anything that way,' Waco advised. 'Or *anybody* and, happen it's *anybody* apologize to 'em humble. They *might* be married.'

'You've got a low mind, boy,' the Kid growled, wishing that he had been able to fetch along his Winchester Model of 1866 rifle without arousing the deputies' curiosity. 'They don't do them sort of things at a fancy whoop-up like this.'

'They *don't*?' grinned the youngster, turning in the direction allocated to him. 'Then I'm right pleased I didn't let you-all talk me into coming sooner.'

Separating from his companion, Waco made his way swiftly across the garden. The half-moon overhead gave sufficient light for him to be able to see where he was going. As he made his way towards the perimeter wall, meaning to follow it round to his destination, he decided that the von Farlenheims might have designed the layout of their garden with the needs of ambushers in mind. However, he also considered that the proliferation of decorative bushes and statues made his and the Kid's task easier.

Having profited from instructions given by his *very* proficient Indian-dark *amigo*, who had learned the art from Chief Long Walker of the *Pehnane* Comanche, Waco possessed considerable skill in the matter of moving without attracting attention or letting himself be seen. It was soon apparent that he would need to make use of his ability. While the Kid had taken the side of the mansion which was most poorly illuminated and could offer the greatest advantage to anyone entering with evil intentions, he would have to go by the well lit end and the open french windows of the ballroom.

Moving from cover to cover with little more disturbance than a shadow, Waco kept on the alert. He felt sure that, if von Farlenheim had guards patrolling the grounds, one of the deputies would have mentioned them. For all that, he wanted to avoid attracting the attention of any of the guests who might be outside the mansion. He could easily explain his presence and Dusty would verify his *bona fides*, but having it done would not help him accomplish his mission should assassins have already penetrated the grounds.

As Waco was drawing level with the french windows, although the width of the garden separated him from them, he noticed something which he decided was worthy of further scrutiny. Halting behind a flowering dogwood bush which was Mrs. Frieda von Farlenheim's special pride, he watched another member of the floating outfit emerging from the ballroom escorting – as yet he did not know her name – Charlene, *Comtesse* de Petain.

'Whooee!' Waco breathed, his eyes roving over the French woman's voluptuous attributes with frank admiration. 'Wouldn't you just *know* that sneaky ole Mark would get hisself tied in with a right good looking gal. I wonder if he's figuring on showing her the "golden horseshoe nail" for sh—'

The youngster's thought that the blond giant might be employing a hoary and frequently successful ploy to lure an unsuspecting female into a stable,[8] or somewhere else equally private, were brought to an abrupt end as a movement farther along the garden caught the corner of his eyes. Turning his gaze from where Charlene and Mark were approaching an ornamental pool Mrs. von Farlenheim had had constructed, he located two masculine figures among the bushes. A moment's study warned him that, while they were exposed to his view, the foliage would be keeping them beyond his *amigo's* range of vision.

For a moment, noticing a couple of flickers of white around the chests of the otherwise black-clad shapes, Waco decided that they could be no more than guests engaged in spying upon the activities of the other people at the reception. Even as close as thirty or so yards he could not tell for sure, but he believed they were dressed suitably for the occasion.

Then the youngster caught a glimpse of something metallic which was appearing in each of the figures' right hand!

Instantly Waco knew that the pair were up to no good!

Even if they were private detectives who had contrived to

8. An occasion when Mark Counter used the ploy is told in: TOWN CALLED YELLOWDOG. – J.T.E.

gain entrance to the reception with the intention of obtaining evidence for divorce against the woman at Mark's side on behalf of her husband, it was unlikely that they would have bothered to arm themselves. In fact, doing so might endanger their chances of completing their assignment without drawing attention to their presence. Guests noticed lurking in concealment might be passed over for the reasons that the youngster had originally envisaged, but not if they were seen to be armed.

So there did not seem to be any reason for the men to be drawing weapons!

Unless—!

Watching the pair as they started to raise the firearms, Waco's deductive intuition began to supply *very* alarming possibilities!

'Oh god!' the youngster breathed, hands diving towards staghorn butts of the holstered Colt 1860 Army revolvers and remembering other occasions when a similar error had occurred. 'They've come to kill Dusty, but it's Mark they're after!'

'Good heavens!' Charlene, *Comtesse* de Petain gasped, employing an expression she had always found useful for emphasizing her 'girlish innocence' and indicating the ornamental pond without relinquishing her grasp of Mark Counter's right arm. 'I never thought I'd see one of *these* in America.'

'I've heard tell they're getting right popular for housing these goldfish critters that've been brought over from Europe for a fair spell now,'[9] the blond giant replied, a little annoyed by his companion's apparent belief that there was nothing but an uncivilized and primitive wilderness on the west side of the Atlantic Ocean.

'Oh dear, this *isn't* my night for being tactful!' Charlene gasped. She was looking around but could not locate that which she sought. Sensing Mark's feelings, she wanted to smooth them over rather than take the chance of having him

9. Bred for centuries in the Far East as a pond and ornamental species, the goldfish, *Carassius Auratus* (L), was first brought to Portugal in the early 1600s, spreading from there to the rest of Europe and, eventually, to the United States of America. The first purely American variety, the long-tailed, fast-swimming 'comet' was first produced during the 1880s in ponds near Washington, D.C. – J.T.E.

decide to return to the ballroom. 'What I said appears to have annoyed you.'

'Shucks, no,' the blond giant said cheerfully, also wishing to prevent their acquaintanceship from ending before he could satisfy his curiosity about her.

'I have so. And you've been so kind that even a little is too much,' Charlene groaned. Squeezing his arm gently, her voice took on a seductively promising timbre as she continued, 'But perhaps I can make amends to you?'

'Why there's not the teensiest bit of need for that,' Mark declared, but in a way that suggested he considered there was cause for some form of apology. 'But, if you want to, it's a pity you're not an American lady.'

'Why's that?' Charlene inquired, genuinely puzzled.

'Well now,' Mark drawled, eyeing her in a conspiratorial manner. 'Happen you-all was an American, I'd be able to take you to see the golden horseshoe nail.'

'The *what*?' Charlene said, her interest aroused as it always was by any reference to the controlling passion of her life which was the reason for all her endeavours, gold.

'It's something *real* special,' Mark announced, sounding – as he invariably did when employing the ancient trick – as if he was not only speaking the unvarnished truth, but letting the girl into a secret. 'You see, every time a stable's built over here, they always put in a golden horseshoe nail for luck.'

'Good heavens! I've never heard of such a thing!' the *Comtesse* gasped. She threw another rapid glance about her, wondering whether the men she had ordered to be sent had arrived, then continued, 'Does it *always* work?'

'Why sure,' Mark replied and felt the hand on his arm tighten a little. 'Every time. Unless—'

'Unless what?' Charlene asked hurriedly, worried by the possibility that the big Texan had stopped speaking because he had duplicated a discovery she had just made.

In the course of her brief scrutiny of the garden, the *Comtesse* had found that the arrangements she had made were being carried out to her entire satisfaction. The two masculine shapes she could see moving among the bushes to her left were clad so as to pass for guests in the poor light. However, as one of them had raised his left hand in a brief wave on catching her eye, she knew differently. They had remembered and acted upon the instructions she had given by en-

56

suring that she was aware of their arrival before commencing their work.

When the man who had hired the killers for Charlene had warned that there would be objections to the safeguard she had insisted upon, she had promised to help reduce the risk involved in carrying it out. Not only would she do all she could to distract their victim, but she would hold on to his arm and prevent him from defending himself if he should detect their presence prematurely.

Watching the men as they continued their cautious advance, the *Comtesse* experienced a sensation of delight and satisfaction. Once again, she had demonstrated her ability as a strategist and justified the faith that had been placed in her when she was given command of the operation. All was going exactly as she had planned. Although she was confident that the blond giant had not the slightest conception of his peril, she retained her grip on his arm. However, she was also ready to release him and collapse in a 'swoon' which would take her out of the line of fire when the time came.

'Well now, this's the way of it,' Mark was saying oblivious to the designs the woman by his side had upon his life. He was watching for her reaction to his words rather than his surroundings as he went on, 'That old nail works best when a feller takes a right pretty lil gal in front of it and she lets him cuddle up comfy and have a – kiss. Only, if she says, "No", it just jumps out of—'

It was a pity, Charlene told herself as she listened to the explanation, that she would not get to see the 'golden horseshoe nail'; nor even hear what happened in the event of the girl refusing to be kissed. Not with the two men coming closer and holding their weapons ready to be used.

The *Comtesse's* summation proved correct!

But not for the anticipated reasons!

'Guns to the left, Mark!'

Up until the four words being shouted from the couple's right, everything had been progressing to Charlene's satisfaction. However, she had failed to take two completely unexpected factors into consideration.

The deductive ability which had brought Waco on the scene at just the right, or wrong – depending upon one's point of view – moment.

And the speed with which Mark responded to the warning.

Hearing the youngster's voice, the blond giant did not waste an instant in wondering what had brought him on the scene so fortuitously. In spite of having a fondness for playing practical jokes, Waco would never use such a subject for one. The very urgency in his voice was proof that he was in deadly earnest and the danger he was giving warning of must be close at hand.

Long years of hazardous living had taught Mark the value of thinking and acting fast in an emergency. So his responses were in motion almost without the need for conscious thought. Instinctively, he realized that his first priority was to liberate himself from the *Comtesse's* grasp and put her out of harm's way. With that in mind, he gave her a powerful shove and, as her hand left his arm, sprang in the opposite direction.

Caught totally unprepared for such a sudden and vigorous reaction, Charlene felt herself being pushed away from the blond giant with considerable force. Despite her squeal of alarm, her major emotion was relief. It was brought about by the realization that she was being propelled from the area towards which lead would soon be flying. Then she noticed where she was going. Her squeal turned into a furious howl, but there was nothing she could do to stop herself. Passing over the edge of the ornamental pool, she plunged face forward into the stagnant green water.

Even as the *Comtesse* was going beneath the surface, the thunder of shots came to her ears.

CHAPTER SIX

SOMEBODY HAD TO LET THEM IN

Despite hearing the furious shriek emitted by Charlene, *Comtesse* de Petain, and the splash as she fell into the ornamental pond, Mark Counter could not spare her so much as a glance. He had seen the cause of Waco's warning and, identifying the type of weapon held by one of the men, was trying to reach whatever shelter would be offered by the nearest stone statue.

As he went down after thrusting the woman into what proved a watery and uncomfortable safety, and even as he was turning and starting to move on his own behalf, the blond giant's right hand passed behind his back and beneath the tails of his jacket. While he had spoken the truth regarding his reasons for leaving off the *buscadero* gunbelt, his misgivings with respect to Charlene had precluded any elaboration on the subject. He might have mentioned that, if not as adequately armed as he would have been with the matched ivory-handled Colt Cavalry Model Peacemakers in their contoured fast-draw holsters, he *was* armed.

Although the white waistcoat concealed it at the front, a stout leather belt encircled Mark's waist and was held firmly in place by loops attached for that purpose to his trousers. He did not require such an aid to keep the excellently tailored nether garments from slipping down. At the rear, it supported a holster – which was set horizontally instead of, as was more usual, vertically – carrying a Colt 'Storekeeper' Model Peacemaker. What was more, when the dress clothes were being tailored, the back of the waistcoat had been shaped so that it would not impede access to the weapon.

For all the thought that had gone into the design and construction of the concealment rig, it did not offer the same facility for really fast withdrawal of a revolver that could be attained with the blond giant's even more carefully manufactured *buscadero* gunbelt. So he knew that he could not liberate the short-barrelled Colt[1] with the extreme rapidity the situation demanded.

Knowing that his big *amigo* was armed, Waco was just as conversant as its owner with the concealment holster's limitations. So, even as he was yelling his warning, he sprang forward. He too had noticed that one of the attackers was armed with what could only be a sawed-off shotgun and he appreciated the full lethal potential of such a weapon.

Aware that only good fortune would allow him to make a hit in the prevailing conditions, the youngster opened fire as he advanced at a run. Nor was he deterred by realizing how his actions would almost certainly place his own life in jeopardy. Raised at shoulder height and arms' length, first his left and then the right hand Colt 1860 Army revolver bellowed, to be thumb-cocked on the respective kicks of the recoil. Still aimed by the same rough alignment rather than with the sights, each spoke again in concert with the opposite foot taking a step.

Firing on the run was not conducive to extreme accuracy, but Waco's fourth attempt produced a result that was both lucky and unfortunate. Knowing where the greater danger lay, he was making the man with the shotgun the primary object of his attentions. Flying by its intended target, the ·44

1. Introduced in 1873 as the Colt Model P 'Single Action Army' revolver, but more frequently referred to as the 'Peacemaker', production was continued until 1941 when it was taken out of line to make way for the more modern military weapons required in World War II. Over *three hundred and fifty thousand* were manufactured in practically every handgun calibre – with the exception of the ·41 and ·44 Magnum, which did not come on the scene during the production period – from ·22 Short rimfire to ·476 Eley. However, the majority fired either the ·45, or the ·44·40 which allowed the same ammunition to be used in the Winchester Model of 1873 rifle.

The barrels were from three inches in the 'Storekeeper' Model – which did not have an extractor rod – to the sixteen inches of the so-called 'Buntline Special'. The latter was offered with a detachable metal skeleton butt so it could be used as a carbine. The main barrel lengths were: Cavalry, seven-and-a-half inches; Artillery, five-and-a-half inches; Civilian, four-and-three-quarter inches.

Popular demand, said to have been caused by the upsurge of action-escapism-adventure Western series on television, brought the Peacemaker back into production in 1955 and it is still in the line. – *J.T.E.*

'Army' calibre bullet[2] ploughed into the left breast of the second would-be assassin and knocked him in a screaming, spinning pirouette. Throwing aside his revolver, he crashed dying to the ground.

With the shotgun starting to lift, the first hired killer had been startled by Waco's intervention and the speed with which the blond giant was responding to the danger. In spite of the latter, he could not prevent himself from wavering in his intentions. He did not doubt that – dress clothes notwithstanding – 'Dusty Fog' would be armed in some way, but considered that the approaching youngster posed an even greater and more pressing threat to his well-being. So he was contemplating turning his weapon in the latter direction when he felt the wind of the bullet which struck his companion.

From the beginning, the man with the shotgun had not approved of the orders he and his partner had received. Going up against a *pistolero* of Dusty Fog's calibre, whom he knew only by reputation, was sufficiently precarious without the restrictions which had been placed upon their actions. If the woman with their intended victim had deviated in the slightest from the arrangements, they would have handled the matter in a way that offered them a greater safety factor; even if in doing so they had put her in peril.

From what he heard and sensed, the man concluded that his partner had been rendered *hors de combat*. Taking that and the other factors into consideration, he decided that discretion was more sensible than valour. A killer by profession, he did not believe in taking unnecessary chances and felt that the situation had deteriorated to the point when it was no longer tenable. Instead of taking the couple of seconds required to cut loose with his shotgun at the smoke-wrapped, flame-spurting, bullet-throwing young cowhand, he spun on his heel and fled as fast as his legs would carry him.

Sliding free and cocking the Colt 'Storekeeper', Mark

2. Although the military sometimes claimed derisively that it was harder to kill a soldier than a sailor, the weight factor of the respective weapons had accused the naval authorities' decision to employ a revolver of ·36 and not ·44 calibre. The weapon would be carried on a seaman's belt and not – handguns having originally and primarily been developed for use by cavalry – on the person, or saddle, of a man who would do most of his travelling on the back of a horse. Therefore, ·36 became known as the 'Navy' calibre. – *J.T.E.*

skidded to a halt in profile behind an exceptionally well developed statue of an unclad 'Greek goddess'. 'Her' proportions and construction were ample enough to shelter him adequately as long as he remained sideways on. They were capable of stopping a bullet from a ·50 calibre Sharps 'Old Reliable' buffalo rifle, much less a ·32 buckshot ball. However, he realized that he could not remain in the safety of his concealment. The use of the sawed-off shotgun implied that his assailants were professional killers. So, by dashing to his aid, Waco was being exposed to their retaliation. Nor would they overlook the youngster's threat to them.

Even before the unmistakable sound of lead striking into human flesh and the cry of a man in mortal pain came to his ears, the blond giant was moving. Bringing his left hand to cup under and support the Colt-filled right, he twisted himself from behind the statue. Searching along the stubby barrel as he swung the weapon at shoulder level, he saw the stricken man going down and the other turning to flee.

Squeezing the revolver's trigger, Mark's shooting instincts warned that he was going to miss. Responding without the need for conscious guidance, his trained reflexes were more attuned to the weight and feel of the considerably longer and somewhat heavier Cavalry Model Peacemaker he generally carried. So he over-corrected the motions of the weapon. Although he appreciated his error almost instantly and tried to rectify it, he failed by a fraction of a second. Slight though the misalignment had been, it proved sufficient to prevent him from achieving his purpose.

Coming so close on the heels of the near-miss which had dealt so severely with his companion, and having the blond giant's bullet almost scrape his head as it went by only added to the hired killer's desire to depart. A few more strides carried him into the welcome concealment offered by the garden's prolific decorative bushes. Aware of what had happened to Charlene, he mumbled a profane hope that she was drowned by the fall into the ornamental pond; but did not let that divert his attention from the pressing matter of escaping. Instead, he concentrated upon a rapid, swerving sprint which was intended to make him a more difficult target in the poor visibility.

Twice more before the man reached the end of the building and was hidden from his assailants' view, lead winged its way not too far from his ears. Goaded to greater efforts by the eerie 'splat!' sound of the bullets splitting the air in very close proximity to him, he made the final strides which carried him beyond the shooters' range of vision. A head, its coloured face registering alarm, appeared at the open door of the kitchen and, after taking one look at him, disappeared again. He did not anticipate any impediment to his flight from that source, but was ready to deal with it should the need arise.

Gazing ahead, the man breathed a sigh of relief. To reduce the chances of their unauthorized presence being detected prematurely, he had had his partner close the back gate through which they had gained admittance. However, appreciating the advisability of ensuring that they could depart without delay, it had been neither locked nor bolted. As he drew nearer, he was pleased to find that the omission had not been discovered and rectified. Once he had gone through, he would use the key with which he had been supplied and which had been left in the lock to at least delay any pursuit until he could reach the horses that were waiting not too far away.

On reaching the gate, the man found his confidence regarding the lack of interference from the kitchen was justified. However, it soon became apparent that he was not to complete his departure from the grounds without challenge.

A figure dashed into view at the other end of the building from which the hired killer had come. He decided that it was a cowhand, dressed all in black and carrying what could only be an old Colt Dragoon revolver.

Being in no mood to trifle, the man started to swing up his already cocked shotgun. The distance was somewhat greater than the most effective range of his cut-down weapon, but he felt it would be adequate against an antagonist who was armed in such an archaic and cumbersome fashion.

Attracted by the commotion, the Ysabel Kid had restrained the anxiety he felt for his companions' welfare and set out to deal with any of the intruders who tried to escape. While running towards the rear of the mansion, he had twisted free his four pounds-one ounce, thumb-busting old Colt 1848 Dragoon Model revolver. His instincts had suggested that, in the absence of the Winchester Model of 1866 rifle, it would be better suited to his needs than the bowie knife.

Passing around the back corner, the Kid discovered that his summation was correct.

There was, however, no time for self-congratulation!

Studying the weapon which was being directed at him by the man at the gate in the back wall, the Indian-dark Texan was in no doubt of what it might be. Nor was he ignorant of its full potential, particularly when it was being wielded in such an exceptionally competent manner.

Possibly no white man could have saved himself!

As always in time of great peril, the Kid reacted after the fashion of a Comanche *tehnap*;[3] and those very capable fighting men had few peers in any aspect of waging warfare.

By the time the flame of the muzzle blast was erupting from the shotgun's right hand barrel, the Kid was already going down in a diving forward roll. He heard the hissing as at least some of the nine buckshot balls flew near by, but he was unscathed. What was more, showing the superlative agility acquired in a lifetime of riding and coping with unexpected, or deliberate, departures from a horse's back, he ended the evasive action on his knees.

Up swung the old Dragoon Colt, grasped by both its owner's hands, until it was aligned with rock-like steadiness. Rearwards pressure on the trigger liberated the sear and the hammer whipped around to strike the base of the percussion cap on the uppermost nipple of the cylinder. Ignited by the spurt of fire that reached it, the fifty grain powder charge in the chamber thrust at and, to the accompaniment of an awesome bellow, ejected a ·44 calibre ball of soft lead from the seven and a half inch long barrel.

Flying true and entering between the would-be assassin's eyes, the bullet burst out again from the back of the head. Killed instantly, he was flung from his feet and his shotgun's second load erupted harmlessly into the air.

Letting out a yell to inform his *amigos* that he was not harmed, knowing that they – hearing the two kinds of revolvers had informed him that at least one more member of the floating outfit could be involved in the fracas around the corner – would be worried by the shotgun's second detonation coming *after* the sound of his Dragoon, the Kid rose and went to the back gate. One glance told him there was nothing to fear from the man he had shot. Standing to

3.*Tehnap:* an experienced warrior. An adolescent boy is a *tuinep*, a young brave a *tuivitsi* and an old man a *tsukup'*. As with the word *Pehnane*, these are the nearest phonetic spellings of the Comanche language. – J.T.E.

one side, he jerked open the gate and, after a moment, went through in a sudden bound that took him into the deep shadows thrown by the wall. Almost invisible in his dark attire, he stood and gazed around. Although he located two horses left in a clump of trees some distance away, there was no sign of other human beings. Concluding that the man he had killed did not have companions in the vicinity, he removed the key from the outside of the gate and returned to the rear of the mansion. Paying no attention to the coloured men who were emerging from the kitchen, he went to find out how his friends had fared.

'Sounds like Lon's got the other one,' Waco drawled, joining Mark as the Kid's *Pehnane* war whoop rang out.

'Sounds that way,' the blond giant agreed, then indicated the body of the second hired killer. 'Let's hope he took his alive enough to talk. This one's cashed in and wolf-bait.'

'Had I known that's what you-all wanted,' the youngster replied, 'having him able to talk, I mean, I'd've let him shoot you a couple of times while I was taking more careful aim.' A mischievous grin came to his face as his gaze flickered to his *amigo's* erstwhile strolling companion and he went on, 'Tell you though, Mark. I don't reckon you'll get to show the lady the "golden horseshoe nail" tonight.'

Swinging his eyes towards where a very bedraggled Charlene – who no longer looked attractive with her hair and gown ruined – was sitting waist-deep in the ornamental pond and spluttering furious profanities in French, the blond giant was inclined to agree.

'Way I figured it, there was only one reason why that foreign jasper's *amigos* needed to shoot him,' Waco said, hoping he was sounding more at ease than he felt with so many eyes on him. 'It was because they recognized Lon 'n' me, so didn't want us to find out who he was trying to hire us to kill.'

Half an hour had elapsed since the gun battle in the grounds of the mansion.

Displaying his usual competence and ability, Sheriff Timothy Farron had taken charge of the situation. Asking the other guests to return to the ballroom and continue with the reception, he had waited until they did as he requested before commencing his investigation. In the interval, he had arranged with Mrs. Frieda von Farlenheim for Charlene,

Comtesse de Petain, to be taken upstairs where she could get out of her sodden garments and bathe after her involuntary incursion into the ornamental pond.

When only the people involved remained, Farron had learned what happened. An examination of the dead men and search of their belongings had supplied little information. Nor had either the peace officer or the OD Connected contingent been able to identify them. There had been little the sheriff could do about learning who the pair were beyond arranging for a check to be made on the reward posters in his office and questions to be asked around Brownsville. He had decided to postpone both until after he had conducted an inquiry on the spot.

At Farron's request, Ludwig von Farlenheim had once again placed his study at the disposal of visitors. In addition to himself, the sheriff and his nephew, Alex, the Governor of Texas, the local justice of the peace, Dusty Fog, Mark Counter, the Ysabel Kid and Waco were present. When they were all seated, the sheriff had requested an explanation.

It had fallen upon a clearly worried Waco to tell of what had happened. For all his courage and capability, he found standing in front of such a distinguished assembly something of an ordeal. However, he had acquitted himself admirably. After having covered the events which preceded the shooting, apologizing to the sheriff for having left the scene before the arrival of the local peace officers, he had commenced to give his reasons for considering such an action was necessary.

'Do *friends* kill each other in this country?' Alex von Farlenheim put in, not caring for what he was hearing and hoping to cast doubts on the youngster's story. 'I mean isn't it more likely that whoever killed this man was his enemy?'

'He sure didn't act like they were,' Waco countered. 'As he was going out of the saloon, he started to wave to whoever he saw. Which I don't reckon he'd've done happen he got cause to reckon they were after his scalp.'

'I can understand that his companions, if *that* is what they were, would not want you to learn the name of the man he wanted killing,' Alex conceded, seeing that the rest of the gathering were accepting the story. 'But surely, having learned what he wanted you to do, you should have found out who he was.'

66

'That was what we aimed to do,' Waco explained, puzzled and irritated by the young Bosgravnian's attitude of thinly veiled hostility. 'Only we figured on getting him off some place where we could make sure he told us, whether he wanted to or not.'

'I don't know what it's like where you-all come from, *hombre*,' the Kid put in. 'But over here, some folks get sort of shy and backward when it comes to telling their names when they're trying to hire a killing done.'

'You said that the man was a foreigner, Waco,' Governor Stanton Howard remarked, feeling that an intervention was required. 'Have you any idea of his nationality?'

'Not for certain,' the youngster admitted. 'But he sounded like some of the Germans I've come across.'

'Have you any German enemies, Captain Fog?' Alex almost barked.

'Not that I know of,' Dusty answered, eyeing his challenger – and the way in which the question had been put made it seem like a challenge – speculatively for a moment.

'He might've been German,' Waco growled, indignant as always when considering somebody was showing disrespect to his hero. 'But the jasper who was with him dressed, looked and talked like a city feller from up North.'

'And what happened to this "fellow"?' Alex demanded.

'He left just after we'd finished fussing with the tinhorns,' Waco answered. 'Looked as if the other jasper was telling him to go and he didn't take kind to the notion, what I saw.'

'What made you-all think it was me this jasper wanted you to kill, Waco?' Dusty inquired.

'A lot of little things,' the youngster replied. 'He got to asking about whether we was bothered that you-all would be riled over the fuss and if we was scared of you. We started making it sound like we didn't cotton to you for a joke. Then we kept it up seriously when he asked if we'd kill for money, allowed the sheriff'd want to know who he had in mind. Thinking about how he was dressed, which was mighty fancy for a place like the Running Iron but not up here, after he was killed, I figured why he'd been made wolf-bait and there didn't seem anybody else he could be wanting gunned down.'

'But surely Captain Fog has many enemies who might want to kill him,' Alex protested, growing perturbed by the accuracy of the young blond's deductions. 'And, learning that he would be attending the reception, they would see the chance it would offer.'

'They might see it,' Dusty conceded. 'But getting a chance to take advantage of it's a horse of another colour.'

'How do you mean?' Alex inquired and he was genuinely puzzled.

'The deputies said that those two jaspers didn't come through the front gate,' the small Texan elaborated. 'And that the back entrance was locked and bolted on the inside.'

'It always is,' Ludwig von Farlenheim confirmed, as the small Texan paused and threw an interrogatory glance at him. He was puzzled by his nephew's behaviour, but put it down to nothing more than an over-inflated sense of superiority to the Texans. 'Amos attends to it every night and I've never known him to miss, much less would he on a night like this.'

'Then *somebody* had to let them in,' Dusty pointed out. 'Sure, I know that Lon found a key in the lock on the *outside*, but turning it wouldn't have drawn the bolts. That could only be done from the inside.'

'You insult my uncle's guests—!' Alex began, oozing indignation in the hope of diverting attention from such dangerously accurate reasoning.

'I don't see it that way!' von Farlenheim interrupted firmly, giving his nephew a prohibitive frown. 'And when somebody who I have invited is abusing my hospitality in such a manner, I want to know not only *who* but *why*.'

'That's understandable,' Alex admitted, taking the hint. Then, seeing another way in which he might discredit the theory, he went on, 'Perhaps the men were merely thieves and not hired assassins after Captain Fog's life. After all, it was Mr. Counter they saw in the garden.'

'That's true enough, Dusty,' the Governor agreed. 'Why would they try to shoot Mark if it was you they were after?'

'They could have been wanting to get rid of all the floating outfit,' the small Texan guessed.

'Or they made a mistake,' Mark went on and his gaze turned to the young Bosgravnian. 'The same one you made when you introduced me as Dusty to the *Comtesse*.'

'*Gott im himmel!*' Alex shouted, coming to his feet and, in his alarm, producing what could have been regarded as a natural reaction from one of his arrogant class who felt he

68

was the subject of an unjustified accusation. 'If you're saying that the *Comtesse* and I are—'

'Pull in your horns, friend,' Mark drawled, showing no concern over the other's menacing attitude. 'All I'm meaning is that somebody else could have heard what you told her and when I didn't say you were wrong, made the same mistake that you had about who I am.'

'It's happened before,' Dusty supplemented, drawing similar inferences as von Farlenheim had respecting the young Bosgravnian's behaviour. 'And, if those two hired guns didn't know me either, they'd go for the feller they'd been told was me.'

'Then it is a pity that they were both killed before they could be questioned,' Alex commented, drawing the only consolation he could from the whole affair. 'Now you may never know who hired them.'

'My ole Grandpappy Long Walker used to allow there's always a way a man can find out anything he wants to know,' the Kid drawled, sounding as mild and innocent as only he could. 'All he has to figure out where – and *who* to ask.'

'And *you* know where – and *who*?' Alex said, not offering to conceal his disdain.

'Let's put it this way,' the Kid replied, showing a similar dislike to anybody who knew him as well as his companions did, even if the young Bosgravnian failed to recognize it as such. 'Was I to want to find a preacher, I'd look in a church. Should I need a saddler, I'd go look for his shop.'

'So?' Alex asked, in what was nearer to a snort than a word.

'So happen I want to find me a hired gun when I'm in Brownsville,' the Kid elaborated, rising in a smoothly flowing motion. 'I know just where to go and look for him.'

CHAPTER SEVEN

AS SOON AS I SHOOT, KILL *HIM*

'*Saludos, Cabrito,*' greeted the burly Mexican bartender behind the counter of what had once been Francisco Castro's *cantina*, with such a friendly air that the welcome might have been genuine. His cold eyes went from one to another of the four Texan cowhands whose noisy arrival had led him to assume, wrongly he now decided, that they were drunk. 'It's good to see you and that you should bring your *amigos* as customers.'

'Tomás, *hermano*,' replied the Ysabel Kid, speaking the Mexican-Spanish border dialect just as fluently. 'Seeing's they are my *amigos*, this rat-hole's the last place I'd take them as customers.'

Having elaborated upon his cryptic comments regarding how to locate hired killers in Brownsville, the Kid had received unqualified permission to put his scheme into operation. As astute a peace officer as ever donned a badge, Sheriff Timothy Farron had raised no objections and offered whatever assistance might be required. He was aware that the methods to be employed were unorthodox, but were more likely to succeed than anything he attempted in his official capacity.

Even with the departure of its owner for a safer region, Castro's *cantina* still retained its usual clientele and continued to afford them certain safeguards necessitated by their unsavory ways of earning a living. Among the precautions were a circle of permanent watchers through which no local peace officer could hope to pass undetected and without having his presence in the *barrio*, the Mexican section of the town, announced before he could reach the establishment.

To circumvent the precaution, the four members of the OD Connected's floating outfit had arrived in a fashion intended to avoid arousing the look-outs' suspicions. Knowing that honest cowhands occasionally visited the *cantina*, they had ridden through the *barrio* openly. Of course, before doing so, Dusty Fog and Mark Counter had returned to Farron's house and changed into raiment suitable for the deception. Wearing their normal working clothes and armament, they had accompanied the Kid and Waco through the streets giving the impression that they were no more than a bunch of slightly drunk cowhands looking for fun.

Although the hour was close to midnight, Castro's *cantina* was still fairly well filled when the Texans entered. Its clientele, a mixture of hard-faced, well-armed Mexicans, white men and half breeds engaged in eating, drinking, gambling or otherwise availing themselves of the establishment's facilities, studied the newcomers with open interest that was not entirely free from hostility. However, a whisper announcing the quartet's identity passed around swiftly. So nobody, not even the garishly and scantily dressed girls who were mingling with the customers, either spoke or offered to approach as they walked across the room. After a quick stare, Tomás hissed something to his smaller assistant who turned and went through a door behind the counter that appeared to give access to a storeroom.

'Ha, *Cabrito*,' the bartender boomed, the joviality in his voice still not reaching his eyes. 'You *never* change. Always making with the jokes. Can I give you and your *amigos* a drink on the house?'

'Only if you wash the glasses you're going to put it in where we can see you and take a long pull out of the bottle yourself,' the Kid replied. 'Who-all's running the place for good old 'Cisco?'

'I am,' Tomás declared, taking a bottle of top quality bourbon from beneath the counter. 'Don 'Cisco made me his *jefe* when he left for Cuba.'

'I mean the *mero gallo*,' the Kid corrected. 'Which *you* don't have the brains to be, even though you're offering free drinks like you thought you was. Is the main boss in 'Cisco's office there?'

'I don't—!' Tomás began, darting a worried glance at a door at the right of the counter.

'If you don't know,' the Kid drawled. 'I reckon we'd best go and take a look.'

'Why don't you stay here and talk over old times with your amigo, Lon?' Dusty suggested. 'And you, Waco. It only needs Mark and me for what we've come to do.'

'Now that's a right smart notion,' the youngster stated, turning to stand with his back against and elbows resting on the counter. 'Was I asked, that is.'

'You *wasn't* and aren't likely to be,' Mark commented, then glanced at Tomás. 'Is it all right if we take a rain-check on that drink?'

'They'll have to,' Dusty warned. 'I don't go for the hired help drinking when they're working. Let's go and see the *mero gallo*, Mark.'

Giving a sigh of resignation, Tomás watched as the small Texan and the blond giant turned to the right and strolled away. He consoled himself with the thought that he had carried out the instructions he had been given earlier in the evening and had done all he could to prevent intrusion. It was now in other hands to deal with the matter. Furthermore, a glance at the Kid and Waco told him that he need waste no time nor effort upon trying to keep them placated. He would not even need to expend one of the drinks from the excellent bottle of bourbon as they were in no mood to appreciate it.

As Dusty and Mark were walking towards the door beyond the end of the bar, they studied the four men who sat around the table alongside it. From all appearances, the quartet were persons of importance. They were drinking from bottles of the best whiskey and *tequila*, while a like number of the most attractive girls the *cantina* had to offer moved away as the Texans approached.

Two of the favoured quartet were Mexicans. Big, power-ful, their unshaven and brutal faces were at odds with the elegant silver-filigree decorated *charro* clothes they wore. More in keeping with their villainous aspects were the plain wooden handled knives and Colt 1860 Army revolvers each had at his waist.

Of the other pair, whose origins were clearly north of the Rio Grande, the elder's attire was that of a professional gambler. Tall, slim, handsome in a pallid faced, black-haired fashion, he carried an ivory handled Colt Civilian Peace-maker in a well-made cross-draw holster on the right side of his waist-belt. He conveyed an impression of being capable of swift and deadly movement when necessary.

Not quite so tall, heavier built and maybe fifteen years younger, the second white man sported range country attire as smart and dandified as that worn by Mark. However, to experienced eyes, the blond giant's garb was strictly functional and the good looking youngster's tended to be more decorative, but there was nothing fancy about the black *buscadero* gunbelt which carried his low-tied brace of rosewood handled Artillery Peacemakers just right for a fast draw.

'Well howdy, Mr. Raffles,' Dusty greeted. 'How's Fort Worth these days.'

'No worse than usual, Captain Fog,' the older of the white men answered, watching the two Texans continue their steady advance, and making no attempt to rise. 'The "gentlemen's" room is through the door at the other end of the bar.'

'I'm right obliged for being told,' Dusty declared and nodded towards the entrance to the owner's office. 'Only I wasn't counting on finding any *gentlemen* in there.'

'That's lucky for you,' stated the younger white man, coming to his feet and placing his back defiantly against the door. 'Because Mr. Turtle told us he didn't want disturbing. Which Buck 'n' me aim to see he ain't.'

'Mr. Turtle, huh,' Dusty drawled, although seeing Buck Raffles had suggested the identity of at least one person in the private office. 'It'll be good seeing him again.'

'Only you ain't going to,' stated the younger man, oozing truculence. 'So you can just haul your short-arsed butt back to the bar, or get the hell all the way out of here.'

Studying the speaker as he and Mark came to a halt some fifteen feet away, Dusty drew pretty accurate conclusions. The young man's character and type was as plain as if he had it written in large letters across his chest. A typical range country hard-case, determined to build himself a reputation, he could be dangerous under the right conditions. Tough enough, although less so than he clearly imagined, he would regard any hesitation in dealing with him as being caused by weakness or fear. If he thought that, his truculence would increase.

One thing Dusty knew well. Where the young man and the other occupants of the bar-room were concerned, any hesitancy would prove fatal. So he had no intention of showing the slightest.

'He kin of yours, Mr. Raffles?' the small Texan inquired, in tones which implied commiseration if the answer should be in the affirmative.

73

'Name's Jack Sutter,' the gambler-dressed man introduced, easing himself erect and keeping both his hands ostentatiously in plain view. Glancing to where the two Mexicans were not yet duplicating his actions, he continued just as blandly, 'We're not kin, but we work for Mr. Turtle.'

'Only you're closer to being the boss,' Dusty drawled, making the comment a statement rather than a question. 'Which being, tell him to move aside.'

'You-all know what fellers his age are like, Captain,' Raffles answered. 'They just don't take to anybody *telling* them to do anything. You could try *asking* him to move, if you're so minded.'

'I could,' Dusty admitted. 'But he won't. Which you and I both know.'

'You can bet your sweet damned life I won't!' Sutter confirmed, taking two steps forward and halting on spread-apart feet, with his right hand rising to hover over the butt of the off-side Colt.

'You see what I mean, Mr. Raffles?' Dusty asked, not showing the slightest indication of being aware of the young hard-case's presence and menacing attitude. 'Now it's all up to you-all.'

'In what way?' Raffles wanted to know.

'I aim to go in and talk to your boss,' Dusty explained. 'And your *amigo* figures on using that fancy gun to stop me.'

'So?' Raffles asked.

'So I'm still going in there to see your boss,' Dusty declared, still in the same even drawl. 'Which I'd advise you-all to make him step aside and let me through.'

'I'd say that's up to him,' Raffles objected, knowing the younger man had designs on his job and wanting to find out exactly what kind of threat was posed.

'Have it your way,' Dusty drawled. 'Only bear this in mind. Happen he tries to stop me, I'll do the same to him. And that means gun-play. There's a real good reason why *you* don't want *that*.'

'What'd it be?' Raffles challenged.

'See Mr. Raffles there, Mark?' Dusty inquired, without taking his eyes from the younger hard-case.

'I see him,' the blond giant confirmed.

'Could be I'm going to have to throw down on his *amigo*,' Dusty warned. 'As soon as I shoot, kill *him*.'

74

'Yo!' Mark replied, giving the traditional cavalry assent to an order with no more show of emotion than if he was saying, 'Good evening' to a stranger.

Having delivered his order and had it accepted, in the silence that had dropped on the whole of the room, and could almost be felt, Dusty took a step forward.

Like most of his kind, Sutter was far from intelligent and used a fair ability at handling a gun to offset a lack of more desirable qualities. So, although he had listened to the conversation, he failed to understand all that it implied. All he knew for certain was that his challenge had been taken up.

Only not, apparently, by the insignificant person at whom it had been directed!

In some way which the young hard-case could not understand, the small Texan seemed to have taken on a size and heft until he loomed above the blond giant at his side and looked more what Dusty Fog should be.

Puzzled by the extraordinary metamorphosis, Sutter could think of only one thing to do. In spite of having a sneaking suspicion that he was making the wrong decision, he dropped his right hand to the butt of the holstered Colt.

And learned that the suspicion was valid!

Even before his companion commenced the hostile movement, Sutter anticipated it would happen and appreciated what effect it might have upon him.

Spending so much of his time in Dusty Fog's company, Mark Counter's full potential as a gun-fighter tended to go unnoticed by most people. However, Raffles was *not* among their number. While he had not been involved and no shooting occurred, he had been at the Bigfoot Saloon in Austin when the blond giant was compelled to throw down on the dangerous outlaw, Churn Wycliffe.[1] The movement had been carried out with the smooth, effortless-looking rapidity which set the truly fast apart from the average performer. Nor was it attained, or very rarely, without a corresponding accuracy in planting the bullets and Raffles did not think that Mark could be one of the exceptions to the rule. Furthermore, he would carry out the order given by the small Texan if the need arose.

With those considerations in mind, especially the latter, Raffles did not hesitate when he saw his judgement of how Sutter would react was justified.

1. Told in: RANGELAND HERCULES. – *J.T.E.*

As soon as the young hard-case commenced his draw, his companion kicked him behind the left knee. Thrown off balance as the leg buckled beneath him, his hand missed the butt of the revolver and he stumbled. Nor was he given a chance to recover his equilibrium.

Gliding forward swiftly, Dusty demonstrated the ambidextrous prowess which he had developed as a child to help distract attention from his lack of height. The right arm rose in a back hand blow which caught Sutter on the jaw and knocked him in a helpless spin from his feet. Simultaneously, the left flashed across to slide the off-side Colt from its holster. Its barrel turned from one to the other of the burly Mexicans as they belatedly tried to rise.

'Stay seated, *señores*,' requested the small Texan, although he no longer looked small to either of the men he addressed in their native tongue. 'There's no need for you to stand on our account.'

'In fact, we insist you *don't*,' Mark went on, also in Spanish, having verified the gambler's recollection of his speed by producing his matched brace of Cavalry Peacemakers almost as rapidly as Dusty's weapon had appeared. While the long barrel of one was lined on the larger of the Mexicans, the other was pointed at the centre of the white man's chest and he reverted to his native tongue, 'There's some would say what you-all did was a mite sneaky, Mr. Raffles.'

'I'd rather be sneaky than get shot,' the gambler replied, glancing around as there was a slight commotion along the bar.

At the first sign of trouble, Waco thrust himself from his lounging posture. Almost before he was fully erect, he had an Army Colt in either hand and his blue eyes searched the room for signs of hostility.

'This's private, folks,' the youngster announced, the cheerfulness in his voice underlaid by a grim warning.

'*Don't!*' the Kid commanded, still employing border-Mexican despite knowing that the man he was addressing could understand English, as he saw Tomás dart a look at something beneath and farther along the counter. His left hand grasped the bottle of bourbon by the neck and lifted it. 'I might just think you was after that old sawed-off shotgun you keep down there and whomp you on the head with this.'

For a few moments, the room fell even more silent and its occupants stood or sat as if turned to stone.

Then the door of the office opened and a man stared into the muzzle of the Colt which seemed almost to leap into Dusty's right hand.

Big, heavily built, the newcomer was clad after the fashion of a Mississippi riverboat gambler of the pre-Civil War vintage. His florid features had the bristling moustache and jolly look of a Bavarian innkeeper. However, as the small Texan knew, the joviality was more apparent than actual. Head of a family which had been prominent in law-breaking circles even before Texas had gained independence from Mexican domination back in 1836,[2] his name was Rameses Turtle.

Showing no sign of alarm at being confronted by Dusty's Colt, Turtle swung his gaze around the bar-room. He took in the sight of the men who were supposed to prevent intrusion. Three were covered by the small Texan and the blond giant, while the fourth sprawled dazed and helpless on the floor. Nor, if their constrained attitude was anything to go on, did any of the other customers seem any better able to lend a hand.

'Good evening, Captain Fog,' Turtle greeted, after having directed a scowl at and received a 'What else could I do?' shrug from his boss gun. 'Do you want to see me?'

'That's the general notion,' Dusty confirmed.

'Did you have to get rough to do it?' Turtle protested.

'That yahoo of yours wouldn't have it any other way,' Dusty replied. 'Now we can talk here, or inside. But *talk* we're going to. And I reckon you'd rather do it in private than where these good folks can hear.'

'It's just a point,' Turtle said, exuding a calm which he did not feel and doing what he could to prevent himself from too great a loss of face over yielding to what he knew was inevitable. 'But have you any *legal* authority to say you can insist on talking.'

'Shoot, I clean forgot!' Dusty answered, in tones of mock exasperation, twirling away his right hand Colt so he could extract and display a five-pointed star badge. 'Uncle Tim, Sheriff Timothy Farron of Cameron County to you-all, ap-

2. An example of this is given in: OLE DEVIL AND THE CAPLOCKS. The family continued to retain their prominence through the Pro-hibition era (1919–33) as is explained by inference in: 'CAP' FOG, TEXAS RANGER, MEET MR. J. G. REEDER, up until the present day. – J.T.E.

pointed us deputies at the request of the Right Honourable Stanton Howard, Governor of the Sovereign State of Texas. Happen you've a mind, you can come down to the jailhouse *now* and verify that he did.'

'That won't be necessary,' Turtle declared, knowing exactly what was meant by the emphasis placed upon the word '*now*'. 'I was just going to *invite* you in.' Telling the two Mexicans in their own language that *everything* was all right, the way he spoke clearly meaning more to them than the mere words expressed, he spoke to his boss gun in English, 'See to Sutter, Buck.'

'Sure, boss,' Raffles assented.

'Waco, Lon!' Dusty called, returning his second weapon to its holster and having his amigos duplicate his action. 'Don't figure on standing there propping up the bar all night. Come on with us.' His gaze flickered to the burly master criminal and he went on, 'It's surely hell trying to get good help these days, isn't it?'

'It is!' Turtle agreed, throwing another scowl at his employees. 'All right, folks, get back to whatever you're doing. Everything's fine.'

CHAPTER EIGHT

IT'S SIGNED 'BEGUINAGE'

'We're not interrupting anything important, are we?' Dusty Fog inquired, as he led his men on Rameses Turtle's heels into what was as much a luxurious sitting-room as a place of business.

'No,' the master criminal said shortly, walking forward.

Looking around, the Ysabel Kid found little had changed since his last visit. What was more, considering that Francisco Castro had fled the country to escape his and other people's vengeance, the furnishings and fittings had continued to be maintained in very good order. In fact, the whole room gave the impression of having been given a thorough cleaning recently.

The large desk in the centre of the room, which could serve as a dining table when required, was glossily polished. There was nothing on it except for a large glass ashtray with several butts and two half-smoked thick cigars, an open humidor and a gasogene.[1] Only two of the half a dozen comfortable upholstered chairs were pulled up to the desk. A tray with two empty glasses and a bottle each of the best quality *tequila* and bourbon was standing on the big, closed Chubb safe in the right hand interior corner. Underfoot, the thick carpet was what, in later years, would be termed 'wall to wall'. On each side, heavy drapes hung from ceiling to floor as if to cover the windows – none of which were visible – and ensure the privacy of whoever might be inside.

'Hey now,' the Indian-dark young Texan drawled, strolling almost leisurely towards the drapes which were suspended down the centre of the left side wall. 'Either this fancy carpet's new, or they managed to wash the blood off the old one.'

1. Gasogene: A figure 8-shaped glass vessel, the upper part fitted with a handle and nozzle like a modern day soda syphon. Gas generated by a mixture of acid crystals and soda passed from the upper into the lower chamber, which was three parts filled with water. This was aerated and used to mix with drinks. – *J.T.E.*

'Huh?' Turtle grunted, turning his head as he was on the point of taking the seat at the rear side of the desk.

'Maybe you-all don't know it – although I reckon you *do*,' the Kid drawled, indicating the wall with his left hand while the right twisted the Colt Second Model of 1848 Dragoon revolver from its holster. The amendment to his comment came as the startled expression which passed across the master-criminal's face informed him the news he was going to impart would not come as a surprise. 'Pappy 'n' me was in here with Belle Boyd just after the War.[2] And I'll swan if she didn't show us that this here curtain, or whatever you call the son-of-a-bitch, isn't just hung there to match the one on the other side. Fact being, there's a door behind it and, dog-my-cats, iffen every time I come in here some jasper don't come jumping out uninvited through it. Got me so jumpy, I sort of killed the last 'n'. And, to make sure it don't happen tonight, I reckon I'd best just toss a bullet through the curtain.'

'There's no call for *that*,' Turtle stated. 'The bartender came through to let u – me know you'd come in, but he'd better have gone back to his work by now.'

'I wouldn't want you-all to think I'm misdoubting you,' the Kid answered, reaching around to raise the edge of the drape and ensure the door was closed. 'Only it's like Dusty says, you can't get hard-working help these days.'

'What do you want, Captain Fog?' Turtle asked, sinking into the chair with an air of proprietorship.

'Well now,' Dusty replied, taking the seat opposite the master criminal while his companions formed a rough half-circle behind him so they could cover all the three entrances to the room. 'We came to see Castro's *mero gallo*, is he here?'

'What Cap'n Fog means, him being so well brought up and all,' the Kid drawled, 'is how come you're making yourself to home in here so comfy, Mr. Turtle?'

'For a good reason,' the master criminal answered coldly. 'This's *my* place. I'm the owner.'

'For how long?' Dusty inquired, as his uncle had not mentioned any change of ownership when being told of the proposed visit.

'What is it you want?' Turtle said evasively.

'How long have you owned the *cantina*?' the small Texan

2. Told in: BACK TO THE BLOODY BORDER. – *J.T.E.*

80

repeated, his attitude showing that he intended to be given the information.

'I've just now concluded the deal,' Turtle replied sullenly.

'With the gent who was drinking the *tequila* and helping you-all smoke all them fancy cigars?' Waco wanted to know, stepping forward and taking up one of the still burning pair. 'Whooee, Dusty. These're just like the real expensive kind Judge Blaze gets sent over from Havana.'

' 'Cisco Castro, as I live and breathe!' the Kid ejaculated. 'So that's why Tomás was so edgy. Good ole 'Cisco's come back from Cuba, has he?'

'Only for a *short* visit,' Turtle admitted, restraining himself from glancing at the back door.

'It'll be a whole heap shorter should we come up against each other,' the Kid warned, with an angelic mildness which caused the master criminal to wish that – in the interests of saving the purchase price for the *cantina* – he and the former owner would have the meeting. 'Only you-all can tell him that I'm not hunting his scalp – *yet* and, happen we get what we've come after, won't start so long's he's headed back to Cuba by sundown tomorrow.'

'I'll pass the word,' Turtle promised, having no doubt that the warning would be acted upon. 'Now, Captain Fog, I reckon we're both busy men. So how about telling me what's brought you here?'

'I want to know who hired those two *pistoleros* who tried to gun me down out to the van Farlenheim place earlier tonight,' Dusty obliged.

'*I* didn't!' the master criminal ejaculated, showing what the small Texan felt sure was genuine surprise.

'And *I* never thought *you* did,' Dusty declared. 'But I'd say it's pretty near certain that whoever did it came here to find his men.'

'Not through *me*,' Turtle insisted, still exhibiting a convincing sincerity.

'You got religion?' drawled the Kid sardonically.

'Not especially,' Turtle replied. 'Hell, I won't try to tell you that I *wouldn't* have fixed it – providing I could be sure you'd *all* go under and there was *no* way it could be brought back to *me*—'

'Mister,' Waco growled, incensed by the frank revelation. 'I could right easy get *not* to like you-all.'

'I don't know this young feller, Captain,' Turtle remarked, throwing Waco a quick yet all-embracing look and returning his gaze to Dusty. 'Is he good?'

'I'd put him close after Mark,' the small Texan replied. 'Which makes him a whole heap better than *anybody* you might throw against him.'

'Huh huh!' the master criminal grunted, sounding impressed. Then he shrugged and went on, 'Like I was going to say, young feller, I wouldn't lie. But I'm also way too old and wily a bird to let somebody come after you-all while I'm in town secretly to do a deal with 'Cisco Castro. Because I'd *know* that happen things went wrong, which'd be *real* likely with you floating outfit boys, you'd do just what you're doing now.'

'I'd sort of got that notion myself,' Dusty admitted.

'Unless you figured on running a double bluff,' Mark suggested, beating Waco to it by a fraction of a second. 'Had too good an offer to turn down and took it thinking that, should it go wrong, we'd think it like you told it. Only, afore you say so, I don't reckon it was that way either.'

'Could've done it to save paying Castro, though,' Waco drawled. 'Counting on ole Lon here drifting in and whittling his head to a sharp point with that itty-bitty toad-sticker of his'n.'

'You've got a real sneaky mind, boy,' Dusty said. 'Only—'

'Only, happen that'd been the way his trail drive was pointed,' the youngster finished for the small Texan. 'His boys'd've known to let us come through instead of trying to hold us off for so long that Castro had time to light a shuck out of the back door. So, should you-all be willing to forgive me for being that mistrusting, Mr. Turtle, could somebody've heard about your deal with Castro and figured on having it spoiled by getting us all riled at you for something *he'd* set up?'

'It could be,' the master criminal conceded, frowning pensively. 'Dink Sproxton's had his eye on this place for a spell and wanted to buy it.'

'And would the said Dink Sproxton be around town at the moment?' Waco inquired.

' 'Cisco and I've got boys out asking if he is and where he's at,' Turtle replied and a frown creased some of the joviality from his face. Moving towards the right side of his black cutaway jacket, his left hand paused as he realized he was doing something that could be misunderstood. 'Can I reach inside?'

'If you're worried about *me*,' the youngster grinned, realizing he had been the cause of the question. 'I don't reckon you'd be *loco* enough to take the wrong kind of thing out.'

'You've got a smart young feller there, Captain Fog,' Turtle praised, extracting and opening out a sheet of folded paper. There was a touch of admiration in his glance as he went on, 'This could have something to do with what you just now said—'

'Waco,' the youngster supplied to the unasked question.

'Waco,' Turtle repeated, then turned his gaze to the writing on the paper. 'It says, "Dear sir, as Europe's premier assassin, I have been employed to remove a certain distinguished personage who will soon be arriving at Corpus Christie. I trust that you will afford me the professional courtesy by refraining from accepting commissions of a like nature against this personage. I appreciate that this may incur you some loss of revenue, for which I tender my apologies. However, I would also point out that if the visitor should be killed by the crude methods you Americans invariably adopt, he is of such great importance that your Government will make the United States far too hot for similiar activities for a long period." '

'Writes real fancy, if a mite long-winded,' Waco commented, as the burly man paused to ascertain what effect the message was having upon his far from welcome visitors. 'I could be wrong, but it sounds to me like the jasper's saying, "Stay the hell off of my range." Only, happen that's what he's doing, I'd've figured him to warn you-all of what'd happen if you didn't.'

'There's a postscript,' the master criminal admitted, his admiration increasing with the further evidence of the youngster's astuteness. ' "If you doubt my ability to enforce what I assure you is a *demand*, the demonstration I have arranged at the Lone Star Hotel tonight will give you convincing proof of it." '

'We haven't heard of *anything* happening down to the Lone Star tonight,' Waco stated. 'Have we, Lon?'

'Nary a thing, boy,' the Kid seconded.

'That's because they don't let low, ornery young cusses and sneaky border smugglers in there,' Mark pointed out, breaking the silence during which he had been enjoying the youngster's handling of the questioning, and knowing that the establishment was Brownsville's most expensive hotel. 'But *I* haven't heard anything either.'

'Nothing *has* so far,' Turtle announced. 'When Tomás came and said that this's been found pinned to the kitchen door, I had 'Cisco send some of his *hombres* out into the *barrio* to see if anybody'd seen it being put there and told two of my boys to go find out what had come off at the hotel. Nobody'd seen who left the note—'

'Now hold hard there a dog-gone minute!' the Kid growled. 'Are you-all telling *me* that some fancy dude from Europe could come through the *barrio* even after sundown and nobody'd notice him?'

'I wouldn't have thought it possible myself, except that it happened,' Turtle replied, having considered that aspect already. 'And I don't reckon any greaser would've dared take the chore, or if he had he'd've let 'Cisco's *mero gallo* know about it. Anyways, one of my boys came back to say nothing had happened at the hotel. The other stayed on in case it did and he's not showed up so far.'

'Is there anything to say *who* wrote the letter?' Dusty inquired, extending his right hand as the master criminal offered him the document for examination.

'It's signed "Beguinage",' Turtle replied. 'But that doesn't mean a thing to *me*. Which means he's *never* worked in Texas, at least not under that name, or I'd've heard about it. And if he's – how's he put it – "Europe's premier assassin", I'd've likely got word happen he'd worked anywhere else in the United States. Anybody who's *that* good's sure to get talked about.'

'How soon do you-all expect to find out some more about this "Beguinage" *hombre*?' Dusty drawled, sounding almost casual, as he looked up from studying the neat handwriting and the excellent quality of the paper.

'I had one of my boys send a telegraph message to an *amigo* in New York,' the master criminal answered, the question having informed him – although he had already known – that not only the blond-haired youngster could draw accurate conclusions. 'And if he doesn't know anything, he'll pass the word to somebody in Europe who will.'[3]

'Like the "Ox", maybe?' the Kid suggested.

'Y— How the hell did y—?' Turtle spluttered, momentarily taken aback. Then his face became bland again and he nodded, 'Of course, it was you last year—'

'It was me,' the Kid agreed. 'I hope there wasn't no hard feelings towards Belle Starr come out of it.'

'So do I!' Mark Counter declared, his handsome face taking on a grim aspect.

'Not from me,' Turtle said reassuringly, having heard of the intimacy which existed between the lady outlaw and the blond giant.[4] 'And I passed the word to the Ox there'd better not be from him.'

'Gracias,' Mark drawled and, as he was confident that the warning would be respected by its recipient, he was willing to let the matter drop.

'You'll let the sheriff know what you hear, so he can pass it on to me,' Dusty put in, bringing the discussion back to current events rather than considerations arising out of the Kid's association with the international criminal known as the 'Ox'.[5] His words were a command rather than a request. 'We'll have pulled out before you hear, most likely.'

'Happen you-all shouldn't,' the Kid went on, in the deceptively angelic and mild manner which all of his audience knew meant that he had never been more in deadly earnest. 'Well, I'm sorry to hear about the fires.'

'Which fires?' Turtle inquired, seeing that the words had been directed at him.

'The ones I'll be calling around to light here,' the Indian-dark Texan replied, still looking and sounding as if butter

3. After an abortive attempt in 1858, the first successful telegraph cable across the Atlantic Ocean became operable in 1866 and a second, partially laid on the previous year was also brought into use. A third cable, linking the United States of America with France, was put down in 1869. Only fifteen letters a minute could be sent over the first cable and the minimum cost of a message was one hundred dollars. However, by the time of this narrative, in spite of every message needing to be handled by six different operators, the service had speeded up. According to Alvin Dustine 'Cap' Fog's researches, Turtle's message had been, 'Wish to buy Beguinage ferret,' what is ability, bloodline. If not known, consult European agents.' – J.T.E.

4. New readers can find more details of Mark Counter's association with Belle Starr in Footnote 6, APPENDIX TWO. – J.T.E.

5. The 'Ox'; Octavius Xavier Guillemot, see: THE QUEST FOR BOWIE'S BLADE. – J.T.E.

would have a hard job melting in his mouth. 'And at all your *other* places.'

'By golly!' Turtle boomed, with an amiability he was far from feeling. 'I think you'd do it, too.'

'Nope,' the Kid corrected. 'You know's sure's sin's for sale in Cowtown[6] I would.'

Unpalatable as the realization might be, the master criminal knew that he was hearing a plain statement of fact and not an idle boast.

While it did not attain the heights reached by Alphonse 'Scar-face Al' Capone in Chicago during the Prohibition era,[7] Rameses Turtle could claim to wield some considerable power in the Sovereign State of Texas at that time. While the Governor, Stanton Howard, and the majority of the senior persons at the captial were beyond his reach, he had control over a few reasonably influential members of the Legislature. He had also a limited number of civic and county officials who were dependent upon his bounty and so could be compelled to do his bidding. There were even a certain number of local law enforcement officers who had had so many benefits that they could not refuse to jump to his commands.

However, as Turtle grudgingly told himself, the same did not apply to the four undesired callers who had inflicted themselves so forcefully upon him. They had intelligence of a *very* high quality, in spite of their light-hearted comments, gun skill far beyond anything he had ever been able to hire and, as he had seen at first hand in the case of Dusty Fog[8] – or, by repute, where Mark Counter was involved – two at least had great competence in defending themselves with their bare hands. Although the Ysabel Kid also could do so if necessary,[9] he preferred more permanent and effective tactics if trouble should be forced upon him. Nor did the youngster, Waco, strike Turtle as being any less able to look after his interests in similar conditions.

Furthermore, the quartet were backed by a clan whose

6. 'Cowtown'; the colloquial name for Fort Worth, Tarrant County, Texas, at which Rameses 'Ram' Turtle currently had his headquarters. – *J.T.E.*

7. See: CAPONE, The Life And World Of Al Capone, by John Kobler, Michael Joseph Ltd., London, 1972. – *J.T.E.*

8. Described in: SET TEXAS BACK ON HER FEET. – *J.T.E.*

9. One example is given in the *'Little Throat-Cutter'* episode of CUCHILO. – *J.T.E.*

influence extended beyond the State's Legislature and Capital building at Austin. It reached to the very uppermost corridors of power at Washington, D.C., General Jackson Baines 'Ole Devil' Hardin might be permanently tied to a wheelchair, but he was still a major force to be reckoned with even outside the borders of the State he had taken a major part in moulding. His reputation for backing the men in his employment was well-earned and deserved.

In every *democracy*, the properly appointed and conventional law enforcement agencies are at a disadvantage when dealing with the intelligently guilty. Those very rules and regulations which were framed for the protection of the innocent were used by malefactors to avert the consequences of their misdeeds. There were many things a properly commissioned peace officer could not do where criminals were concerned, because if he did it would cost him his employment.

Such considerations did not affect the members of the OD Connected's already legendary floating outfit. Faced with a problem while they were acting as they did as Ole Devil Hardin's hands and feet, they were ready, willing and exceptionally able to apply whatever methods might prove necessary to attain their ends. They knew that, providing their cause was just, their grim-faced employer would bring to bear the full weight of his authority in their support.

Of all the members of the floating outfit, as Turtle was all too painfully aware, there was none more willing to cross the bounds of conventional white man's behaviour than the Kid. Once, on learning that a woman had ordered a hired killer to cut Dusty's throat and bring back his ears, that baby-faced quarter-Comanche had returned the man to her in that identical condition.[10]

So, if the Kid threatened to burn down Turtle's saloons should the need arise, he would keep that promise. Nor, with his *Nemenuh* training to help, would he be easily prevented from carrying out the threat.

'Thing is, Mr. Turtle,' Dusty commented, almost politely, indicating the sheet of paper. 'Do you-all think this *is* genuine?'

'It doesn't strike me that *anybody* would take the chance of doing it as a joke,' Turtle answered, making a mental note to pass on such details as his telegraph message produced. It

10. Told in: A TOWN CALLED YELLOWDOG. – *J.T.E.*

87

would not elevate him in the four young Texan's estimation, but it might save him considerable grief in the future if he complied with what he knew to have been an *order* and not a suggestion. 'But I'll tell you better *after* I hear what, if *anything*, happens down at—'

There was a knock on the door and it opened.

'Boss!' Raffles said, looking across the threshold. 'Joel's just come back from you know where.'

'And so do *we*,' Dusty said dryly. 'Which you can stop playing all cagey and tell us *all* what he said.'

'He doesn't know how, except that it sounded painful and bad,' the boss gun obliged after receiving a nod of authorization from his employer. 'But a feller's just now been killed at the Lone Star Hotel.'

CHAPTER NINE

I DO NOT THREATEN IDLY, BEGUINAGE

Charlene, *Comtesse* de Petain, was in a vile mood as she slammed the door of her temporary accommodation in Brownsville behind her. Taken all in all, she was anything but pleased by the way in which the evening's events had turned out.

Although Charlene had been granted every facility available at the von Farlenheim family's mansion, it was far from sufficient to repair the ravages caused by her involuntary plunge into the green and stagnant waters of the ornamental goldfish pond. Lacking the services of her capable and well-trained maid, who had taken advantage of her attending the reception to go out for an evening's entertainment, she had been unable to undo the effect of the dousing upon her previously immaculate hair. What was worse, without the aid of her make-up box, her face proclaimed her actual age and real nature far more accurately than was otherwise the case. Nor had all the ministrations it had received been able to render her sodden ball gown wearable. Being compelled to make use of a much less flattering garment belonging to her slightly shorter, considerably plumper and not so daring, hostess had done nothing to redress the undesirable state of affairs.

Nor had the thought that she would be required to explain what had happened in the garden at least once, but more likely several times, if she returned to the ballroom enamoured the *Comtesse* of the prospect. It was too much like twisting a knife in a wound for her to have to do so. What had made matters worse was her ever growing realization of how badly her plans had gone amiss.

Alex von Farlenheim's explanation of what had been revealed during Sheriff Timothy Farron's preliminary investigations had convinced Charlene of one thing. Attempting to usurp the task of the far more competent local man, Franz Zapt had set in motion the train of events which had ruined everything. Nor had the realization that, because of young Farlenheim's misconception, she had wasted time in luring the wrong man out to be killed made her feel any better disposed towards the world in general and her male fellow conspirators in particular.

Listening to the young Bosgravnian's boastful discourse upon how he had tried to circumvent and discredit Waco's summations, the *Comtesse* had been much less delighted than he had expected. Having revised her earlier belief that her faction would only be opposed by simple, poorly educated and uncouth yokels, she had been worried in case suspicions were aroused by his ill-advised behaviour.

On top of all else, Charlene was in no frame of mind to regard the smugly self-righteous, 'I told you so' attitude displayed by Walter Scargill with anything like the favour he had clearly anticipated. In fact, she had regretted her inability to come up with an excuse to avoid it when he had insisted upon accompanying her on her return to the Lone Star Hotel where they had adjoining rooms. Only an appreciation of how dangerous it was to leave him in the arrogant and hot-tempered von Farlenheim's company had prevented her from giving a direct and uncompromising refusal. After the way he was behaving and the hostility he had already aroused in the young Bosgravnian, there could have been an open confrontation without her restraining influence. Or at least, injudicious comments could have been passed to worsen a situation which was already quite bad enough.

In the interests of averting further problems, it had been mandatory for Charlene to let Scargill travel in the carriage which the von Farlenheims had put at her disposal. However, despite having led him on in the past, the last thing she had wanted under the circumstances was to have him try to force his attentions upon her. So, on reaching the hotel, she had pleaded fatigue after what had happened and, without as much as a kiss on the cheek as a reward, left him and entered her first floor quarters.

Gazing around, the *Comtesse* found that apart from a sheet of paper that had been placed upon the gossamer-thin nightgown her maid had laid out ready for her return, everything seemed to be exactly as when she left. Stalking across the room, she picked up the paper and noticed that it was written very neatly in French.

'*Comtesse*,' Charlene read. 'I know that you are a money-hungry bitch and have been promised the estates of Baron Goeringwald as payment for your endeavours in the plot to overthrow the house of Relphstein, but I have been employed to assassinate the Crown Prince Rudolph of Bosgravnia. I do not tolerate opposition, nor competitors, in the work I am paid to carry out. As you value your life, leave the task to me. You will soon have proof that I do not threaten idly. Beguinage. P.S. To show I bear you no ill will personally, the one I have selected is he who is of least use to the furtherance of your scheme.'

On reading the signature on the letter, the *Comtesse* felt as if she had been touched by an icy hand and she barely paid any attention to the postscript. Not only had she believed that her aspirations towards ownership of the third largest estate in Bosgravnia were a secret shared only by two other people, she had heard of 'Beguinage'.

The knowledge was not such as to allow the message to be discounted as nothing more than a joke, or an attempt to produce an over-dramatic fright.

Nobody had ever lived long enough to describe, or identify, Beguinage!

As Charlene knew all too well, there was no more cold-bloodedly efficient and deadly professional assassin in Europe.

Even as that alarming thought was striking the *Comtesse*, before she could even start to wonder from whence Beguinage had obtained the confidential information, much less located and gained access to her room, the scream of a man in terror rose from next door.

Being anything but pleased over his curt dismissal by the *Comtesse* de Petain, Walter Scargill's temper was little better than that of hers during the journey from the von Farlenheim family's mansion. Putting all the fury of his outraged ego into slamming the door of his room, he glared around him. The mess in which he had left his quarters had been tidied up by a conscientious maid. She had put his clothing and other property away, but on the bed were two items which had not been in the room when he had set off for the reception. However, the condition he was in prevented him at first from noticing the additions.

As always when the drinks were free, Scargill had imbibed

more than was good for him and he had a poor head for liquor. However, while drunk, he was not so bad as he might have been. Estimating his character accurately, the von Farlenheim's butler had signalled to the other attendants. Not only was his source of supply reduced, but the drinks with which he was served were much weaker than those being supplied to the other guests.

Never the most considerate of men towards those of a lower social status, except where his writing was concerned, Scargill peeled off his jacket and dropped it on the floor as he slouched towards the bed. Divesting himself of his cravat, collar and shirt in the same way, he came to a teetering halt.

For a moment, Scargill stared uncomprehendingly at the two foot square wooden box upon the bed. There was a sheet of paper resting on its lid. Slowly his eyes managed to focus at the words printed neatly on the paper.

'Please accept this tribute to a man many regard as the new Charles Dickens,' Scargill read.

Picking up the paper, the young man stared owlishly at it. While he concurred with the writer's summation of his abilities, it never occurred to him to wonder who might have delivered it and the present. His sole interest was to discover the nature of the gift. Allowing the document to slip from his fingers, he gave the box a shake in his eagerness to raise its lid.

Even before the box was open and the light from the lamp overhead flooded in, there was a rustling sound followed by a hissing which reverberated from the wooden container almost like a railroad engine discharging steam.

If Scargill had been less drunk, he might have had a better understanding of what he saw in the box. It looked like a fat, pulsating, loosely coiled piece of rope that was brownish in colour, but slashed with lighter bars and blotches. Then one end of it rose into an S-shape and shot forward so swiftly that the eye could barely follow the motion.

A flattish, diamond-shaped head rushed towards Scargill's right arm. Between the eyes and the nostrils were the twin holes, giving access to the heat-locating Jacobson's organ, which gave the *Crotalidae* snakes the title, 'pit-vipers'. The coloration and absence of the warning rattle would have told a more knowledgeable person that it was a copperhead, accounted by many authorities as the most lethal of its viviparous kind, and not a rattlesnake. It had a full measure of all the qualities which made the *Viperidae*, to which the sub-species belonged, the most efficient of the venomous snakes.

Unlike the *Elapidae* – which included the cobras, kraits and mambas – whose neurotoxic poison killed by paralysing the action of the victim's heart and lungs, the hemotoxic venom of the *Viperidae* destroyed the blood cells and ruptured the blood vessels. However, the latter's mode of injection was vastly superior. The majority of the *Elapidae* could only open the mouth to about forty-five degrees and needed to chew on whatever was being bitten, so that the poison could flow in via the grooves in the short, modified teeth. On the other hand, the jaws of the *Crotalidae* in particular could gape to a good *one hundred and eighty* degrees. This allowed the long fangs – which were folded back when not in use and operated like hypodermic syringes – to stab in deeply and inject the noxious fluid instantly. Also, unlike a cobra which could only strike at a downwards angle, the pit-vipers could attack in almost every direction including straight up.

Pure instinct rather than any conscious appreciation of what was happening brought a reaction from Scargill, but it was not the wisest one he could have made. A shriek of horror burst from him as he felt the fangs burying themselves into his forearm. Snatching back his hand, he dragged the copperhead from the box. His attempts to shake it off merely made a desperate situation worse. Like all of its kind, the snake could regulate the amount of venom it discharged and, having no wish to waste the limited supply, had only delivered what it considered sufficient for its needs. Feeling its captive struggling, it did not release its hold. Instead, it tightened its jaws and, as the man staggered across the room screaming in horror, sent more of the deadly liquid through its fangs.

Although the commotion brought several of the hotel's other guests to the door of Scargill's room and, in collapsing, he dislodged the copperhead, he was as good as dead long before any help could reach him.

On being told what had happened, Charlene retreated to her quarters. She was shaking with fear as she burned the note she had found.

Beguinage's promise of supplying proof had been fulfilled.

'So you don't know of any reason why anybody would want to kill Mr. Scargill, ma'am?' Sheriff Tim Farron asked.

'I'm afraid that I do not know, *m'sieur*,' Charlene de Petain replied, glancing from the peace officer to Dusty Fog in a none too successful attempt to discover what they were thinking. When granting the interview, she had decided her attitude should be that of a member of the nobility who, in spite of being distressed by the evening's events, was willing to render every assistance to the forces of law and order. 'Of course we are little more than chance acquaintances. We had never met until we were on the ship coming here.'

Just under an hour had elapsed since Walter Scargill's screams had aroused the other occupants of the Lone Star Hotel.

Summoned from his home, where he had gone to change into more suitable clothing for the performance of any duties which might arise out of his nephew's activities, Farron had hurried to the hotel. His arrival was shortly after the four members of the OD Connected's floating outfit had come on the scene. Already there, the town marshal had done the preliminary work. The copperhead snake had been killed and, along with its victim, removed from the premises. All the guests had been induced to return to their rooms and order was restored.

Taking charge of the situation, the sheriff had listened to the marshal's report and Dusty's description of what had occurred at Francisco Castro's *cantina*. Then he had set about organizing the investigation into Scargill's death. Knowing that Mark Counter, the Ysabel Kid and Waco had all served as peace officers and were competent in such work, he had assigned them to help the marshal in trying to discover how the poisonous reptile had been brought into the building. Then he and his nephew had gone to interview the *Comtesse*. They had found her awake and, although haggard in appearance, she had expressed her willingness to be questioned straight away rather than in the morning.

'Did he mention that anybody might be wanting to take his life, ma'am?' Dusty inquired, studying the woman's face with as great an interest as she had examined his own.

'Not in so many words,' Charlene replied, conscious of the scrutiny and, having drawn very favourable conclusions with respect to the small Texan's intelligence, not caring for it. 'Of course, like all these liberal-intellectuals, he probably believed that the sinister secret police of what they refer to as the "Establishment" were after him. He did hint of it, I seem to remember.'

'Huh huh!' Dusty grunted non-committally, producing two documents he had been concealing behind his back and holding them towards the woman. 'Then I shouldn't reckon there's any chance you'd know this handwriting?'

Having all too unpleasant recollections of an identical sheet of paper, it took every bit of the *Comtesse's* will power to accept the two she was being offered. Nor could she refrain from glancing at the ashtray in which she had dropped the burned remnants of the letter she had received from Beguinage.

'I've never seen i—' Charlene began automatically, then realized that the small Texan was following the direction in which she was staring. 'That was a rather indiscreet letter an – admirer, but *not* Mr. Scargill, sent to me. I thought it should be destroyed.'

'It's often the wisest thing to do, ma'am,' Dusty conceded, in a flat and neutral voice and held out his hand.

'As I said,' the *Comtesse* went on, just a trifle hurriedly, wanting to divert the two men's thoughts from the ashes and her explanation. Instead of returning the documents, she made a gesture with them. 'I don't recognize the writing, but I may still be able to help you. It is my belief that, like myself, whoever wrote them was French.'

'*Both* of them, ma'am?' Dusty said, deceptively mildly, knowing that the letter delivered to Rameses Turtle was underneath and she could not have read the signature.

'Aren't they *both* from the same person?' Charlene countered, alert for traps and sufficiently recovered to think with her accustomed rapidity. 'As the paper appears to be identical, I assumed they were.'

'They are, ma'am,' the small Texan confirmed, still in a lazy drawl which gave no indications of his true feelings. 'Why'd you-all think the writer's French, like you?'

'French, almost certainly, but hardly of *my* class,' Charlene corrected stiffly, drawing herself up and becoming every inch the offended *grande dame*. 'The writing is the standard script taught mainly in Jesuit schools to those who will become clerks, or take up similar occupations. I'm afraid that *I* did not have such an education.'

'Is "Beguinage" a French name, ma'am?' Farron put in, when his nephew made no response, making the word sound like, 'Begu-in-age'.

'Begu—?' Charlene began, guessing what the sheriff had tried to say despite his pronunciation of the name.

'That's how the letter's signed, your ladyship,' Dusty pointed out.

'Ah!' the *Comtesse* ejaculated, wondering if the small Texan's apparent politeness and employment of the incorrect honorific was really sarcasm. Failing to decide, she made a needless examination of the second sheet. 'It is pronounced, "Beg-win-*arsh*", *m'sieur*. Yes, it *could* be French, but I've never known *anybody* who was called it. Certainly poor Walter never mentioned it to me. It is so unusual I would not have forgotten.'

'French, huh, not German?' Farron asked, then looked at his nephew. 'They found who that *hombre* down to the Running Iron Saloon was, Dusty.'

'Which man is this, *m'sieur*?' Charlene inquired, in spite of having a good idea.

'A German called "Zapt", ma'am,' the sheriff replied. 'He was killed as he left the saloon, right after he'd tried to hire two of Dusty's own cowhands to kill him.'

'Good heavens!' Charlene gasped, her left hand fluttering to her breast in a convincing display of 'horror'. 'So much shooting and killing. No wonder they call this the "Wild West". But this Zapt could not be Beguinage, could he?'

'If he was,' Dusty drawled. 'He surely didn't act like "Europe's premier assassin", which is what he claims to be in the letter.'

'The letter?' Charlene repeated, with well simulated innocence. 'Oh! You mean this *other* one. To whom was it sent? I don't need to ask about the one on top.'

'It went to a man called Ram Turtle,' the sheriff explained, as the *Comtesse* started to read the second message. 'You wouldn't know hi—'

'*Sacré bleu!*' Charlene yelped, genuinely surprised by the warning and knowing some reaction would be expected. 'But this – this threatens to assassinate Crown Prince Rudolph of Bosgravnia when he arrives in Corpus Christie!'

96

'You-all didn't know he was coming, ma'am?' Dusty drawled.

'Of course I knew!' Charlene snapped, her irritation growing more obvious. 'Really sheriff, I find this suspicion very annoying!'

'I wouldn't call it suspicion, ma'am,' the small Texan objected, looking even smaller and more insignificant. 'It's only that I'm a mite slow in picking things up.'

'That was *very* well done, Captain Fog,' the *Comtesse* praised. 'But I'm afraid I know *your* reputation too well to be fooled. However, to satisfy your curiosity, we of the European *nobility* usually know where we are going. Besides, I have the honour of Rudy's – His Highness, Crown Prince Rudolph's acquaintance.' She darted a coyly conspiratorial glance at the men as she made and corrected the 'error', continuing. 'It was not kept a secret that he would be coming to hunt in Texas. In fact, that is why I am here.'

'You arranged to meet him,' Dusty guessed.

'Not in so many words,' Charlene corrected. 'But he gave me to understand that my presence would not be unwelcome.'

'Have you-all any notion why Mr. Scargill came over here, ma'am?' Farron inquired. 'Was it to meet the Prince?'

'I shouldn't imagine so,' the *Comtesse* replied. 'His kind want to overthrow all kings, princes and established Governments to take over the ruling themselves.'

'His *kind*, ma'am?' Dusty prompted.

'Surely you met him?' Charlene challenged.

'Nope,' the small Texan countered. 'I didn't have time to do much socializing at the reception.'

'Then you have read his books, no?' Charlene asked.

'No, I can't say I have,' Dusty confessed, although he could have guessed at the content of the dead man's works.

'They are filled with "social conscience" and descriptions of the evils of class distinctions and hatred of everybody who has something he has not,' Charlene explained, with a bitterness that was not completely assumed. 'In fact, it was rumoured around Paris that he is – or *was* – involved with a group of international anarchists. I thought that might have been why he came to the United States, to escape from them, or the police.'

'Like you said, he's not the kind of jasper who'd get invited to meet somebody like the Prince,' Dusty drawled.

'Only he might have had notions to make him the *late* Prince. Which being, that Beguinage *hombre* strikes me's the kind of old he-bull who doesn't take kindly to anybody else stepping on his range.'

'I don't under—!' the *Comtesse* commenced, then brought off another of her simulations of enlightenment bringing horror. 'Good heavens! Do you mean that this Beguinage creature thought poor Walter intended to try and assassinate Rud – his Highness – and murdered him to stop him?'

'That's how it looks to me,' Dusty stated. 'How'd you-all read the sign, Uncle Tim?'

'I reckon I'll float my stick along with you, Dusty,' Farron declared. 'That being so, and as the Countess can't tell us anything more, we'll leave her to get some sleep. Would you-all want me to have a deputy stand guard outside your room tonight, ma'am?'

'Do you think that Beguinage might come after me?' Charlene gasped, then gave a shrug. 'But what reason would he have to do so. I promise you that I have no desire to kill Rud – His Highness. Rather the *opposite*, in fact.'

'Then you *should* be safe enough, ma'am,' Dusty drawled, taking back and pocketing the letters. He picked up and donned the hat he had removed on entering, going on, 'Good night, ma'am. Thank you for being so understanding.'

'That's all right,' Charlene replied, wondering if there had been any significance behind the slight emphasis on the word 'should'. 'I only wish I could have been more help. Perhaps I would feel safer if I knew you had a man outside, *m'sieur.*'

'I'll have one there and another covering the window from the alley, ma'am,' Farron promised, also donning his hat. 'Let's go, Dusty.'

The hopes that the two men were nourishing of being able to compare notes ended as they left the room.

'I was just coming to fetch you-all,' Mark Counter declared, striding along the passage followed by Waco and the Kid. 'Ram Turtle just sent Raffles to tell us that they've found Dink Sproxton, but are leaving him for us to handle.'

Listening at the door, Charlene felt alarm. If Sproxton was captured alive by the peace officers and induced to talk, he would expose her as the person who had commissioned him to hire the men sent to kill Dusty Fog – and more!

98

CHAPTER TEN

BEGUINAGE'S DONE IT AGAIN

'Well, yes sheriff,' agreed the night clerk of the Seamen's Temperance Hotel, staring sleepily from the peace officer who had disturbed his slumbers to the four young men in cowhand clothing. 'We *do* have a guest answering that description, but *his* name isn't "Sproxton".'

'It wouldn't be "Smith", for shame?' the Ysabel Kid asked dryly.

'I'll have you know this isn't *that* kind of hotel, young man!' the clerk protested, his plump – if bleary-eyed – features registering righteous indignation. 'Mr. Abercrombie is a most respectable gentleman, if a Catholic, of temperate habits and would *never* think of bringing a woman to—'

'It's all right, Mr. Warbanks,' Sheriff Timothy Farron put in soothingly, being aware that the hotel prided itself upon maintaining a high standard of morality and catered mainly for members of the seafaring fraternity who neither drank nor womanized after the fashion of many of their contemporaries. 'My deputy didn't mean anything. Which room is – "Mr. Abercrombie" in?'

On being told by Buck Raffles where Dink Sproxton could be found, although not by what means the discovery had been made, the peace officer had waited only long enough to arrange for a watch to be kept on the quarters of Charlene, *Comtesse* de Petain. Then he had set off with the members of the OD Connected's floating outfit to carry out what he hoped would be an informative interview.

As he had explained to Dusty Fog, Mark Counter, the Ysabel Kid and Waco, Farron could understand why Sproxton would select such a hiding-place if he wished to avoid making his presence in Brownsville known. For all the desk clerk's protestations, 'Mr. Abercrombie' was anything but respectable. Nor, generally, was he of temperate habits and if he did not bring members of the opposite sex to the hotel, it was for convenience rather than because of a disinclination towards such company.

'W – Why do you want to know?' Warbanks asked querulously, having worked in less salubrious establishments and knowing what such a visitation by peace officers frequently portended.

'We want to ask him a few questions,' Farron replied.

'B – But can't it wait until morning?' the clerk wanted to know.

'Time's way past midnight, friend,' Waco drawled. 'It's morning already.'

'This can't wait,' the sheriff went on. 'Which room is he in, *please.*'

'N – Number Six, along the corridor at the end and back,' Warbanks supplied, having noticed the way in which the peace officer's last word had been uttered. Sheriff Farron was liked and respected by law-abiding citizens all through Cameron County, but he was known to be very determined in the performance of his duties. 'Shall I come and announce you?'

'Last gent like you's did *that* for us got his head blowed off,' warned the Kid.

'Wh – What—?' the clerk gobbled, fright replacing the indignation.

'Go back to sleep and leave it to us, Mr. Warbanks,' Farron requested, darting a disapproving frown at the Indian-dark Texan. 'We'll try not to make too much of a disturbance, but the man you know as "Mr. Abercrombie" is a dangerous criminal and we have to take him unawares.'

'A *criminal*?' the clerk repeated, aghast at the thought of such a person gaining admittance to the hotel. Then he stiffened and went on in a firmer tone, 'Do you want me to give you a pass-key, sheriff?'

'No thanks,' Farron replied. 'He could be a light enough sleeper to hear the lock click and wake up.' Turning his attention to the cowhands, he displayed his knowledge of the geography and layout of the town's business premises by continuing, 'Number Six is a corner room, with two windows. One at the back and the other on the alley. You and Waco take them, Lon. We'll give you-all five minutes to get into place.'

'Yo!' the Kid assented, appreciating that there was no time for levity.

So did Waco, but as he and his companion were setting off, he could not resist remarking, 'You'll notice who-all gets sent out into the cold night air, *amigo*?'

'Why sure,' agreed the Kid. 'Only, like you-all told the gent behind the counter so knowing, it's morning now.'

'That only makes it *worse*,' the blond youngster pointed out. '*Morning* air's even worse'n night air. Especially when it's *this* early in the morning.'

In spite of their light-hearted comments, the sheriff had not the slightest misgivings over the task to which he had assigned the Kid and Waco. He knew that he could rely upon them to behave responsibly and intelligently once they set about their duties. Any doubts he might have had would have been removed by seeing them separate on reaching the street. By taking the longer route, the Kid would reach the rear window without having to pass the one in the alley and perhaps disturb the man they were after.

Taking out his watch, Farron glanced at it. Then he nodded reassuringly at Warbanks. Shaking his head sadly, the clerk continued to lean on his desk and stared along the passage towards Number Six.

'Let's go,' the sheriff ordered, returning his watch at the end of the five minutes. 'I'll be first in.'

'Mark and I've worked together, Uncle Tim,' Dusty objected. 'Let us do it.'

'This isn't the time, or place to argue, sheriff,' the blond giant went on, before Farron could protest.

Going by his considerable experience as a peace officer, the sheriff knew that the two young men were making good sense. So he nodded his concurrence. Approaching their objective, each had drawn and cocked a Colt before arriving. Crossing to the opposite edge of the passage, Mark watched Dusty halt at the right and Farron go to the hinged side of the door.

Receiving a nod from his *amigo*, the blond giant strode forward swiftly. Turning ahead his left shoulder, he drove it into the centre of the door with all the weight of his enormously muscular, two hundred and twenty pound frame. Instantly, there was a screeching as the hinges' screws were torn from their settings and the bolts burst asunder, followed immediately by the crackle of wood being splintered.

However, in spite of having been successful in opening the door, Mark found himself in a potentially precarious predicament. Before retiring for the night, the occupant of Room Six had augmented the security offered by the lock and bolt with the back of a chair rammed under the door's handle.

Although the force of Mark's charge not only tore the door from its hinges, but caused the legs of the chair to buckle and crumple, the collapse was not complete. Carried onwards by his impetus, he was tripped and felt himself going down. His training and the instincts, developed by a lifetime of riding, allowed him to partially control the fall; but he knew that he might be in considerable danger from the man they had come to interview.

At such a moment, a peace officer's very existence depended on having a competent partner who could be relied upon implicitly to take the appropriate action.

Dusty Fog was all of that!

Hearing the destruction of the chair and correctly deducing what it implied, the small Texan realized that his *amigo* was almost certain to be in difficulty. So, even as Mark was being precipitated across the threshold, he went into action.

Almost before the blond giant was landing on the floor, Dusty sprang to the left over him and into the room. No less aware of the situation and its ramifications, the sheriff followed in an identical fashion except that he leapt in the opposite direction. On alighting, each of them was slanting his weapon towards the bed. The way they had behaved was intended to confuse the occupant and, brought from sleep by the commotion, render him uncertain as to which of them posed the most immediate threat.

Laudable as the precaution had been, it proved needless.

The room was in darkness, but some light came in from the passage. Sufficient, in fact, to illuminate the bed – and the motionless figure sprawled half in, half out of it!

'What the hell?' the sheriff growled and, despite considering there would be no need for caution, advanced without relaxing his vigilance.

'Are you all right, *amigo*?' Dusty inquired, also walking forward.

'Don't worry,' Mark answered to the small Texan's back, coming to his feet. 'I've only bust three ribs and both arms.'

102

But I should be able to keep anybody who we've woke up from interfering.'

'Good for you,' Dusty called back over his shoulder, keeping his attention upon the man on the bed. Then his gaze went to a glass which lay alongside the motionless figure's hand and he asked, 'Is it Sproxton, Uncle Tim?'

'Looks like him,' the sheriff replied, taking out a match and lighting the bedside lamp. Having done so, he knelt and raised the corpse's head. For a moment, he could barely recognize the agony-distorted and almost empurpled features. Lowering the head, he nodded grimly. 'It's Sproxton all right. But he sure didn't die peaceably or natural. Fact being, I'd say Beguinage's done it again.'

'All the windows in the room were closed and fastened, as well as the door being locked, bolted and having a chair stuck under the handle,' Sheriff Timothy Farron told the men who had gathered by his request at his home. 'According to the desk clerk, nobody came looking for Sproxton and he didn't see any strangers. Which there're two ways Beguinage could've got in without needing to pass the desk, even if he'd been at it all the time.'

In spite of the lateness of the hour, the peace officer had conducted the preliminary investigation into yet another murder which had presumably been perpetrated by the European professional assassin they knew only as 'Beguinage'. Beyond discovering that the cause of death had almost certainly been poison administered in a bottle of wine, which was standing half empty on the bedside table, he had learned nothing to help him locate the killer. Realizing that it was unlikely any more could be achieved at that time, he had decided to call it a day. While accompanying the four young Texans to his home, he had passed on all he had learned about the 'German' who was shot outside the Running Iron Saloon. He had also promised that he would not bring together the others who were interested before noon, so that the quartet could get some sleep. There had been no objections raised to his suggestion.

At the appointed time, the men who were requested to attend had arrived and were seated in the sheriff's sitting-room. With one exception, they were the same group who had come together following the abortive attempt to assassinate Dusty Fog the previous evening. After Ludwig von

Farlenheim had apologized for the absence of his nephew without realizing that the small Texan for one was pleased about this, Farron had told of Sproxton's murder and what little had been learned about it.

'Waco,' Governor Stanton Howard said, at the conclusion of the sheriff's far from informative narrative. 'What do *you* make of it?'

'Well, sir,' the young blond answered, blushing just a trifle as every eye turned his way. He threw a glance redolent of, 'Why *me*?' at Dusty and, squaring his shoulders slightly, went on, 'Way I see it, any *hombre* up to what Sproxton was in town'd be mighty careful who he opened his door to; particularly after dark.'

'Nobody's gainsaying *that*,' the sheriff declared, when the youngster paused.

'So he'd have to know whoever it was could be trusted, or figure so,' Waco elaborated. 'Which, happen Turtle told us the truth about Beguinage never having worked in Texas – and I don't reckon he was lying, for once – that seems to cut him out. Does, or *did*, Sproxton have him a regular and steady gal down here?'

'I've never heard of one,' Farron admitted. 'Fact being, he had a reputation for casting a wide loop and not tying into any gap permanently.'

'Not that it means anything, though,' the youngster sighed. 'I'd say a woman of any sort'd be apt to get herself noticed and remembered in that kind of holier-than-thou place.'

'What're you getting at, *amigo*?' Dusty asked, the term 'boy' being reserved for when only the other members of the floating outfit were present.

'Only that this whole damned game's got me licked to a frazzle,' Waco confessed. 'He was killed in his room, with all the windows and doors fastened on his side. Which I know whoever gave him that poisoned wine didn't need to be on hand when he drank it, but he'd have to be pretty damned sure he could trust 'em afore he'd pull the cork, or even get close enough to hand it over.'

'Have your men found where the bottle came from, Tim?' the local justice of the peace inquired, having no doubt that such a point had not escaped the sheriff's notice.

'Nope,' Farron replied. 'There wasn't a label on the bottle, nor anything to even suggest where the wine came from. I've had a *Chicano*[1] friend look it over. He allows it could be a local brew, but without tasting it there's no way he can tell for sure and he couldn't do *that*.'

'Depends on how good a friend he is whether you'd tell him to or not,' the Ysabel Kid remarked, then became serious. 'This "Beguinage" must be one hell of a smart son-of-a-bitch, though. He goes through the *barrio* without *anybody* noticing him. Then he gets an *hombre* who likely wouldn't trust his own mother to open up 'n' take a bottle of wine from him. All I know is, that's one jasper I'd hate like hell to have riled up at me.'

'Maybe Beguinage is Spanish,' von Farlenheim suggested. 'If he is and was dressed in the right clothes, he could go through the *barrio* without attracting attention.'

'Trouble being, the *Comtesse* de Petain allows the way he writes makes her think he's French,' Farron pointed out. 'Of course, the Jesuits run schools in Spain. But my *amigo*'s looked over both messages and allows it's not their style of script.'

'Talking about the *Comtesse*,' Dusty put in, grateful for the opportunity to satisfy his curiosity and not in the least surprised to have found out that his uncle had had the documents checked by somebody who would know the difference in styles between French and Spanish educational methods. 'How'd she and Scargill get to be invited to the reception?'

'Don't tell me that you suspect *her*?' von Farlenheim barked.

'I've got no reason to,' Dusty said, so blandly that he might have been speaking the truth. 'It's just that he didn't strike me's being the kind of man who she'd go around with.'

'There's no accounting for taste,' von Farlenheim growled, having wondered about the same thing. 'Anyway, she came over on the *Atlantic Star* with my nephew. At least, Alex got to know her on the boat. When my wife heard he had, she insisted that he invited her. When she said that she'd made arrangements to have dinner with Scargill, Frieda told her to bring him along.'

'She couldn't't've been mixed up in it,' the local justice of the peace protested. 'Why she could've got killed along with Mark out in the garden.'

1. *Chicano*: a native of Texas who was of Spanish, or Mexican, parentage. – *J.T.E.*

'Huh huh!' Dusty grunted, making use of a non-committal sound he had frequently found useful. Then, with the air of one who wants to change a subject, he looked at von Farlenheim and continued, 'Has your nephew come over to help set up the hunting trip for the Prince?'

'Not exactly,' the burly man answered, looking embarrassed. Then he gave a shrug of resignation and went on, 'This is confidential, of course, gentlemen, but Alex is here under something of a cloud. He got in some trouble. Not too serious, but it caused him to have to resign from the Bosgravnian Military Academy. His father sent him here in the hope that he might ingratiate himself with the Crown Prince, or that a successful hunt organized by me would persuade His Highness to have Alex reinstated.'

'Let's hope that we can give him one then,' Dusty drawled. 'Have you-all heard of a feller called Franz Zapt?'

'I can't say that I have off-hand,' von Farlenheim replied, showing relief over the matter of his nephew having been shelved. ' "Zapt" is a pretty common name in Bosgravnia, though, like "Smith" over here. In fact, as far as I can remember, that's what it means in true Bosgrav, although the more generally used language spoken there is German. Does he say he knows me?'

'He's not doing any talking at all now,' the Kid commented dryly.

'That's the name of the man who tried to hire Lon and Waco to kill me,' Dusty elaborated.

'The one who was killed outside the Running Iron Saloon?' asked the justice of the peace. 'How'd you find out who he was, Captain Fog?'

'I didn't,' Dusty corrected. 'Uncle Tim told me.'

'I had my deputies start asking around town,' the sheriff explained, as the others looked at him. 'They traced him to the Seamen's Temperance Hotel. The trouble was by the time they did, somebody – it might have been the feller from up North he'd checked in with and who's lit a shuck² out of town – had gone through his room and taken everything

2. 'Lit a shuck': left, generally hurriedly. In trail drive, round up and other night camps, 'shucks' – dried corn cobs from which the grains had been removed – were available to supply illumination for anybody who had to leave the firelight and walk in the darkness. As the 'shuck' burned quickly, a person using one had to move fast if he wanted to benefit from the light it gave. – *J.T.E.*

that would've identified him, or told us what he was up to. We only found out who Zapt was because the day clerk's German and, hailing from near Bosgravnia, had recognized his accent and got to talking with him, but not about anything that helped.'

'Do you know anything about the other man, Tim?' asked Howard.

'Only that he signed the register as Gustav Breakast, of Newark, New Jersey,' Farron answered. 'I've telegraphed the police there to ask if anything's known about him, but haven't had a reply yet.' His gaze flickered to his nephew and he grinned. 'Which, afore it's brought up by any of you smart-alicky young Rio Hondo varmints, I've seen what Ram Turtle had to tell. Allows he doesn't know the name, but he'll ask around and see what he can find out. That could maybe come out more than the Newark police'll know. Had him along to look at those two *pistoleros*, too. Give me their names, for all the good it'll do and said he'd try to learn who they was working for.'

'From what I've heard, Ram Turtle isn't usually *this* obliging to the law,' the Governor remarked. 'Don't tell me he's seen the light at long last.'

'Not so much *seen* it, sir,' Waco drawled, throwing a glance at the Kid. 'He just doesn't take to the notion of having it touched off – under where he's sitting.'

'I think I'd rather *not* know what *that's* supposed to mean,' Howard stated, having heard something of the tactics Ole Devil Hardin's floating outfit had employed on occasion when dealing with recalcitrant or unco-operative malefactors. 'The thing is, gentlemen, what can we do about preventing this Beguinage – whoever he is – from trying to carry out his assignment?'

'We'll have to find out who he is and where he is before we can do anything about stopping him,' the justice of the peace declared. 'Which shouldn't be all that difficult. There can't be all that many foreigners freshly arrived from Europe around town.'

'Not too many,' Dusty agreed, but with reservations. 'Which's why we're likely too late to catch him.'

'How do you mean?' the justice of the peace demanded.

'Happen we're smart enough to have figured it out that way, you can bet he has too,' the small Texan replied. 'And, seeing's how he's done what he came here for, there's no

107

reason for him to stay on and take a chance of being found out.'

'Hell, yes!' Waco ejaculated, following his *amigo*'s train of thought and cursing himself silently for having failed to draw a similar conclusion.

'But he *hasn't* done what he came here for,' the justice of the peace protested, puzzled by Dusty's line of reasoning. A large, plump, capable man of staid appearance and demeanour, he did not approve of the Governor associating in such a free and easy manner with the OD Connected's hired hands and hoped to show that they, the youngest in particular, were not infallible. 'His Highness hasn't even *arrived* here yet.'

'No, sir, he hasn't,' Waco conceded, having deduced that he did not meet with civic official's approval. 'Fact being, from what *I've* been told, he isn't coming to Brownsville at all.'

'Hot damn, you're right!' von Farlenheim ejaculated, slapping a big hand against his thigh. 'He's landing at Corpus Christie and will be heading north after the hunting trip. It was never intended that he'd come here. All the arrangements, your official reception for him, Governor, and the rest, are to take place up at Corpus Christie.'

'Probably Beguinage didn't know that,' the justice of the peace suggested.

'If he *didn't*,' Waco drawled, refusing to be deterred by the official's coldly disapproving glare. 'He's not as smart as he's *proved* he is. Or the folks he's working for haven't told him all they *know*. Which *they're* likely to have done. So, was I asked, I'd say he *knew* the Prince wasn't coming here.'

'Then why did *he* come?' demanded the justice of the peace, intrigued despite his misgivings.

'To warn, scare, or kill off anybody else who might have the same notion where the Prince was concerned,' Mark Counter suggested, seeing the point his *amigos* had been making which was still – apparently – eluding the local man.

'Or who had the know-how to get it done for somebody's didn't know this neck of the woods well enough to fix it themselves.' Waco supplemented. 'Which's why he left the message at 'Cisco Castro's *cantina*, it being a place where hired guns and such can be got to and taken on.'

'You mean that he thought just giving the warning would

frighten somebody like Castro off?' the justice of the peace asked.

'Maybe not scare 'em so bad they'd go hide in a dark corner,' the youngster replied. 'Could be's he'd got word that Castro 'n' Ram Turtle was meeting up and talking trade over the *cantina*. So he figured neither of 'em'd want a fuss that'd raise too much dust and, 'specially after they'd seen what he could do when he'd a mind, they'd take what he said to heart and do like he asked.'

'And killing Scargill wouldn't "raise too much dust", as you put it?' the justice of the peace challenged.

'Not so's it'd blow over *them, sir*,' Waco answered, his voice taking on an edge even if it was only obvious to the other members of the floating outfit. 'There wasn't anything to tie the killing in with them, or so he figured. What he didn't count on was Ram Turtle showing *us* the letter.'

'I'll tell a man that there Beguinage *hombre's* one real lively son-of-a-bitch,' drawled the Kid, wanting to turn some of the civic official's attention away from the youngster. 'Going around warning off Ram Turtle 'n' good old 'Cisco Castro. Then after he's made wolf bait[3] of that Zapt jasper who was—'

'Hold hard there, *amigo!*' Waco commanded. 'Let's us have some good old Texas fair play. We can't go blaming Beguinage for *that*. Unless I'm wrong, I'd say it was Dink Sproxton who did it.'

'You've likely got good reasons for saying it,' Farron stated. 'Why him?'

'*Somebody'd* hired those two yahoos who tried to gun Mark down, thinking he was Dusty,' the youngster explained. 'Which doesn't seem to be Beguinage's way, he likes something with less chance to it. And, seeing's how it wasn't Ram Turtle or Castro's did the hiring, that sort of sets Sproxton on top of the deck to be dealt. For one thing, he was living at the same place's Zapt and that Breakast jasper. Then he'd likely recognize Lon and me when he saw us with Zapt and know that having us asked to gun Dusty down was going to blow the whole shebang apart at the seams. Which, being newly arrived from Europe 'n' all, it's not likely Beguinage would, smart's he is.'

3. 'Made wolf bait': cowhand term meaning to kill. Derived from the practice of shooting an animal and, having poisoned the carcass, leaving it as a means of ridding a range of wolves. – *J.T.E.*

'That sounds like pretty good figuring to me,' the sheriff conceded, hoping that the justice of the peace would take the hint. 'But why'd he kill Scargill. Not just to prove a point to Ram Turtle, surely? Wiping out Dink Sproxton'd've been a better way of doing *that*.'

'The *Comtesse* allowed that Scargill was a liberal-intellectual suspected of being in cahoots with European anarchists,' Dusty reminded his uncle, wanting to avoid having his own thoughts mentioned upon the subject of who the Englishman's murder had been intended to warn. 'Could be he was tied in with those soft-shells[4] who're plotting to take over Bosgravnia. So Beguinage put him under to scare off the rest of them.'

'It could be,' Farron agreed. 'His room'd been gone through and everything that might've told us anything taken. At least, the maid who went in to turn down his bed allowed somebody'd been in and tidied it up after she'd left, which makes it look that way. I'll tell you, one way and another, that Beguinage's a real bad *hombre*.'

'He is,' the Governor seconded, nodding grimly. 'And, I don't care *how* it's done, I want him *stopped*.'

'Dusty,' Mrs. Farron said, entering the room with a buff-coloured telegraph message form in her hand. 'This has just come for you.'

'Damn it!' the small Texan ejaculated, after reading the message. 'I was afraid *this* might happen. There's some trouble come up back to home and Uncle Devil wants me to go help take care of it. You and the boys will have to handle things here, Mark, but I'll have to head for home this afternoon.'

---

4. Soft-shell, derogatory name for a liberal-intellectual. – *J.T.E.*

CHAPTER ELEVEN

YOU BOYS GO AND STOMP HIM GOOD

'Beguinage, *Beguinage!*' Alex von Farlenheim snorted, glaring almost contemptuously at Charlene, *Comtesse* de Petain, as they were walking towards the open doors of the big stable at Kelly's Livery Barn with the intention of hiring horses to go for a ride. 'To hell with him and his warnings. *I'm* not afraid of him, no matter who – or *what* you say he is!'

'Then you're a bigger fool than I thought!' the woman spat back, speaking the young man's native tongue with considerable fluency. Although she was afraid of Beguinage, after the convincing demonstration given by Walter Scargill's murder, she did not care to be reminded of her fear. 'And *do* try to hold your voice down to less than its usual roar. There may be somebody inside who speaks German.'

Only an early riser when there was no other choice, Charlene had still been in bed when von Farlenheim arrived at the Lone Star Hotel shortly before noon. Disturbed by the events of the previous night, although she felt neither regret nor grief over the Englishman's death, she had slept badly. In fact, she had only dropped off as the first light of dawn was creeping into the sky. So her first inclination had been to send word for the visitor to go away. However, wanting to find out if there had been any further developments, she had changed her mind. Deciding that she would prefer to hear of these in privacy, she had decided against asking the Bosgravnian to her rooms. Instead, she had suggested that they went for a ride and put themselves beyond the reach of possible eavesdroppers.

Having donned what she considered to be suitable raiment, after having the ravages of the previous night repaired by her maid's ministrations, the *Comtesse* had joined von Farlenheim in the lobby of the hotel. Immediately she had revised her intention of taking lunch before leaving. Showing

111

a complete lack of tact and common sense, he had started to discuss what had happened to Scargill in a loud and carrying voice. Realizing that Beguinage might be a guest in the hotel and within hearing distance, she had insisted that they set off immediately. Eager to gain whatever information he might have to supply, she refused his offer of collecting mounts from his uncle's mansion and insisted that it would be quicker to hire horses at the nearest livery stable.

Listening to von Farlenheim as they were walking to the livery barn, Charlene had regarded what he was saying with mixed feelings. While pleased at having an opportunity to talk with him, she felt that he might have occupied his time more advantageously in accompanying his uncle to the meeting at the home of Sheriff Timothy Farron. Like her own, the young Bosgravnian's sole sentiments over Scargill's murder were that he might have left some incriminating documents in his room. However, from what her maid had said while attending to her make-up and hair, she had guessed that any he had had in his possession were found and carried off when – apparently tidying up the mess he had left while working – Beguinage had conducted a thorough search prior to leaving the lethal 'present'.

'He was right about one thing,' von Farlenheim had remarked, when Charlene mentioned the contents of the note she had received as part of her description of the events preceding Scargill's death. 'He did get rid of the one who was least use to us.'

'In one way,' the *Comtesse* had replied. 'But with him gone, we won't have such a readily available scapegoat upon whom to lay the blame for the Prince's assassination.'

'We can still make it look like the work of his anarchist scum,' von Farlenheim had stated. 'After all, we know that they too want His Highness dead and are hoping to do it while he is hunting over here.'

If Walter Scargill had been alive to hear that part of the conversation, he would have been mortified and infuriated. Far from having won over the beautiful French aristocrat with his personal charm, he had been no more than a dupe she was leading on to take the blame for the assassination.

There had been a further irritation, although at the same time it was also some slight consolation for Charlene when she listened to what von Farlenheim had to tell her about the killing of Franz Zapt and Dink Sproxton. While she found it interesting, there were aspects which aroused her contempt and anger.

Showing more initiative than the *Comtesse* would have given him credit for, the young Bosgravnian had risen early that morning to conduct inquiries. He had visited the pre-arranged rendezvous to which the man they knew as 'Gustav Breakast' had been sent the night before by Sproxton. From 'Breakast', the representative of a criminal organization based in New York which had been hired by her associates to provide local assistance, he had found out what had led up to the shooting of his countryman.

Assigned by the leaders of the conspiracy to work as a go-between, Zapt had grown impatient on hearing that Sproxton was having difficulty in obtaining the men who were needed to kill Dusty Fog. He had announced to 'Breakast', after Sproxton had left to resume the search, that he would attend to the matter personally. Unable to dissuade him, or even to stop him dressing in a manner which would allow him to lurk in the grounds of the von Farlenheim family's mansion without arousing suspicion, the New Englander had taken him to the Running Iron Saloon in the belief that he would be unable to achieve his purpose there. When it had seemed that he might, 'Breakast' had gone to fetch Sproxton. On the local man identifying the proposed 'hired killers', they had both considered it was vital that Zapt be silenced before he could say too much.

'Breakast' had declared that there was nothing more he could do in Brownsville with Sproxton dead. As he had warned from the beginning, the only other source known to him was Francisco Castro's *cantina*. Acting upon the owner's instructions, its *mero gallo* had already declined to become involved. When the proposal had been put, without the exact nature of the affair being disclosed, he had said that his employer was engaged upon negotiations which were so delicate it was considered inadvisable to have the local law enforcement agencies aroused. He had also intimated that grave exception would be taken if anything untoward oc-curred and caused Sheriff Timothy Farron to start an inves-tigation. Announcing that he was leaving for Corpus Christie and would start making arrangements there, 'Breakast' had promised he would do all he could to learn Beguinage's identity before the arrival of their quarry.

113

It had been the further reference to the mysterious and deadly efficient professional assassin, or rather Charlene's expression of her misgivings and concern, which had provoked the bitter exchange.

Hoping to learn something informative, the *Comtesse* had asked if von Farlenheim could suggest which of their associates might have gone behind their backs and hired 'Europe's premier assassin'. He had been unable to suggest anybody, stating that he attached no importance to the appointment. When she had tried to point out the danger of having such an obviously selfish and determined person involved in their affairs, he still had been inclined to shrug the matter off. Her attempts to point out that Beguinage's participation could not be dismissed so lightly had aroused all his feelings of masculine superiority.

Never one to yield submissively to displays of male condescension, particularly when it originated from a person she considered to be of inferior status and far less intelligence, Charlene had angrily flared back. She knew it was neither tactful nor wise to do so, but she had been unable to resist.

'Whee-dogie, Simp, Dickie-Boy!' a drawling and somewhat slurred male voice said, as the couple were entering the stable far from on the best of terms. 'Will you-all just look at the shape of that gal there.'

Clad in a manner suitable for attending the 'meet' of any fashionable European 'hunt', the *Comtesse* was aware that she presented a most attractive sight. Coming to a V-shaped point at the front, the tight fitting bodice of her Wedgwood-blue riding habit was buttoned from the bottom to its high, rounded neckline without concealing the contours of her magnificent bosom and slender midriff. Its straight sleeves had turned-back cuffs closed by two silver buttons and was edged with a white lace frill that was matched around the neck and along the front to the top of the voluminous skirt. She had on thin black leather gloves and carried a riding-crop. Encircling the base of her masculine black silk top hat, a muslin veil dangled down the back and was pinned for security to her waist.

While Charlene had never been averse to finding herself the object of male admiration, she had no liking for hearing it expressed in such an open and inelegant fashion. That was even more the case when the person who had made the comment clearly belonged to what she regarded as being a far lower class of society to her own.

Like the pair to whom he had spoken, the man who had passed the remark was a young Texas cowhand. Tall, reasonably well made, tanned and moderately handsome, his general appearance suggested – as did that of his companions – he had spent the previous evening enjoyably if not wisely.

Slightly shorter, but somewhat more heavily built, the other two had a family likeness about their rugged features. Not only did they and the speaker convey the impression that they were slightly the worse for drink, but the state of their clothing suggested it had been worn while they were sleeping on the straw of the empty stall from which they were emerging. Some of their impromptu bedding still clung to their garments and even over the revolvers each had holstered on his belt.

'She sure's hell's real pretty to look at,' confirmed the elder of the men who had been addressed, ogling Charlene with the air of one who was conveying a compliment.

'I'll tell you-all though, Brother Simp, Okie,' commented the younger, confirming the sibling link suggested by the pair's features, looking at von Farlenheim. 'I've *never* seen a feller's was's fancy got up's that 'n'.'

'Whooee-hoo!' chortled the older brother, now turning his derisive gaze to the Bosgravnian. 'Ain't *he* the fairest flower on the green prair-ee?'

A dull flush of anger came to von Farlenheim's cheeks at the words. Apart from the white straw 'planter's' hat, purchased shortly after his arrival as being suited to the local climatic conditions, the way in which he had dressed that morning was the epitome of European male equestrian fashion. He considered that the tight-fitting, waist long and skirtless brown jacket, frilly bosomed white silk shirt, maroon cravat of the same material, figure hugging white riding breeches and well-polished Wellington boots[1] set off his manly physique to its best advantage. So he took grave exception to the way in which he was being discussed. It was

1. 'Wellington boot': used in this context, not the modern rubber, waterproof variety, but the style of footwear – with the legs extending to knee-level at the front and cut lower at the rear – made popular during the Napoleonic Wars by Arthur Wellesley, Duke of Wellington (1769–1852) – *J.T.E.*

not an attitude he considered seemly, nor was willing to accept, from an untidy and obviously drunken trio of what he regarded as obvious peasants and underlings.

'For whom do you work?' the Bosgravnian demanded, stalking forward with a military precision and slapping his riding-crop angrily against his right thigh with each alternate step.

'How's that again, fancy pants?' Okie inquired, taking a couple of long strides away from his companions and running a disdainful gaze over the elegant European riding attire.

'God damn it, are you deaf?' von Farlenheim barked, his bearing such that it would have aroused alarm if directed against a peasant from his homeland who would have known that incurring an aristocrat's wrath could bring about instant dismissal. 'I want to see your master.'

'Now *that'd* be right difficult,' Okie stated, showing not the slightest apprehension over the request nor the approaching man's threatening demeanour; effective as it would have been against a Bosgravnian peasant. 'The son-of-a-bitch hasn't been *born* yet.'[2]

'Schweinehund!' von Farlenheim bellowed, in his best parade ground manner. He was so infuriated by the mocking reply and the sniggers from the brothers that he lost all control of his never too even temper. Still speaking in his native tongue, he went on, 'You need a lesson in respect for your betters!'

Raising his right arm, the young Bosgravnian increased his pace. It was his intention to supply the lesson with his riding crop. His decision was opening the way for him to discover a very important difference between the United States and his homeland. What he failed to realize was that he would be dealing with a different kind of man from those he was accustomed to before he had crossed the Atlantic Ocean.

Despite the various reforms which Crown Prince Rudolph was instituting – they were the main cause of two en-

2. The author does not claim that this conversation was the basis of the joke told by the late – details of his death are given in: THE PROFESSIONAL KILLERS – Deputy Sheriff Thomas Cord, of the Rockabye County Sheriff's Office, which is recorded in Part One, 'The Sixteen Dollar Shooter' of THE SIXTEEN DOLLAR SHOOTER, but it could be. – *J.T.E.*

tirely different factions' desire to depose him[3] – no peasant would have dared to do other than accept a blow from one of the aristocracy, or at the most back away from it. Retaliation would have been unthinkable, as any attempt would have resulted in even more severe punishment.

So von Farlenheim did not anticipate the response he was about to receive.

In spite of being unable to understand German, watching how the young Bosgravnian was behaving, Okie realized that chastisement was intended against his person. Throwing up his left hand deftly, he pushed aside the other's arm as it was directing the riding crop at his head. Having done so, displaying an equal precision in taking the offensive, he shot out his clenched right fist.

Hard knuckles impacted with some force against the centre of von Farlenheim's face. They snapped back his head and turned what should have been a vengeful advance into an involuntary retreat, with blood gushing from his nostrils. Managing to retain an upright posture, but only at the expense of dropping the riding crop, he succeeded in bringing his withdrawal to a halt after taking about half a dozen paces. Instinctively, he raised his right hand to the source of the pain. Glaring at the blood which he had wiped on to the back of it, he let out a howl of almost animal-like fury and charged into the attack again.

Once more, the tactics proved ill-advised!

Side-stepping von Farlenheim's bull-like rush, Okie drove a punch into his stomach and folded him at the middle like a closing jack-knife. Then, pivoting with a grace that was at odds with his earlier more languid movements, the cowhand delivered a kick to his rump and sent him sprawling face downwards into the empty stall.

'You boys go and stomp him good!' Okie requested of the brothers, who had moved aside to let his victim pass. Jerking his thumb over his shoulder, he gave a chuckle filled with lechery and continued, 'I'll just go on over there and get better acquainted with that fancy-looking gal.'

3. The faction supported by Charlene, *Comtesse* de Petain and Alex von Farlenheim were opposed to the reforms, which would reduce their domination over the working classes, and the liberal-intellectuals had no wish for a beneficial régime as this would reduce their chances of stirring up the population against the ruler and Government as a prelude to gaining control themselves. – *J.T.E.*

117

Watching the cowhand as he turned and started to cross the barn, Charlene felt alarm. She was prepared to defend herself with some of the very unladylike methods she had learned during her impoverished and tomboy formative years.[4] However, having seen how effectively he had dealt with von Farlenheim, she realized it was not going to be that easy. In fact, she could find herself in serious difficulty and in a situation over which she had no control. Not only was she, the Bosgravnian, and the three cowhands apparently the only occupants of the building, but she had not noticed anybody in the vicinity. Nor was there a human habitation close enough for her screams of help to be heard.

Nearer came the leering cowhand!

Sucking in a breath, the *Comtesse* gripped her riding crop tighter!

'Maybe the lady doesn't want to get better acquainted, *hombre!*' said a drawling, yet hard and threatening voice from the doorway at the left side of the barn. 'So why don't you-all go look for some calico-cat who might reckon you're worth knowing?'

After the way in which she had been tricked the previous evening, Charlene had never thought she would want to as much as hear Mark Counter speaking again. Yet, listening to the way he was addressing the approaching cowhand and looking at him as he stepped across the threshold, she felt a surge of relief. No matter what happened next, her safety was assured.

Curiosity caused the *Comtesse* to remain instead of taking flight immediately. While grateful for the blond giant's intervention, she still felt bitter over the way he had led her astray and helped to ruin her scheme to remove Dusty Fog. So, before taking her departure, she wanted to see what punishment might be inflicted upon him.

'What the—?' Okie yelped, coming to a halt several feet away from the woman. His head snapped around to stare at the newcomer.

'Hey now!' Simp growled, lurching to confront Mark. 'Just who in hell do you-all reckon you're talk—?'

Moving with speed similar to that he had displayed when drawing his Colts at Castro's *cantina*, but horizontally instead of towards the ivory butts, the blond giant shot out his

4. And had not forgotten how to carry out, as is shown in: BE-GUINAGE IS DEAD! – *J.T.E.*

hands. They clamped on and bunched up the front of the elder brother's calfskin vest in a way which immobilized his arms. Then he felt himself being lifted, swung and released so that he hurtled across the barn. Running into and tripping over a bale of hay, his progress was halted more abruptly than he would have wished. However, every cowhand was an accomplished horseman. So he contrived to break his fall and land without injury.

'Why you big son-of-a—!' Dickie-Boy howled, jumping forward.

Family loyalty demanded that the assault upon Simp was avenged, but the way in which the younger brother went about it was ill-advised. His furious comment served to warn the intended victim of his intentions. Which was no way to achieve success when dealing with a man of Mark's ability.

Having turned his back on Charlene, Okie had seen how easily the blond giant coped with Simp, and doubted whether Dickie-Boy would pose any greater problem than his sibling. So, on seeing that his judgement was correct, and realizing that he would be the next recipient of the interloper's attentions, he dropped his right hand to the butt of his low-tied Colt.

Deducing what the second of the brothers was up to – but unaware of what was happening behind him – Mark set about countering the threat. He made a swift turn. Not only did it bring him face to face with his would-be assailant, but it gave an added impetus to the way his right arm was swinging around. Meeting the oncoming cowhand, the back of the clenched fist sent him in a rapid, twirling spin after his brother. For all that, in one way at least, Dickie-Boy might have considered himself fortunate. Possibly because of the speed with which it was delivered, the blow caught him at the top of his arm. If the contact had been made against the side of his head, he might have suffered a serious injury. As it was, in following Simp over the bale, little harm was done. He did, however, alight on his brother in a way which obviously left them too winded and stunned to rise and resume hostilities.

Ever a fast thinker, Charlene realized that the blond giant was not to receive the thrashing she had hoped to see administered. So her first inclination on noticing what Okie was up to was to let him go ahead. It was revised

119

immediately. Considering the intelligence and capability shown by Dusty Fog, she felt that it would not come amiss to have a source of information close to him. Either as a willing accomplice or as an unsuspecting dupe, provided she would win Mark over, he would fill the requirements admirably.

But not, the *Comtesse* told herself, if the cowhand in front of her did what he clearly intended.

With that in mind, Charlene stepped forward and her right hand whipped around. Her speed of thought was demonstrated in a practical way by the target she had chosen. Deciding that Okie's leather vest would offer greater protection, she aimed the lash of her riding crop across the somewhat tightly stretched seat of his Levi's pants. Coming so unexpectedly, the blow elicited a yelp of pain which was followed by a savagely profane exclamation and he made as if to turn back upon his assailant.

'Hold it there!' Mark commanded, his right hand dipping.

To the *Comtesse*, it seemed that the long-barrelled Peacemaker appeared in the blond giant's grasp out of thin air. More experienced, Okie needed only the sight of the weapon being directed his way and the sound of its hammer being drawn back to fully cocked to produce an instant compliance.

'That's better,' Mark declared. 'Tell the lady you're sorry and go 'tend to your *amigos*.'

'Sorry, ma'am,' Okie responded sullenly, rubbing at his stinging rump with a cautious hand, then went to the bale of hay.

'Thank you, Mr. Counter,' Charlene said, walking forward. Her gaze went to where von Farlenheim was rising, his face smeared with blood, in the empty stall. 'Why, Alex, you're hurt!'

'Where are the swine?' the Bosgravnian demanded in his native tongue and lurched forward with his fists clenched.

'Over there,' Mark replied, guessing rather than understanding what had been said. 'But, was I you-all, I'd leave 'em be and go have a doctor look at your hurts.'

'Good heavens, yes,' the *Comtesse* agreed, exuding a concern she was far from feeling. 'You *must* go straight away. I'm sure that Mr. Counter will escort me back to the hotel so you can do so without delay.'

'Whooee!' Simp remarked, 'recovering' after the trio –

albeit reluctantly in von Farlenheim's case – had left the barn. 'Now what do you-all reckon that was all about?'

'Don't ask me,' Okie replied, as his fellow members of the OD Connected's trail crew came to their feet, and he rubbed his rump tenderly. 'Cap'n Dusty said do it, so we have. You pair had the *easy* part. I've come out of it with one hell of a sore butt.'

CHAPTER TWELVE

THE NAME'S *RAPIDO* CLINT!

It was unlikely that many of the people with whom Dusty Fog had come into contact during his most recent visit to Brownsville would have recognized him as he swaggered arrogantly through the main entrance of the Binnacle Tavern in Corpus Christie. His whole appearance and bearing made him much more noticeable than was usually the case. Apart from the other three members of the OD Connected's floating outfit who had accompanied the small Texan to Brownsville, only one trusted married couple and such diversely separated members of society as Governor Stanton Howard, Sheriff Timothy Farron, master criminal Rameses Turtle and his boss gun, Buck Raffles – with all of whom it had been necessary to share the knowledge of what was intended – were aware of the transformation which had been effected upon him.

Although travel-stained, the small Texan's new-looking range-style clothing was of a far superior quality to any which an ordinary working cowhand could legitimately afford. What was more, it had clearly never been subjected to the kind of wear and tear suffered by the garments of a 'saint'[1] on behalf of his employer. Significantly, to experienced eyes – which, despite the nautical implications of the establishment's name, included the majority of the barroom's occupants – the Winchester Model of 1873 carbine dangling from his left hand, his gunbelt and the matched brace of bone handled Colt Civilian Model Peacemakers[2] in

---

1. 'Saint': a cowhand who is conscientious and loyal to his employer. – *J.T.E.*
2. If Dusty Fog had been aware of the situation for which Governor Stanton Howard had required the services of the floating outfit and had anticipated the developments he would have brought along the walnut handles with which his Peacemakers had been equipped on leaving the Colt factory, or the 1860 Army revolvers and their holsters – interchangeable with the pair on his belt – that had been his current weapons' predecessors, as an aid to his disguise. – *J.T.E.*

the cross-draw holsters had obviously been cleaned and made ready for use prior to his entrance.

Being aware that the plotting against the life of Crown Prince Ruldolph of Bosgravnia was even more well organized and complex than he had at first anticipated, the small Texan had laid plans to circumvent whatever might be a-foot. The message he was supposed to have received from his uncle, General Jackson Baines 'Ole Devil' Hardin, had been a fake. It had served the purpose of giving him an acceptable excuse to leave Brownsville and to try and counter what he had believed was the most serious threat to the distinguished foreign visitor. No matter what Charlene, *Comtesse* de Petain and her faction, or the liberal-intellectual anarchists might attempt, he had been convinced that the most deadly danger would be Beguinage. As had been demonstrated, Europe's 'premier assassin' was a master at dealing out unexpected death.

There had been much to do before Dusty could set out for Corpus Christie. He was convinced that Beguinage had already gone there.

One of the matters to which the small Texan had turned his attention had been establishing the exact status of the *Comtesse* de Petain and Alex von Farlenheim. Or rather, as he had had no doubts regarding their complicity, ascertaining who else was involved and what was being planned.

Although neither the woman nor the young Bosgravnian had been aware of it, the Ysabel Kid and Waco were keeping them under observation on the morning following the reception for the Governor. Learning that they intended to go riding, and gambling upon them obtaining horses from Kelty's Livery Barn, because it was more readily available than the von Farlenheim family's stables, there had been sufficient time for Dusty to organize the incident in which Mark Counter had 'rescued' Charlene from the three 'drunken' cowhands. The ploy had been so successful, as had the blond giant's subsequent association with her, that there was now an extra factor in a position to keep an eye upon her activities.

Confident that Mark was capable of handling his part of the scheme and leaving the sheriff to watch out for any of the anarchist faction who might appear in Brownsville, Dusty had concentrated upon contending with the major menace to the Crown Prince's safety.

From what the small Texan had already seen, he realized that Beguinage was no ordinary hired killer. So he believed that only by playing upon one aspect of the assassin's habits could he hope to get to grips. Knowing that nothing short of a maximum effort would be of any use against such an intelligent and wary opponent, he had made his preparations for the campaign with great thoroughness and attention to small as well as large details.

There had, admittedly, been a few fortunate factors which had helped Dusty in his proposed attempt to deceive and trap Beguinage. However, as he had learned to do while building his reputation as one of the Confederate States' Army's best cavalry raiders, he had not hesitated in turning every available resource to his advantage.

From Ram Turtle had come much vitally important information and the promise of the assistance that was requested. A desire to serve the ends of law and order had not motivated the willingness to help. Knowing how much his authority depended upon having his desires respected, he had been furious at both Dink Sproxton and Beguinage for having aroused Brownsville at a time when his orders were for it to be kept peaceful while he was negotiating with Francisco Castro. While even his European contacts had been unable to identify the assassin,[3] he had given orders that Dusty was to receive every co-operation.

Unlikely as such an occupation might be for Lou Bixby, formerly of the Texas Light Cavalry, who prior to enlisting and becoming a sergeant in Dusty Fog's Company 'C' had been a successful professional gambler, he was now a barber. He had gone into the business on marrying a lady's hairdresser at the end of the War Between The States. Remembering what they owed to the financial aid given by the Hardin, Fog and Blaze clan, they had put their combined specialized skills at his former commanding officer's disposal. As a result, using a dye which they had perfected, the small Texan had hair as black as that of the Ysabel Kid.

Obtaining suitable clothing had been even easier to accomplish. Nor had the finishing touch posed any greater difficulty. Okie's home was close to the border with New

3. According to 'Cap' Fog, the return message had been, 'Beguinage ferret best of its kind. Bloodline not known.' – J.T.E.

Mexico and one of his mount[4] in the trail herd's *remuda* carried a West Texas brand which was in no way associated with the OD Connected. He had agreed to loan it as willingly as he had played his part in the deception at Kelly's Livery Barn.

By the time Dusty had ridden north to Corpus Christie, he had all he needed to establish himself with a new identity and, as befitting the trade he was pretending to follow, personality. Apart from a letter of authority signed and sealed by the Governor of Texas, which he was carrying in the concealed pouch fitted at the back of his gunbelt, he had nothing to show who he really was. Only in the most dire and urgent of circumstances would he display the document as long as Beguinage was alive. For the rest of the time, he must stand on his ability to convincingly play the role he had selected.

Crossing the room with the carbine in his left hand and carrying his saddle – with a bed-roll, but *no* rope, attached – over his right shoulder, conscious of being the focus of everybody's interest, the small Texan was about to start the deception in earnest. Paying no apparent attention to the scrutiny to which he was being subjected, he came to a halt at the bar. It was devoid of other customers, so he set down his right hand burden and laid what he carried in his left upon the top of the counter.

'Howdy, you-all,' Dusty greeted the burly, hard-faced bartender as he came along, frowning at the carbine on the shiny surface. 'Pour out two glasses of whiskey and take something for yourself.'

'*Two?*' queried the man behind the counter, glancing around automatically.

'They're for *me*, so don't bother wig-wagging up no she-male company,' Dusty drawled, his tone flat and threatening. 'I'm a two-handed drinker. Which they'll both be paid for. So that'll cover the cost of washing two glasses, taken with the one you'll be having.'

For a couple of seconds, the bartender's frown deepened. He was used to young hard-cases, or would-be hard-cases, arriving and trying to show that they were wild, woolly, full of fleas and never curried below the knees. Over the years,

4. 'Mount': the Texan's name for the horses allocated to a cowhand for the performance of his duties. In the Northern cattle-raising States, these are referred to as a 'string'. – *J.T.E.*

he had developed various effective methods of coping with them. However, he had also learned the value of caution. It was always advisable to assess the quality of the opposition before deciding how to handle it.

With the latter consideration in mind, the bartender turned his calculating gaze upon the latest arrival. The conclusions he drew were not comforting and suggested that he should proceed with caution.

Small though the newcomer might be, there was a width to his shoulders and more than a hint of a muscular development beyond the norm that was not at first apparent. Nor was the evidence of physical strength belied by the ease with which he had been carrying the heavy double-girthed[5] saddle and its attached bed-roll one-handed. Unless he had saddled his horse at the hitching-rail outside, which seemed unlikely, he must have brought the rig at least from the livery stable about a quarter of a mile away. Yet he showed no signs of distress nor strain over having done so.

Furthermore, there was a suggestion of his true potential to be obtained from the small Texan's face and voice. There was nothing weak, or bombastic, about the tanned features. His accent was that of one who had had a good education. Not every formerly wealthy family had regained its fortune since the end of the War. Even those which had were known to have their black sheep. Some of the most deadly gunfighters belonged to one or the other of those categories.

'No, sir,' the bartender told himself silently. 'This's one *hombre* I'm not fixing to take lightly.'

'Would Ram Turtle be here?' Dusty inquired, after the man had filled and set two whiskey glasses in front of him.

'Who?' the bartender inquired, so blandly that he might have been genuinely puzzled by the question.

'Are you-all new here?' Dusty demanded, noticing the other make an almost imperceptible motion with his head and was moving the glasses so that one was in front of each hand.

'Huh?' the bartender grunted, watching three men rise and, spreading out, approach in a casual-appearing manner.

5. Because of its Mexican connotations, being derived from the Spanish word, *cincha*, Texans prefer the word 'girth' – pronouncing it 'girt' – and not 'cinch' for the short, broad band of coarsely woven horsehair, canvas, or cordage, strap, terminating at each end with a metal ring, which together with the latigo fastens the saddle on a horse's back. – *J.T.E.*

'All right, so play innocent,' Dusty drawled, keeping the trio under observation via the reflection in the mirror behind the bar, but giving no sign of being aware that they were coming. 'That's likely what you've been told to do. I admire a man's does what he's told, show's he's got the right spirit. Which I'm telling you that, happen the Ram's not here, you-all can go fetch out his *mero gallo* for me.'

'Yes, sir,' the bartender assented, trying to sound submissive and throwing a glance that was also a signal at the three large men who were converging upon the much smaller new customer. It was unlikely they would all be needed in his opinion, but they invariably employed much the same tactics when dealing with recalcitrant visitors. 'Who-all shall I say wants him?'

'The name's *Rapido* Clint,' Dusty supplied, using the alias he had decided upon before leaving Brownsville.[6] He too was measuring the distance between him and the approaching trio. In as casual a fashion as they were acting, he took one of the brimming glasses between the thumb and forefinger of each hand. 'They call me "*Rapido*" because of how fast I can move.'

As the three men started to lunge in his direction, the small Texan demonstrated how the speed of his actions would have justified the granting of the name in the Spanish-Mexican idiom. Working with the smooth co-ordination granted by his ambidextrous prowess, his hands jerked outwards. The contents of each glass flew straight to where it would best serve his purpose.

On the point of grabbing their 'unsuspecting' victim, the man to Dusty's right and left received a quantity of the raw whiskey in their faces. Splashing into their eyes, the liquid stung with a fiery sensation that had a disastrous effect on the vision of each. So neither saw that the object of their attention was taking further steps to avoid letting himself be grabbed by them.

Watching as '*Rapido* Clint' thrust away from the bar, letting the now empty glasses slip from his hands, the bartender considered that at last he was committing an error in tactics and it was going to cost him dearly. His withdrawal was taking him backwards into the arms of the third

6. Details of another and later Rapido Clint's career are given in 'CAP' FOG. TEXAS RANGER, MEET MR. J. G. REEDER. – *J.T.E.*

bouncer. Once they wrapped around him, his treatment of the other two would be repaid in full.

A similar point of view was held by the last of the trio until he was about to enfold the small Texan in the reverse bear-hug which had become his favourite method for such situations. Before he could do so, he learned that the only mistake was on his and the bartender's part.

Being fully aware of the third man's presence and proximity, Dusty had already decided upon the most suitable means to remove the threat he posed. Making a twisting motion with his torso to supply an added impetus, the small Texan sent his bent right arm behind him as he had been taught by Ole Devil's Japanese valet. As with the other lessons in unarmed combat he had received from Tommy Okasi,[7] coming so unexpectedly, it proved very effective. Propelled by all the power from a body with the muscular development of a Hercules in miniature, his elbow caught the man in the solar plexus.

To the recipient of the attack, it seemed that he had been kicked by a large and unusually vigorous mule. Not that he was capable of expressing any coherent thoughts on the matter for something over a minute. Driven backwards by the force and pain of the blow, he lost his balance and collapsed on to his rump in a way that did nothing to help him recover the breath that had already been driven from his body.

Spluttering curses and knuckling his eyes in an attempt to clear his vision, one of the first pair collided with his similarly occupied companion. Instantly, drawing an erroneous conclusion, he swung a blow that knocked the other sprawling backwards to the floor. Then, contriving to focus his gaze for long enough to discover his mistake, he made another in trying to rectify it. Swinging around, he sprang at the cause of his misfortunes. He was in no condition to tangle with such an agile and competent foe. Avoiding him without the slightest difficulty, Dusty kicked his legs from beneath him as he went by and he alighted with a bone-jarring crash supine on the floor.

Behind the counter, the bartender was taking in the sight as if unwilling to believe his eyes. Then, realizing that the

7. New readers can find some details regarding the career and special qualifications of 'Tommy Okasi' in Footnote 16, APPENDIX ONE. – J.T.E.

128

proposed victim might consider him as the instigator of the abortive attempts at assault, he made a lunge in the direction of the sawed-off shotgun that was kept on a shelf for use in emergencies. As far as he was concerned, the situation now came into *that* category.

Alert for any further danger, Dusty only needed to see the bartender begin to move and he took counter measures. Displaying another facet of his *'rapido'* qualities – the word implied motions of exceptional speed – his hands crossed to fetch out the matched Colts.

'Leave it be!' the small Texan commanded, cocking and aligning the left hand weapon at the burly man while allowing its mate to dangle ready for use in other directions if required. 'Come back this way with your tiny little fists where I can see them *all* the time.'

No fool, the bartender obeyed. He drew conclusions from the unmoving way in which the Peacemaker was pointing at him. That was not the handling technique of a beginner, nor a young show-off with a little ability trying to demonstrate his toughness, but the deadly efficiency of a top hand *pistolero valiente.*[8] What was more, *'Rapido* Clint' no longer struck him as being small, but seemed to have taken on height and width in an amazing fashion. Although the bartender knew that the effect was brought about by the force of the other's personality, without being able to express the sentiment in so many words, he drew little consolation from the thought.

'Hey now!' called a booming voice, as the door of the private office was thrown open. 'Where away's the squalls?'

Glancing at the two men who were emerging, the bartender gave a sigh of relief and hoped that his own responsibilities were at an end. The speaker had been his immediate superior, the big, heavily-built, bearded and nautically dressed Bos'n Crumper. However, the other was of an even higher standing in Ram Turtle's organization.

'Well howdy you-all, Buck,' Dusty greeted, returning the Colts to their holsters as swiftly as they had been extracted and with an air of considering they would no longer be needed. ''Lonzo back to Cowtown allowed you and the Ram'd be either here or at Brownsville.'

'The boss's down there, *Rapido*,' Buck Raffles replied,

8. *Pistolero valiente:* an exceptionally competent gun-fighter, mostly one who sold his skill to the highest bidder. – *J.T.E.*

seeing how well the small Texan had benefited by the description of the bouncers' tactics he had received from Turtle. 'But he sent me up to see how things are going. What the hell came off *here*, damn it?'

'There's no call to go mean-mouthing the gent there,' Dusty objected, indicating the bartender at whom the other's angry words had been directed. 'He was only doing what he's paid to. Which *isn't* to let any yahoo who fancies come in and ride him, I for sure don't hold it against him and hope it'll be mutual.'

'Sure, *Rapido*,' the bartender confirmed, having noticed there was an aura of warning behind the apology. 'And I'll see them three feel the same way.'

'Anyways, Buck,' Dusty drawled, his attitude showing that he regarded the matter was closed and his view had better be respected. 'I'm right pleased to see you-all. Had me a spell of bad luck at the tables over to your place in Cowtown. So I reckoned's how your boss'd taken most of my money, I'd drift along over and ask how he was set to put me in the way of earning more.'

'And how do you want to earn it, me hearty?' Crumper inquired, having noticed the reference to the head bartender of Turtle's Fort Worth establishment and the deference being displayed by the boss gun. 'What kind of work do you do?'

'None that raises sweat, nor calls for heavy lifting and toting,' Dusty replied, making sure his words carried around the silent room and making a small but noticeable gesture to indicate his bone-handled Colts. 'Mostly I do what I'm best at. I kill folks who other folks want killing – and do it for money.'

CHAPTER THIRTEEN

I WANT TO HIRE YOU TO KILL SOMEBODY

'Mr. *Rapido* Clint?' asked the man, in response to whose knock Dusty Fog had opened the door of his hotel room.

'That's me,' the small Texan confirmed, allowing the Colt Civilian Model Peacemaker – which he had picked up on hearing he had a visitor – to dangle in casual-seeming readiness so that the other could see it. 'What can I do for you-all?'

The time was shortly after eleven o'clock on the morning following Dusty's arrival in Corpus Christie. Taken with the appearance of the man in the passage, the use of his alias rather than the name in which he had signed the hotel's register suggested that his pose as a hired killer had been successful. In which case, it might also be bringing about the situation he required.

After having obtained a sizable 'loan' at the Binnacle Tavern, commenting that by doing so he had ensured Buck Raffles would be diligent in producing lucrative employment for him, the small Texan had set off to find accommodation. He had already decided upon using the expensive Portside Hotel, after having discussed the matter with his more knowledgeable co-conspirators in Brownsville. Close to the waterfront district, it was in a respectable area. On both counts, it could be the type of place Beguinage would select as a base for operations. Furthermore, as its general clientele were people connected with the shipping interests, Dusty had felt he was less likely to meet anybody who might know him and inadvertently raise doubts about his new identity.

There had been a slight difficulty with the desk clerk, who had clearly been perturbed by the prospect of a dishevelled cowhand requiring a room. However, Dusty's accent and a display of his finances, backed by the quite true statement that he belonged to a very wealthy and influential cattle-raising family, had gained him admittance. A hot bath, a

131

shave and a change into clean clothing, albeit the attire of a successful professional gambler, had prevented any further objections to his presence.

Returning to the Tavern, Dusty had made a tour of the town in Buck Raffles' company. No matter what his personal feelings on the matter might have been, the boss gun had carried out the task he was assigned by Rameses Turtle in an exemplary fashion. In the course of their wandering from place to place, he had introduced the small Texan to a number of people. Most of them would have been considerably alarmed if they had known the truth about ' "*Rapido* Clint" from out Amarillo way'.[1]

So successfully had Dusty played the part that, just before they parted company at midnight, Raffles had confessed he would have been convinced if he was not in on the deception. However, as they had both known, the fact that Ram Turtle's boss gun was personally performing the introductions had been a major factor in establishing the small Texan's character. In fact, falling into the spirit of the thing, Raffles had built up a considerable reputation for '*Rapido* Clint' which Dusty had had to uphold once by demonstrating his effective bare-handed fighting skill and later via a display, on a target and bloodlessly, of his superlative gun handling abilities.

Although the various audiences might not have heard of '*Rapido* Clint' prior to that evening, by the time the small Texan had returned to the Portside Hotel, nobody doubted he was other than had been claimed.

Nothing had happened to disturb Dusty's sleep. However, with the arrival of the vessel carrying Crown Prince Rudolph of Bosgravnia likely to take place within the next three days, he had not anticipated there would be too much delay if news of his ability and desire for gainful employment had reached any of the interested parties. It was also possible, he knew, that word of his availability had come to Beguinage's attention. If so, he would have to be constantly on his guard. With that in mind, he had armed himself when the knock on

1. None of them ever found out. Having given an assurance to Rameses Turtle that he would neither disclose nor make use of any confidential information he received, unless it pertained to Beguinage or other assassination bids, Dusty Fog kept his word. The insight he undoubtedly gained into the criminal circles of Texas has never been divulged even to the other members of his family circle. – *J.T.E.*

his door had announced he was about to receive a visitor.

One glance at the middle-sized, neatly attired, be-spectacled and clerkly-looking caller had told Dusty that he was in all probability the man who had gone under the name of 'Gustav Breakast' in Brownsville. So, unless there had been some new developments since his arrival at Corpus Christie, he was more likely to be an enemy than an agent of Beguinage.

'Can I come in?' the visitor asked, darting a glance to where two women wearing the black and white habits of nuns were approaching along the passage. 'My business is of a private and confidential nature.'

'Come ahead,' Dusty offered, concealing the Colt behind his back before it could be seen by either of the women. Apart from taking the precaution, he paid no more attention to them than they were showing in either him or 'Breakast'. Allowing the man to enter, he closed the door. 'Go sit and rest your feet while you're talking.'

'Thank you,' the visitor replied and complied. His New England accent was a further clue to his identity. Watching the small Texan return to the unmade bed and replace the revolver in its holster, he continued, 'I've been given to understand that you're good at your specialized line of work—'

'Not just *good*, the *best*,' Dusty corrected, strapping on his gunbelt. 'And don't waste my time talking 'round in circles. We both *know* I'm a hired killed and that's what you've come to see me about.'

'I'm not sure—!' the man began, unused to such candour.

'In that case, you'd best haul your butt the hell out of here while you still can,' Dusty interrupted coldly, picking up his black cutaway jacket but not starting to put it on. 'Because, *hombre*, I've not ate yet this morning and I'm only willing to hold off from doing it if what you've got to say's worth my while to listen to.'

'Who and what do you think I am?' 'Breakast' challenged.

'Well now,' Dusty drawled. 'You *could* be just some jasper who was around in one of those places I went to last night and came calling to see what it's like talking to a genuine hired killer. Or you *might* be a writer for some fancy Eastern newspaper looking for a story. In either case, you're going to wish you'd never took the notion to come.' He made a brief prohibitive gesture with his empty hand, going on, 'Only I know you're *neither*. So don't start getting fool ideas about bringing out that little old sneaky gun you've got "hidden" up your left sleeve. Instead, let's talk turkey and quit pretending we're anything but what we are.'

'That's reasonable,' the man admitted, both impressed and startled by the discovery that his concealed weapon had been detected. He realized that he was dealing with a man of intelligence and discernment rather than the usual run of semi-moronic hired killers he usually employed. 'I want to hire you to kill somebody.'

'Shucks, *I* knew that all along,' Dusty declared sardonically, donning the jacket. 'First off, though, I always want to know who I'm talking to. It makes things more sociable-like.'

'My name's "Luncher",' the young Easterner obliged, having considered it advisable to adopt a different pseudonym on leaving Brownsville and selecting from a pre-arranged code in case he needed to communicate with his superiors. ' "George Luncher", and I'm from New York.'

'That's likely a "summer name",' the small Texan drawled. 'But I'll accept it, seeing's I wasn't born "*Rapido* Clint" either. At least, we've got around to deciding that you-all want to hire lil ole me.'

'I do,' 'Luncher' confirmed, deciding that a 'summer name' was what Texans called an alias.[2]

'For how much?' Dusty asked and again signalled to prevent his visitor from speaking. 'Once we've got *that* settled, you can tell me who you-all want making wolf-bait.'

'What do you usually charge?'

'That depends on who it is and how important they might be.'

'He's *very* important,' 'Luncher' stated frankly, knowing that to do otherwise would avail him nothing.

'We're starting to merry-go-round in high water again,' Dusty warned, his voice hardening. He went on without troubling to explain that the term was used to describe the dangerous situation when cattle crossing a river started to swim around in an ever tightening circle. 'And I'm running

2. Even in law-abiding circles, anywhere west of the Mississippi River, a person was at liberty to select another name than his or her own to use. The only acceptable way to state disbelief was to inquire, 'Is that your *summer* name?' – *J.T.E.*

shy on patience, so you-all'd best start heading straight across the range. Just tell me who-all it is you want killing and I'll figure out what doing it's going to cost you.'

'He's a prince who's on his way over from Europe,' 'Luncher' stated watching for any indication of how the information was being received.

'Huh huh!' Dusty grunted, contriving to sound non-committal while also giving the impression that the news was what he had expected. 'That means there's *big* money involved. Tell you what, *Mr. "Luncher"*, you-all start off with *your* price. Then we can haggle on *up* to *mine*.'

'Two hundred and fifty—' the Easterner began, remembering what he had been told about '*Rapido* Clint's' financial condition.

'I reckon I'll go and have my breakfast,' the small Texan drawled, withstanding an inclination to say 'Breakast'.

'Three hundred—' 'Luncher' bid quickly, searching the tanned and impassive features for any suggestion of acceptance as he lengthened the pauses between each successive offer. 'Four – Five – Six – Seven-fifty—'

'Who-all do you reckon you're dealing with?' Dusty demanded coldly, when the price's advance was brought to a halt. 'I'm not some two-bit sundowner who's got to sell out dirt cheap because the sheriff's going to start running me west. You're *way* too low, the *others* are offering well over seven hundred and fifty.'

'*Others?*' 'Luncher' repeated, looking genuinely startled.

'That prince jasper can't be any too popular back to his home range,' Dusty elaborated. 'You're not the only one who's going around putting down a bounty on his lil ole scalp.'

'Damn it!' the Easterner complained. '*He* never told me—'

'Likely *he* wouldn't,' Dusty said unsympathetically.

'Who else is after him?' 'Luncher' inquired, all too casually.

'Who-all's putting up *your* money?' the small Texan countered.

'I can't tell you *that*!' 'Luncher' protested.

'And *I* didn't expect you to,' Dusty replied. 'So don't go asking me any more hawg-stupid questions. I'll tell you, though. Way I read the sign, your bunch've more money to spread around than *them* most likely. So this is how I see it.

My price's three thousand, five hundred lil ole iron men, with five hundred in advance and the rest when the prince's made wolf bait.'

'*Three thousand five hundred?*' 'Luncher' repeated. 'That's a lot of money!'

'Not for somebody that important,' Dusty pointed out. He's more than just some back country rancher, or small town politician. Taking him, even when he's out on the range hunting, is going to be trickier than all hell. 'Specially should *your* bunch want it making look like it was an accident as well.'

'They do,' the Easterner admitted, led into indiscretion by his surprise at discovering the extent of the small Texan's knowledge.

'Tell you what I'll do then,' Dusty drawled, adopting an attitude which suggested he considered the meeting had gone as far as it could at that time. 'I've not given *them* an answer yet, seeing's they wouldn't come right out with a "yes" to my price. So whyn't you-all go tell your bunch what I'm asking and see if they'll trail along?'

'I'll do that.'

'Just make sure they know one thing, though.'

'What's that?'

'The horse-trading's over,' Dusty declared, picking up and donning his hat. 'You've got my price. Take it or leave it, I'll get it from you or the others.'

'So now all I can do is wait,' Dusty Fog concluded his description of the meeting with 'George Luncher', as he sat with Buck Raffles in the dining-room of the Portside Hotel. 'Do you-all know who told him where to find me and the name I'm using here?'

There had been no more conversation after the small Texan had delivered his ultimatum. The Easterner had shown no inclination of wanting to prolong the interview. Nor had Dusty considered it was advisable for him to try and do so. If he had, he might have aroused the other's suspicions. As it was, he felt he had achieved as much as was possible from the meeting. By displaying indifference, he had ensured that he would be accepted as an intelligent, coldly calculating, money-hungry professional killer who had already been made an offer by a rival faction. With that much done, all he could do was await the next development.

With the basic details agreed upon, 'Luncher' had left to consult with his superiors. Having made arrangements to meet Raffles at his hotel for lunch, before they had parted the previous night, Dusty had postponed eating until his guest arrived. Apart from the two nuns he had seen upstairs who were now seated engrossed in conversation at the opposite side of the dining-room, they had the place to themselves. Once they had ordered their meals from the waitress, they were at liberty to talk without being overheard.

'I couldn't say for sure,' the boss gun admitted. 'It'd most likely be the Bos'n or one of the bartenders, but it could've been any of the others. I'd passed the word that, having loaned you-all money, the sooner you was found some work the better. But I didn't figure it'd be wise to tell them I wanted to know if anybody showed interest. The Ram lets them make what they can on deals like that, so starting to change it could've got them suspicious.'

'I can see that it would,' Dusty admitted. 'But I'd like to know. You-all could make out that you want to know whether he got it from your boys at first hand, or if somebody's being all sneaky and passing the word to another brand.'

'That'll do it,' Raffles grinned. 'It'll give me a reason to have them tell me if anybody else comes around looking to hire you.'

'Or *anybody* else,' Dusty supplemented.

'Comes to that, I've just now got the word that Schindler's drifted in,' the boss gun remarked. 'Do you-all know him?'

'Can't say I do.'

'He's a better'n fair hand. Was a sharpshooter[3] during the War and works with a Sharps buffalo gun that'll hold true to well over half a mile. They do say he's hit to near on three-quarters, using one of those telescope-sights.'

'Could just be a coincidence,' Dusty drawled. 'Has he been around to see your people at the Binnacle Tavern?'

'Not so far,' Raffles replied. 'Which could mean he's already hired, or he might not be looking for work. I've passed the word to have an eye kept on him, though.'

'*Beuno!*' Dusty praised, glancing to where the nuns were walking out of the room.

3. 'Sharpshooter': used in this context, a sniper. The latter term had not yet come into usage. – *J.T.E.*

137

'What'd you-all make of that jasper who came to see you, Cap'n?' Raffles inquired.

'He's a cagey son-of-a-bitch,' the small Texan replied. 'Which we both know he's good at his work, or he'd not have been sent down here in the first place. Don't you-all know anything about him?'

The arrival of the waitress with the two men's orders brought a temporary halt to the conversation. It was resumed after she had departed and while they were eating.

'Not a whole heap more than you do,' Raffles confessed. 'He showed up at 'Cisco Castro's *cantina*, had proof that he'd been sent by a New York bunch we'd both done business with in the past. 'Cisco's *mero gallo* didn't let on we were involved when he told him we didn't want the town riling up right then and he took off like he was willing to go along with it.'

'How big's this New York bunch?'

'One of the biggest.'

'Have they got any political leanings?' Dusty inquired. 'I don't just mean sneaking their own folks into public office.'

'Not that I know of,' Raffles answered. 'Why?'

' "Luncher", or "Breakast", which isn't his real name either, I'd reckon, showed there're definitely two factions after the Prince,' Dusty explained. 'We'd figured there might be, but it's always nice to know for sure. Would his crowd hire out to a bunch of anarchists?'

'They'd hire out to *anybody* was the price right,' Raffles declared. 'Only, from what I've seen of 'em, anarchists'd rather work through their own kind. Hey though, it's just now hit me. There're two bunches involved. So which of 'em's Beguinage working for, he's killed off folks in both.'

'I've been wondering about that myself,' Dusty admitted. 'At first I thought it might be the *Comtesse's* bunch, but that burned paper in her room makes me think he'd warned her off. So it's either the anarchists, there's a third bunch mixed in it we haven't heard about yet, or one of the *Comtesse's* crowd's trying to cut out the rest. There's only one thing I'm concerned about, though. Stopping *anybody* having the Crown Prince killed. Because it's like Beguinage warned the Ram, happen he's put under, Texas's going to be too damned hot for honest, hard working owlhoots. Which doesn't worry *me* none, but Uncle Devil's going to be madder'n a well-boiled screech-owl – and *that* sure as hell does.'

Before any more could be said, one of the hotel's maids entered. Crossing to the table, she told Dusty she had tidied his room and asked if he had any laundry he wanted attending to.

'I sure have,' the small Texan replied, having requested the service from the desk clerk. Coming to his feet, he went on, 'I'll just go and let the lady have what needs doing, Buck. Order up some coffee, will you.'

'Sure,' Raffles agreed.

'Did you lock up when you came out?' Dusty inquired, having accompanied the maid upstairs, noticing his room's door was standing slightly ajar.

'Well, no sir,' the plump, cheerful-looking woman replied. 'I don't have a master-key and finding the right one on my bunch takes so long. But this's a honest place, sir. There's never a thing been stolen here.'

'Let's hope this isn't going to be the first time,' Dusty said quietly, looking along the deserted passage. 'Did you come straight down to me?'

'Not *straight* down, sir,' the maid admitted. 'We're only allowed to come up the front way when we're with a guest. So I had to go down and around the back.'

'It's my own fault, anyway,' Dusty said soothingly, making sure his right hand was ready to reach across to the left side Colt as he pushed open the door. He knew there would not have been time for anybody to make a thorough search of his room; but, if an attempt to do so was in progress, whoever was making it would probably be ready to fight. 'I should've have left my washing out.'

'Everything's all right, sir,' the maid declared, following the small Texan in and sounding relieved. Then her voice took on a puzzled note and she went by him to cross the room with rapid strides, continuing, 'That's strange, sir. I don't remember putting this box on the bed!'

Being more concerned with searching for any intruder who might be on the premises, Dusty's attention on entering had been directed to the large wardrobe at the left as the only place of concealment. In spite of having placed his saddle, bed-roll and carbine therein, it still offered sufficient space for a man to hide inside. Hearing the woman's comment, he glanced around.

What the small Texan saw and remembered from another hotel room in Brownsville sent him, his right hand fetching its Colt from leather, bounding after the woman.

'Now *where* in the world did this come from?' the maid asked, lifting up the two foot square wooden box without noticing that she broke a piece of black thread that was fastened between a small hook on the lid and one of the counterpane's decorative buttons. 'I *know* it—'

Operated by a spring that the thread had helped to keep under compression, the lid of the box flew upwards. Even as Dusty arrived and knocked it from the woman's hands, her words were terminated in what began as a gasp of surprise and turned into a full-blooded shriek of terror as she caught sight of the contents.

Tumbling out of the box, a copperhead snake fully as large as the one which had killed Walter Scargill landed in the centre of the bed. While it had been content to lay relaxed and motionless in the darkness of its prison, the treatment to which it had just been subjected brought a change of attitude. Instantly the multi-jointed body assumed the so-called 'fighting coil'. As the lower portion tightened like a compressed spring, the upper rose to assume an S-shape from which a strike could be made at lightning speed and for almost half of its length. Rotating, the coffin-shaped head's curved fangs were exposed as the mouth opened and the forked tongue sought to locate the cause of its discomfiture.

Still screaming at the top of a not inconsiderable voice, the maid spun around and dashed wildly from the room. Her first movement set up vibrations which brought the copperhead's attention in that direction and it gave a hiss which was audible despite the noise she was making.

Knowing just how dangerous the aroused creature could be, Dusty did not hesitate in his response. Slanting the Colt into alignment, he fired. Without waiting to see if the shot took effect, his left hand flashed across to force back the hammer and his right forefinger kept the trigger depressed so that the next cartridge was ignited almost instantaneously. Both missed their mark, but the second had drawn closer. So he continued with his efforts.

As the mechanism required cocking manually for every shot, although not conducive to extreme accuracy, 'fanning' was the swiftest method of discharging a 'single action' revolver. Keeping his left hand making the circular scooping motion, while turning the barrel slightly and controlling the recoil as each successive shot was fired, Dusty emptied the Colt's chamber with great rapidity. On the fourth explosion, he saw through the swirling smoke of the consumed black powder that he had achieved his purpose. Struck by the bullet, which passed through two of the coils, the copperhead's body bounced into the air. Landing again, it thrashed spasmodically for a few seconds before becoming still.

Conscious of voices raised in alarm from the passage and the sound of approaching feet, the small Texan bent to look under the bed. To his relief, he found that passing through the thick counterpane and well-stuffed mattress had reduced his 'city loaded'[4] bullets' velocity sufficiently to prevent them from piercing the sturdy planks of the floor and endangering anybody who was underneath.

'What has happened, young man?' asked a feminine voice, speaking with just a trace of a foreign accent.

Straightening up and turning around, Dusty found that the larger of the two nuns had entered followed by two of the male guests. She was well made, about five foot seven in height and had a bland, matronly cast of features.

'It could have been somebody's notion of a joke, ma'am,' the small Texan replied, stepping aside and indicating the bloody, shattered copperhead on the bed. 'Only, happen it was,' his gaze flickered to the men and he realized that either might be Beguinage come to find out how the trap had worked, 'I didn't think it was funny and I'm betting neither did the snake.'

'*Bon dieu!*' the nun gasped, her face registering alarm. She made the sign of the cross and went on, 'I trust you will light a candle to the Virgin in thanks for your salvation.'

'I don't reckon doing it'd do me a whole heap of good, ma'am,' Dusty answered, opening the Colt's loading gate and, setting the hammer at half cock, pushing on the rod beneath the barrel to eject the first of the spent cartridge cases. 'The church I was raised in didn't do that.'

'Then you must give whatever thanks you feel are appropriate,' the nun declared.

---

4. Like most top grade gun-fighters, Dusty Fog loaded his own ammunition. To reduce the danger to innocent bystanders, he reduced the amount of powder in those cartridges which might have to be discharged while in the confines of a town. – *J.T.E.*

141

'Yes, ma'am, I'll do just that,' the small Texan responded politely, but made no mention of his other promise that he would make Beguinage pay for the attempt upon his life, particularly as the means might easily have caused a harmless woman's death.

CHAPTER FOURTEEN

SOMEBODY POINTED BEGUINAGE TO ME

'There's two things you can do for me,' Dusty Fog stated, walking with Buck Raffles towards the Binnacle Tavern. 'Find where that "Luncher" *hombre*'s living, and who sent him to see me.'

Something over an hour had elapsed since the attempted murder.

On his arrival, the manager had been both annoyed and alarmed. It had soon become apparent that he was solely motivated by a desire to prevent any blame for the incident falling on the Portside Hotel. So he had grown more amiable when the small Texan had absolved the establishment of all responsibility.

After Dusty had interceded on her behalf and prevented her from being fired, the maid had admitted that she stopped 'just for a minute' at the kitchen on her way to inquire about his laundry. However, she had insisted that she locked the door behind her and he had seen no reason to contradict her story. He had realized that the delay must have been longer, as the nuns had claimed that they had seen nobody in the passage when returning to their room.

The town marshal who had been summoned was nowhere near as competent as Sheriff Timothy Farron of Cameron County. Nor, according to Raffles, did he have such a high standard of honesty. Catching the signal given by the boss gun, who was present during his investigation, he had shown diligence only in trying to smooth matters over for Dusty's benefit.

When the small Texan had claimed that the attempted murder might have resulted from mistaken identity, the marshal had accepted his reasons. As Dusty had pointed out, not only was he unable to think of anybody who might want him dead, but he had arrived in Corpus Christie and taken the room late the previous afternoon. So the proposed victim could have been the occupant who had vacated it prior to his taking over. Promising to conduct inquiries along that line, the peace officer had gone to make a start.

Having been assured by the manager that the snake's remains would be removed and every item of bedding changed, Dusty had left the hotel with Raffles. Waiting until certain that they were not being followed, they had started to discuss the incident.

'I'll do that,' the boss gun promised. 'He was at the Seaman's Temperance Hotel, but he's not staying at the same kind of place here.'

'I never thought he would be,' Dusty drawled. 'He's too smart for that. But, wherever he's at, you can bet it'll be a place where he'll fit in with the other roomers.'

'I'll keep that in mind,' Raffles promised, having failed to consider such a point as a possible aid to the discovery. 'But it won't be's easy as finding Dink Sproxton. A gal he'd had and thrown over'd seen him going in and passed the word when she heard we were looking for him.'

'We're not likely to be *that* lucky with "Luncher",' Dusty replied. 'But I'd like to know as soon as possible. And who sent him to the hotel. I was only curious before, but now it's urgent. *Somebody* pointed Beguinage at me and knowing who could help me stay alive.'

The same bartender was on duty as had been in attendance when Dusty had made his dramatic first appearance at the Tavern. As with the maid at the hotel, his exculpation of the other's behaviour had created a spirit of co-operation. Setting up two schooners of beer as requested, the man glanced around and lowered his voice to impart some information which he would otherwise have retained for Raffles' ears only.

'Schindler's working.'

'He is, huh?' the boss gun replied.

'Soapy Joe saw him,' the bartender explained. 'He'd heard we was looking for him and passed the word—'

'I told them to say there was a chore the boss wants doing,' Raffles commented.

'And he told Soapy's he couldn't take anything for maybe a week,' the bartender went on. 'So the Soap pulled out and hung around, trailed him down to the waterfront. Reckons he was looking up at windows that face the harbour and went into a couple of places likely to ask if he could go up there.'

'Which means he's working, for sure,' Raffles admitted.

144

'I don't want to sound nosey, *Rapido*,' the bartender stated, guessing the boss gun was wondering why he had made a basically confidential disclosure with the small Texan present. 'And I'm not even asking, but whatever he's come for might cut across the chore I sent that jasper from New York to put to you.'

'It was you who sent him, huh?' Dusty asked.

'Sure,' the bartender confirmed, then a worried look came to his face. 'It was all right, wasn't it? He'd got the usual proof of who he was and everything.'

'It was all right,' Dusty said reassuringly, taking out a twenty dollar gold piece and placing it in front of the man. 'That's for the introduction and there'll be some more happen he meets my asking price. I don't suppose he said where he's hanging out?'

'Only that he'd drop by if he needed anything else,' the bartender replied. 'I didn't push it, his kind don't take to nosey folks.'

'Or tip 'em as good,' Raffles supplemented with a grin.

'That too,' the bartender confessed.

'Just so you don't forget to put the boss's cut on one side,' Raffles drawled, but there was a note of warning under the even tones. 'Anyways, happen he comes again, or even if he doesn't, we want to know where he's living in town.'

'I'll tend to it,' the bartender promised, then glared at a customer along the counter who was banging a glass to attract his attention. 'All right, all right, I'll get to you soon's I'm through here.'

'Best go now,' Dusty suggested. 'He's *buying* his drinks, which helps to pay you. Thanks for sending him along, but there's nothing settled yet. So I'm still open for other offers.'

'I'll mind it,' the bartender declared and went to attend to the customer.

'Well now,' Dusty drawled, watching the burly man resume his duties. 'I'd say nobody else's been asking *him* about me.'

'Nor any of the others – if they're working for us and not themselves,' Raffles answered. 'They'd'd've told him about it if anybody asked. Who-all do you reckon's hired Schindler?'

'How high does he come?'

'He'd pull down close to as much as "*Rapido* Clint" asking.'

'Then I wouldn't want to guess,' Dusty admitted. 'Which

145

'I'm not so naïve that I reckon anarchists wouldn't have that kind of money, so it still doesn't close the corral gate on *them*.'

'What I've heard, they pay's high's anybody,' Raffles admitted. 'Only with the way he'll handle it, whoever's doing the hiring've changed their minds about wanting it to look accidental.'

'Or reckon that making it plain it wasn't one would turn out more to their advantage,' Dusty amended, instinctively drawing the correct assumption with regard to the faction in question's motives. 'I reckon I'll go put on something a mite more comfortable and have me a lil stroll around the waterfront.'[1]

'Do you-all want company?'

'Not particularly.'

'It might be better to have some,' Raffles objected. 'Beguinage's already had one crack at you and it only fell apart because you'd seen the same play afore. Happen he's figuring on trying again, the waterfront'd be a right smart place to do it. Which he might have better luck next time.'

'Would *that* bother you, or the Ram?' Dusty inquired dryly, realizing that the other was perturbed.

'You can bet your life it *would*,' Raffles stated vehemently. 'The boss told me I'd got to make sure's nothing happened to you.'

'I never knew I was *that* popular with him,' Dusty protested.

'You are the way things stand,' the boss gun announced, grinning faintly. 'The Ram's one tough *hombre*, but there's one jasper he doesn't want to get riled at him and that's the Ysabel Kid. He knows's, should *anything* happen to you-all on this chore you're doing, he'd never again dare sleep of a night for fear of waking up and finding that baby-faced *Pehnane* slit-eye lighting a fire on the centre of his chest. Fact being, Mr. *Rapido* Clint, I'm none too took with the same notion myself. So, happen it's all right with you-all, I'd sooner you stayed alive and well.'

'Well now, you won't find me giving any strong arguments on *that*,' Dusty admitted, smiling at the heart-felt and

1. Subsequent investigations proved that the anarchists who had hired Oscar Schindler considered letting the assassination be obvious murder would strengthen their cause. They intended to accuse the aristocratic faction of having arranged Crown Prince Rudolph's death to prevent the liberal changes in the laws he was planning from being ratified. – *J.T.E.*

clearly genuine comments regarding his Indian-dark *amigo's* reputation for taking deadly reprisals when roused. 'Only this's one deal I'd sooner handle on my own. Tell you, though. I'll leave a message to be passed on to Lon should I get killed, telling him that it was my own fault and you're not to blame.'

For all his light-hearted remark, Dusty Fog had not underestimated the perils involved in the reconnaisance he had decided to carry out. Studying the two men who were approaching him and thinking of the third to his rear on the otherwise dark and deserted street, he had an idea that – uneventful as the afternoon and evening had been – the danger he had anticipated might soon materialize. He was so certain that it would, he was pleased that he had set out on his mission in a suitable manner.

One of the reasons that the small Texan had returned to the Portside Hotel before embarking on his quest had been to change his clothes. There might have been a better chance of passing unnoticed while dressed after the fashion of a professional gambler, but the garb had one major disadvantage. The sides of the cutaway coat offered a slightly greater impediment to the freedom with which he could draw the two Colt Civilian Model Peacemakers than he considered acceptable. He was aware that in an emergency, even a fraction of a second could spell the difference between life and death. So he had wanted to have his utmost speed available. Another benefit to be gained from donning the clothes of a working cowhand was that his dark green shirt would present a less obvious aiming point than the frilly bosomed white one which went with the other attire, particularly in the dark.

Nor, grave as Dusty had known it to be, did he take only the menace of Beguinage into account. From what he had been told by Buck Raffles before leaving the Binnacle Tavern, he had decided that Oscar Schindler was a factor which could not be dismissed lightly. Even though his activities had not previously come to the small Texan's attention, he was acknowledged as a master of the killing by hire trade. If he should suspect that an interest was being taken in his affairs, he would be likely to demonstrate his resentment of the intrusion. A man of his calibre would not be put off by the reputation '*Rapido* Clint' had acquired around Corpus Christie. It would merely serve to make him more cautious in his efforts at removing a possible rival.

Dressed as he had been on his arrival, Dusty had slipped out of the hotel – with the connivance of the maid whose life he had saved – by the rear entrance. Before leaving, he had also refreshed his memory by studying the map of the town which Governor Stanton Howard had had the forethought to supply. Long experience in such matters had then helped him to find the area which would be the focal point of everybody's attention when the royal visitor arrived.

Even before the small Texan had learned of Schindler's presence, he had had mixed feelings over one of the precautions to ensure the safe arrival of Crown Prince Rudolph in Corpus Christie. As the draught of the steam-sloop prevented it from coming alongside the quay, it would drop anchor about half a mile out in the bay. From there, the distinguished visitor and his entourage would be brought ashore in boats, to be met by the Governor and other dignitaries. When Dusty had pointed out the dangers of such an arrangement, Howard had agreed that they existed. Against that, it was believed the Crown Prince's popularity in his homeland was causing the plotters to want it made appear his death was accidental. So it seemed likely any attempt would be delayed until the hunting expedition was in progress and offered better possibilities. In which case, the short trip in the open boat should have proved safe enough.

Dusty's deductions with regard to Schindler's arrival had changed all that!

Armed with arguably the world's finest long range, heavy calibre rifle and possessing the skill to utilize its full potential for accuracy, the newcomer could hope to hit the Crown Prince while he was still aboard the steam-sloop at its anchorage and did not, although he probably would, need to wait until his victim came ashore. Powered by one hundred and twenty grains of black powder – which produced a muzzle energy of close to two thousand, three hundred foot pounds – the five hundred and fifty grain .45 bullet would be flying at almost fourteen hundred feet per *second* and could deal out death at an even greater distance if necessary.[2]

2. On June the 27th, 1874, the Battle of Adobe Walls was terminated after a bullet from a Sharps 'Buffalo' rifle in the hands of scout and guide Billy Dixon killed a mounted Indian warrior over a distance of what was later measured at *one thousand, five hundred and thirty-eight yards.* – J.T.E.

Although removing the cause of the threat might have seemed the most obvious course, Dusty had realized that there were going to be difficulties in putting it into effect. Contact would have to be established before Schindler could be arrested or, failing that, warned that the reason for his presence in Corpus Christie was known and would be circumvented. Unfortunately, the news Soapy Joe had brought to the Tavern as Dusty was on the point of leaving suggested that doing so might not be possible. After making the surveillance of the waterfront area, the sharpshooter had eluded his follower and his present whereabouts were unknown.

Considering the size of the area Schindler had covered with Soapy Joe on his trail, Dusty had ruled out one way of dealing with him in the event that he had not been located earlier. It would be impractical to obtain the services of sufficient men to prevent his attempt being made. Not only were there too many points from which he could use his long range weapon to ensure they were all covered, but the presence of so many observers could not be kept a secret. Once the sharpshooter either saw or heard of them, he would withdraw and wait for a more suitable opportunity. Nor, as the date of the steam-sloop's arrival could only be estimated and could not be known for certain until it appeared off the coast, would there be time to get such a large body of men into their respective positions as it was approaching the bay.

Dusty had decided that, in the final analysis, there was only one way to cope with the situation.

Catch Schindler in the act and make sure that he was removed as a threat!

It was risky, but not unacceptably so!

With that thought in mind, the small Texan had followed his usual procedure of trying to duplicate his opponent's line of reasoning. It was a trait he had developed to a high degree and found beneficial on numerous other occasions. While traversing the same general route as Schindler, he had sought out the most likely positions from which an assassination bid with the Sharps 'Buffalo' rifle could be made. While difficult, there had been certain obvious factors to help him make the selection.

Although obtaining a clear line of fire was of vital importance, Dusty had known Schindler would also want a position which offered at least one avenue of escape after he had made his kill and would prefer to have more. By the time night had fallen and brought an end to the quest, Dusty had located three sites which would meet the sharpshooter's requirements. However, as he had anticipated, there were a number more that could serve his purpose only slightly less advantageously. Far too many for comfort, in fact, or to be covered adequately.

All in all, Dusty's investigations and the summations he had formed upon them caused him to feel relieved by the thought of a precaution he had had the Governor take. While it did not offer the whole solution, it made the situation somewhat less precarious and increased the chances of circumventing Schindler.

Throughout much of his perambulations, Dusty had had a feeling that he was being followed. Using every trick he knew, he had still been unable to locate the watcher. So, after night had fallen, he had decided that he would try to lure whoever it might be into view.

Having called at the Portside Hotel to check whether he had had any visitors, he had gone from there to the Binnacle Tavern on learning there had not been. However, he had heard that the Governor had arrived in town and was expecting the distinguished visitor to show up the following day. Under the circumstances, there had been no attempt to maintain secrecy. So it was obvious that Beguinage and Schindler would know that their intended victim might be available in the next twenty-four hours.

The small Texan's visit to the Tavern had proved equally unproductive. Neither the sharpshooter nor 'George Luncher' had been located. Nor had anybody else shown interest in obtaining '*Rapido* Clint's' services. Declining the offer of company on the grounds that to have any would ruin the chance of bringing whoever had been dogging him out into the open, he had warned Raffles against sending anybody to keep watch over him. Although the boss gun had not been too happy by the prohibition, he had gone along with it.

Going on much the same round of places as he had visited the previous night, Dusty had employed a technique he was taught by Belle Boyd to make it appear he was drinking heavily without actually imbibing sufficient liquor to impair his faculties. He had found that the news of the Crown

Prince's visit was creating considerable interest and some speculation upon the chances of profiting from it, but heard nothing to suggest that word of the assassination plots had leaked out.

Shortly before midnight, having been unsuccessful in discovering anybody following him, Dusty had decided to call off his attempt. On starting to walk to the Portside Hotel, his gait and demeanour suggested that he was very drunk. For all that, he had never been more sober and alert as he was passing through a deserted portion of the town's business section not far from his temporary accommodation.

Then, suddenly, the area had stopped being deserted!

Once more using a trick learned from the Rebel Spy, Dusty had stopped as if to look at the display in the window of a gunsmith's shop. Swaying in the fashion of a person under the influence of liquor, he had felt the hair on the back of his neck begin to bristle. A glance in the direction from which he had come was the cause of the sensation.

Stepping warily and carrying a rifle, a man in range clothes had appeared from an alley three buildings further along the street. On noticing the small Texan, he had come to an immediate halt. However, he had not offered to raise the weapon.

Even if the man had behaved less suspiciously, Dusty still would not have ignored him. There was no sign of him wearing a badge and few except peace officers had a legitimate reason for walking the streets at that late hour armed in such a fashion.

Waiting for a few more seconds, the small Texan had resumed his weaving walk towards the distant hotel. By the time he had taken his fifth step, he had sensed that he was in a trap. First a man had emerged from the second alley ahead and then another came out of the next opening beyond him. Like the rifle toter, they wore cowhand attire. Although neither was armed in the same fashion, each had his right hand concealed behind his back – and an empty holster on his gunbelt.

CHAPTER FIFTEEN

I'LL DEAL WITH *YOU* MYSELF, MR. CLINT

'I saw a big-pig Yankee marshal a-coming down the street,
  Got two big pistols in his hands, looked fierce enough to eat,
    Oh big-pig Yankee go away, go right away from me,
    'Cause I'm just a lil Texas boy and scared's I can be.'

Singing a cowhand song that was calculated to start a fight if heard by any Kansas lawman, in a voice that was slurred as if from over lubrication by hard liquor, Dusty Fog continued to walk an uneven route towards the two approaching men. Carefully, he directed his staggering steps in such a way that he kept the leader between himself and the second of what he knew to be potential assailants.

Nearer came the two men, the small Texan was still contriving to prevent the one at the rear from getting a clear shot at him. Allowing his singing to trail off, he strained his ears and was not sorry to discover that the third of his would-be attackers had not taken advantage of the noise to close the distance separating them. Nor, as he was armed with a rifle, was there any need for him to do so, and being in close proximity would put his own life at risk when his companions started shooting.

Swerving so as to retain the *status quo* with the men ahead, Dusty glanced into the alley he was about to pass. To his consternation, he saw a shadowy figure clad in what looked like a Stetson and a long, flowing cloak standing at the far end. However there was neither the time nor the opportunity for him to try to discover whether the dark shape was friend, foe or innocent bystander.

Returning his gaze almost immediately to the front, Dusty realized that he had not done so a moment too soon. The distance between himself and the leading man had been reduced to just over thirty feet. From all appearances, the other clearly thought it was close enough for his purposes. His right shoulder moved as a prelude to bringing the arm from behind his back.

In just under a second, the first of the attackers was dead!

Moving in an almost sight-defying blur, the small Texan's hands swept the Colt Civilian Model Peacemakers from holsters which had been designed to permit the maximum speed. Nor was there anything to get in his way, as there might have been if he had worn his black cutaway jacket. Turning outwards at waist level – as he automatically assumed the legs apart, knees slightly flexed and torso inclined forward stance – the weapons seemed to be moving of their own volition.

There was only one way in which Dusty dared shoot under the circumstances. If he had done otherwise, his own life could easily have been forfeit.

Driven upwards, the two .45 bullets entered beneath the man's chin. However, so accurately had the amount of powder which propelled them been estimated, although they tore his brain apart and killed him instantly, neither penetrated the top of his skull. As he was pitched over backwards, the weapon he had been concealing spun unfired from his lifeless grasp.

In spite of holding his cocked revolver just as readily accessible as the man in front had been, the second assailant was unprepared to use it. In fact, having been completely taken in by the small Texan's simulated drunkenness, he had not even been worried by the way his companion had kept in his line of fire. Believing their intended victim was too intoxicated to be dangerous, as had been the case ever since their current employer had pointed him out, the man was merely holding the weapon as a precaution he did not envisage being necessary.

When his companion toppled backwards in front of him, the man froze at a moment which called for the utmost rapidity of movement. Belatedly, he tried to bring his revolver into operation against the menacing and suddenly somehow enormous looking figure in the gun fighter's crouch beyond the supine and spasmodically twitching body at his feet. While the left hand of the two Peacemakers which had so *very* recently been reposing passively in their holsters was slanting downwards at his companion, the other was being directed at him as if drawn by the attraction of a magnet fastened to the centre of his body. He had a brief view of the muzzle blast's fiery glare, then felt a savage impact against his left breast. Twisting away from the would-be victim, he lost his hold on the unused weapon and joined his companion on the hard, wheel rutted surface of the street.

Remembering what had first alerted him to the possibility of danger, Dusty did not hesitate after having removed the second threat to his life. Even as his right hand was controlling the Colt's recoil kick and thumbing back the hammer, he commenced a swivelling dive which turned him away from his now defunct assailants.

Once again, as so often in the past, the small Texan's superbly attuned reflexes were all that stood between him and death, or at least injury.

In fact, the margin was so slight that Dusty felt the wind of the rifle's bullet along his back as it winged just above his descending body. An instant's delay would have seen it tearing into his flesh.

Ignoring the feel of the hard earth as he came down, the small Texan saw the man advancing and firing on the move. He was pleased that the other lacked the superlative skill of the Ysabel Kid, but did not let himself be lulled into a sense of false security. Twice lead ploughed into the ground, throwing up geysers of dirt and drawing closer, as he prepared to fight back.

Letting the Colt slip from his left hand, Dusty transferred it to cup around and give added support to its mate's butt. Resting his elbow in front of him, in much the same way as when shooting a rifle from the prone position, allowed him to make a much firmer base from which to take his next action. Having done so, he began to align the sights for the first time in the fracas. Nor did he allow himself to be deterred when a third portion of flying lead struck just a couple of feet away and went over in the vicious whine of a ricochet.

Designed as an exceptionally effective close quarters *defensive* weapon, the Colt Peacemaker offered only rudimentary means of taking aim. However, in the highly competent grasp of the Rio Hondo gun wizard, extremely accurate shooting could be carried out with the shallow U-shaped groove milled in the rounded top strap bridging the cylinder and the fixed 'knife-blade' front sight over longer

154

distances than those for which the devices had been envisaged.

Satisfied with his aim, Dusty touched off his shot. The hit he made served his purpose, even though producing a less severe effect than those he had previously discharged against his assailants.

Having come to a halt so as to line his rifle to better purpose, the man had not been too perturbed by what he saw. While he realized that the small Texan had only been pretending to be drunk, he considered himself to be beyond the range at which he would be endangered by the Colt no matter how well it had been handled against his companions. So he received a shock as the bullet it dispatched struck and knocked his own weapon from his hands.

Letting out a startled rather than pained yelp, the last of the trio was in no doubt over what action to take next. Nor did he linger over putting his decision into action. He had a Colt holstered at his right side, but he did not give it so much as a single thought. Even without his stinging hands feeling numb and inoperative, he knew that he was far outclassed by the man he and his companions had been hired to kill. So he turned and dashed away as fast as his legs would move.

For the second occasion in a very short space of time, the third of the would-be murderers might have counted himself fortunate. If his intended victim really was a genuine 'Rapido Clint' and possessed the same skill, he would almost certainly have been shot in the back as he fled. On the other hand, while willing to kill if necessary, Dusty Fog saw no need to do so once he started to run away. While the small Texan would have liked to capture the man and question him, there was insufficient light for the kind of fancy shooting that would be required to bring him down with a bullet in the leg. Confident that there was nothing further to worry over from that source, Dusty was content to let the man depart unharmed.

What was more, the small Texan had not forgotten that there might still be yet a further threat with which he must contend.

The shadowy, cloaked figure in the alley was almost certain to have been involved with the three attackers. Which meant that, even if whoever it was – the loosely fitting garment and hat prevented even a clue as to the sex of the watcher from being shown – had intended allowing the trio to carry out the murder, it was obvious that they had failed. He, or even she, could at that moment be deciding to do his – or her – own dirty work. In which case, the sooner steps were taken to prevent such an eventuality, the better.

Still retaining both hands on the butt of the Colt, Dusty swung his torso and arms until he was lying on his side and pointing the barrel into the mouth of the alley. He was just in time to see a brief flapping of the cloak as the onlooker disappeared around the corner at the rear.

Snatching up the second Colt, the small Texan rose swiftly. If – as he suspected – the watcher had been the trio's employer, he wanted to try to discover who it might be. While Beguinage had never taken help on the previous killings, he could have decided that the failure of the snake to do its work meant he was up against somebody who could not be handled in the fashion which he usually employed. However, there were two other possibilities. Oscar Schindler might have seen him making his reconnaissance and was wanting to remove an interfering rival, but had no wish to become involved personally. Or the trio could have been hired by 'George Luncher', either to try out *'Rapido* Clint', or because he had discovered the deception.

Wondering if he would be able to satisfy his curiosity, Dusty advanced along the alley. Shouts in the distance informed him that the shooting had attracted attention, but he ignored them. He could hear the sound of the third attacker's rapidly departing feet, but nothing to suggest that the mysterious watcher was taking a similar action. For all that, having removed his hat with his still gun-filled left hand, when he arrived at and peered cautiously around the corner, the cloaked figure was nowhere to be seen. Deciding that it would be pointless to try to conduct a search without some indication of where to start, he holstered the Colts and returned to the street.

The man who called himself Beguinage was closer than the small Texan had imagined. Watching the other depart, having taken a similar precaution by removing his hat before peeping around the corner of a nearby building, he breathed a sigh of relief. As yet, little mention of the deadly speed with which Western gun-fighters could draw and shoot had spread to Europe. So he had hardly known whether to credit what he saw as he watched the way in which '*Rapido* Clint' killed the first two of the men he had hired. All he had realized for certain was that anybody with such skill went far beyond what he could achieve where using firearms was concerned. Not that he resorted to such crude methods as a general rule, preferring more subtle means of bringing death to those he was hired to dipose of.

'I should have known better than to trust those three,' the European assassin mused as he was padding silently away. 'Anybody who could survive the snake-box would be too intelligent for the likes of them. So I will deal with *you* myself, Mr. Clint. In fact, I think I'll be able to kill two birds with one stone. What fools these Americans are, to believe they can match their wits with the Beguinage.'

'Who-all brought this?' Dusty Fog inquired, accepting an envelope addressed to him – in writing he did not recognize – by the name he was using at the Portside Hotel.

'Some Mexican street urchin, sir,' the desk clerk replied in a disinterested fashion. 'He came in, gave it to me and ran out again before I could speak to him. I thought that was strange, they usually wait for a gratuity.'

'Could be he wanted to make sure he got himself a good place to watch all the high-toned doings,' the small Texan drawled, pulling open the flap of the envelope, although he too wondered why the boy had not waited at least long enough to collect a tip for delivering the message. 'It's not likely he'll get asked down on the quay with the Governor, mayor, and all the other high mucky-mucks.'

'I should think *not*!' the clerk snorted, eyeing the guest disapprovingly as he did not consider the most important event ever to happen in Corpus Christie was a subject for levity. 'I hope it isn't something that will cause you to have to leave, *sir*. It would be a pity if you couldn't stay for the arrival of our royal visitor this afternoon.'

Two days had elapsed since the gun-fight in the business section. Apart from the surviving would-be killer and the mysterious cloaked observer, nobody else was aware of Dusty's participation. Having no wish to find himself compelled to announce his true identity and purpose to the town marshal, who he had learned enough about to consider untrustworthy, he had left the scene before anybody could arrive and investigate the disturbance. Nor had the local peace officer any idea of what had happened. In fact, when he had met the small Texan in Buck Raffles' company at the Binnacle Tavern, he had stated that he believed the two dead men were killed by the man with the rifle who had then fled.

Although Raffles had identified the corpses as having been hired killers of the cheapest and poorest quality, who were only accepted by his organization to carry out menial tasks that were too poorly paid to attract more competent members of their trade, he had not found out the identity of their last employer. Their movements had been traced until they had left one of the least salubrious saloons in the waterfront district in the company of a woman who had arrived earlier and been given employment by the owner. He had stated that he thought she was some kind of foreigner, but had learned only that her name was Maria. He had hired her because she was slightly better looking than the usual run of female employees he attracted. As she had not returned, Dusty assumed that she must have been a confederate of Beguinage.

'George Luncher' had not revisited the Portside Hotel, but he had sent a note containing a hundred dollars in bills as a retainer and a promise that he would finalize the deal as soon as his principals arrived from Brownsville. In spite of all that Raffles' people had tried to do, they had located neither him nor Oscar Schindler.

Although Dusty had exercised constant vigilance, there had been no further attempts upon his life by Beguinage. Nor had he come any closer to discovering who the assassin might be. He had checked the hotel's register, but could not find anybody other than the two nuns who had moved in since the first day that Beguinage could have arrived from Brownsville. Even they were no longer in residence, having left claiming that the incident with the copperhead snake had frightened them into taking their departure.

The other three members of the floating outfit had arrived with Governor Stanton Howard's retinue, but as yet the small Texan had not met any of them. Having learned how expertly Beguinage could follow and remain undetected, he had no intention of taking the chance of having the deception exposed. If that happened, he would never manage to lure the assassin out of hiding. So he had sent a note to Mark Counter, the Ysabel Kid and Waco informing them of the circumstances. He had told them to keep well clear from him and to exercise unceasing alertness. It was unlikely that

Beguinage would strike at them, but he felt the precaution was worth taking.

At the blond giant's suggestion, although the small Texan did not know of this until later, Charlene, *Comtesse* de Petain and Alex von Farlenheim had been invited to accompany the Governor's entourage. She had accepted, but the young Bosgravnian refused and said he would make his own way there later.

Shortly before noon, a vessel that was obviously a steam-sloop of the United States' Navy had been sighted on the horizon. It had signalled that it would delay entering Corpus Christie Bay until four o'clock in the afternoon. That would allow the welcoming party to assemble and have all ready on the quay to greet the royal passenger. The news had passed around the town with the rapidity of a wind-driven prairie fire and the majority of the population were very excited by the prospect. The desk clerk's response to the small Texan's comment was typical of the general feeling prevalent among the better class of the community.

'It sure would,' Dusty admitted, as he extracted and opened the sheet of paper from the envelope. 'I've never even seen an ordinary for-real prince, much less a *crown* prince. It should be quite a sight.'

'That it should,' agreed the clerk, less huffily as the small Texan had adopted a less bantering tone. He gave a sniff and, full of civic pride, went on, 'So much for *Brownsville* now. It was to Corpus Christie he decided to come.'

On the point of continuing to extoll the virtues of his home town over its rival, the man realized that his audience was no longer paying any attention. So, giving another sniff that registered disapproval of such inconsiderate behaviour, he turned and stumped pompously into his office.

There was good cause for Dusty's preoccupation!

'Mr. *Rapido* Clint,' the message ran. 'If you would avoid having Oscar Schindler deprive you of your fee for assassinating Crown Prince Rudolph of Bosgravnia, go to the Edgehurst Warehouse shortly before the steam-sloop drops anchor. You should have no difficulty in finding it, as it is one of those in which you took such an interest when you were trying to decide from where he would strike. Schindler will be there and intends to kill His Royal Highness the moment He sets foot on American soil.'

There was no signature. However, despite the writing

being different from that of the other notes Dusty had seen, he felt sure the letter had come from Beguinage.

In which case, the message was intended to lead 'Rapido Clint' into a trap!

The vital question was, what form would the trap take?

Thinking of the address he had been given, Dusty did not doubt that he would find Schindler there. It was a place which, after much consideration and study, he had selected as the sharpshooter's most likely choice. The others might be closer, but it was still within the range of the Sharps 'Buffalo' rifle. In addition to the distance, there was another factor which would reduce the chance of it being suspected. At first sight, it had seemed that other buildings were in the line of fire. A closer and more careful examination, both on the ground and with the aid of the map supplied by the Governor had proved this was not so. There was a restricted view from an upstairs window, yet adequate for a man with Schindler's ability, all the way to the point at which the Crown Prince was to come ashore.

Was Beguinage bringing his two rivals together in the hope that one, possibly both, would kill the other?

From what Dusty had seen of the European assassin's work so far, he felt sure something more subtle was planned. Beguinage would never be content to rely upon a scheme that left so much to chance. Having caused 'Rapido Clint' and Schindler to meet, he would be determined to ensure that neither survived the encounter.

One thing above all else had been plain to Dusty's way of thinking. No matter what Beguinage had in store for his *alter ego*, against such a capable antagonist, he would be forced to go alone to spring the trap. Even if any of the other members of the floating outfit were available,[1] unless they were following at such a distance that help could not arrive quickly enough to be of any use, the assassin was almost certain to see them and refuse to put in an appearance. Furthermore, the message had been timed to reach him too late for any elaborate precautions to be taken.

Accepting that he would have to take his chances alone, Dusty had set off from the hotel. Aready the crowds were starting to assemble and the area in which the Edgehurst Warehouse was situated appeared completely deserted. There was nobody in sight as he approached the rear of the

1. Why this was is told in: BEGUINAGE IS DEAD! – *J.T.E.*

building. As Raffles had claimed Schindler always worked alone and having estimated that he would have taken up his firing position by now, Dusty had hoped for such conditions when selecting the route by which to reach his destination.

However, although there was no sign of human life and the rest of the entrances were closed, one small door stood slightly ajar.

And was being drawn open from inside!

On the point of commencing his draw, the small Texan refrained when he saw the person who was coming from the building. Having learned from Raffles what Schindler looked like, Dusty knew it was not him. Nor, if the other's appearance and behaviour was anything to go by, had the sharpshooter changed his methods and taken a confederate to act as a lookout.

Apart from the way in which the emerging man was dressed, Dusty decided that he had rarely seen anybody who struck him as so completely average and ordinary. About five foot ten, his height attracted no notice by being unusually tall or short. His build was neither so good nor so skinny as to draw attention to it. His face was devoid of any distinguishing features and gave no definite clue to his ethnic origins beyond that he was of European stock. Of a brownish tint, his hair was of a colour it was impossible to describe exactly. Equally indeterminate, his age could have been anywhere from the late twenties to early fifties. Only his attire – the loose fitting brown robe, bare legs and sandal-covered feet of a mission *padre* – marked him as being describably different. All else was completely average.

'The Lord be praised!' the man gasped, hurrying towards the small Texan. He pointed in the direction from which he had come, continuing in a voice that – except for holding just the slightest trace of some undefinable foreign accent – matched his wholly average and unnoticeable aspect. 'Can you help me, my son? I fear there has been violence done inside.'

'How do you mean, Father?' Dusty inquired, relaxing a little at the evidence that he was dealing with a member of one of the holy orders.

'I heard voices raised in anger from the upper floor as I was going by,' the *padre* elaborated. 'And, as a man of the cloth, I felt it was my duty to go and try to keep the peace. This door was open and I went in. As I was going across to the stairs, there were the sounds of struggling, blows and the cry of a man in mortal pain.'

'Who was it?' Dusty asked.

'That I do not know,' the *padre* admitted, lowering his head so his face could not be seen and shuffling his feet as if embarrassed by the confession. 'While it is my duty to go and see, I realized that doing so could be very dangerous. If one man had done bodily harm, or worse, upon another, he would not want any witnesses. So my nerve failed me. As some of our order have discovered to our sorrow, not everybody in Texas is a Catholic with respect for our cloth. But you have the appearance of a man of action, my son. Could you come in with me?'

'I've a better idea than that,' the small Texan replied, glancing at the windows of the upper floor. 'You-all stay here and let me go in to take a look around.'

'I have no wish to put you into jeopardy, my son,' the *padre* protested.

'Don't let that worry you, I've been there before,' Dusty drawled. 'Which I'll be *real* careful. Wait here please, Father. Happen you-all hear shooting and I don't yell or come out soon after, go fetch the marshal.'

'I've got you, Mr. "*Rapido* Clint"!' Beguinage breathed exultantly, watching the small Texan going to the open door of the warehouse. 'You're no cleverer than Schindler, or all the others who have let a priest's attire bring about their deaths.'

With that, Europe's 'premier assassin's' right hand went into his loose left sleeve and emerged grasping the hilt of a wicked looking knife. The spear point[2] of its double edged blade had had the coating of *curare*[3] replaced after it had been wiped off while ending the life of the sharpshooter. Showing no more expression than he would if carrying out a normal, everyday function, he stepped silently after his next unsuspecting victim.

2. Spear point: one where the sharpened edges of the blade come together in symmetrical convex arcs. A less utilitarian point than the 'clip', *q.v.*, being mainly used on knives designed purely for fighting rather than general purposes. – *J.T.E.*

3. *Curare*: a highly poisonous blackish, brittle resinous extract of certain South American trees of the genus *Strychnos*, particularly *S. Toxifera*. Sometimes called, *woorali* or *urare*, it is exceptionally fast acting and used by the native Indians as an arrow poison. The author has been unable to discover from where Beguinage obtained his supply. – *J.T.E.*

CHAPTER SIXTEEN

BEGUINAGE IS DEAD

Dusty Fog was half-way across the open floor of the Edgehurst Warehouse, making for the flight of wooden steps which gave access to the upper portion of the building, when the realization of exactly what he was doing struck home.

Ironically, it was a comment made by Beguinage in his eagerness to persuade '*Rapido* Clint' to walk into the trap which supplied the vital clue and triggered off a warning bell in the small Texan's head.

There was not the slightest sound from the upper floor and, as yet, Dusty had not drawn his guns. He was waiting for the first suggestion that he needed them before doing so. Yet for all his appreciation of the probable danger he was facing, he found he was unable to shake off a thought that kept nagging at him. Something had happened recently which was stirring a responsive note in his memory.

Or had been said!

The realization that it was the latter struck home!

Recollecting the '*padre's*' comment about how Catholics were inclined to show respect for members of their creed's priesthood, Dusty began to find that various aspects of the affair which had puzzled himself and his companions were leaping into focus. The implications they aroused were alarming.

Only one kind of non-Mexican person could have passed through the Brownsville *barrio* after nightfall without being observed and remembered.

A man wearing the attire of a Catholic priest or *padre*!

Knowing that he was likely to have aroused the ire of two powerful criminal factions by his intrusion on their domain, Dink Sproxton would have had to have complete trust in whoever was outside before he would open his door – or believe that the caller was harmless. There could be only a

163

very few strangers who would come into the latter category under the circumstances.

Of all the people in the world, Sproxton – a Catholic, according to the desk clerk at the Seamen's Temperance Hotel – would consider it safe to give admission to a representative of the church in whose faith he had been raised. In all probability, the bottle of poisoned wine had been sold to him on the pretence that the money would be donated to one of the visitor's charities.

Brought closer to home, Dusty took into consideration the way in which he personally was acting at present.

Having come into what he knew was almost certainly a trap set by a ruthless, efficient and exceptionally intelligent person, the clothing worn by the *'padre'* had still prevented Dusty from suspecting the truth. Instead, he had turned his back on a complete stranger who had just emerged from the building to which he had been directed by a message he was convinced had come from Europe's 'premier assassin'. Nor had he given the slightest thought to how implausible some aspects of the *'padre's'* story had been.

All in all, Dusty told himself – while also thanking the foresight which had led him to don cowhand and not gambler's attire that morning – he had not only walked into Benguinage's trap, but he had done everything in his power to ensure that it was able to snap closed.

Unaware of the thoughts which were assailing the man who he intended to make his second victim of the day, Europe's 'premier assassin' crept silently across the warehouse. He gave the impression of being some merciless predatory beast stalking his prey and, to all intents and purposes, that was exactly what he had become. While he preferred more subtle methods as a general rule, he was a skilled performer with the knife. He held it with the *curare*-coated spear point protruding ahead of his thumb and forefinger, a way which would allow it to be thrust to its best advantage. One blow was all he would need. Particularly if it went home on exposed flesh, death would be swift and inevitable.

That had been the case with Oscar Schindler!

More successful than Buck Raffles' men had been, Beguinage had kept the sharpshooter under observation. At first, he had intended to terminate his rival the same evening. Learning that there was yet another hired killer becoming involved, he had held off after the copperhead snake failed to remove the newcomer. Nor had there been another opportunity to reach Schindler until the impending arrival of Crown Prince Rudolph of Bosgravnia had offered the opportunity.

Engrossed in making preparations to carry out his assignment, Schindler had been oblivious of Beguinage's approach until it was too late. As he had started to turn, the razor-sharp, needle tipped knife had flashed around and laid his throat open almost to the bone. He was dead in seconds, long before he could even attempt any reprisals against his murderer.

With the first rival removed, all the assassin had needed to do was await the coming of the other. He knew that the Mexican boy to whom he had entrusted the message had carried out his instructions and fled before any question could be put which would have supplied 'Rapido Clint' with the information that a 'padre' had sent it. So, although he was aware that the small Texan was not a Catholic, he had been confident his disguise would prevent his true identity from being suspected.

Not only had 'Rapido Clint' risen to the bait, he had done as Beguinage anticipated by approaching from the rear of the building. In that respect, the assassin had felt just a trifle cheated.

Until the small Texan had appeared upon the scene, nothing Beguinage had seen of them so far had given him any cause to respect the abilities of his American contemporaries. The way in which the insignificant seeming young man – whose appearance must usually serve him as did Beguinage's own – had searched for and selected those places most likely to appeal to Schindler had been impressive. Nor had the knowledge that he had already escaped from the snake trap which had never failed in the past lessened the assassin's appreciation of his potential.

Breaking the rule of a lifetime and hiring the three men to try and remove 'Rapido Clint' had been as much a test of the other's abilities as a way of getting rid of him. Doubting whether the religious aspect would serve the purpose, Beguinage had decided to use the local hired killers. Guessing that his proposed victim had close associations with the only source of good quality men, he had been compelled to take what was available. Seeing how the small Texan coped with

165

them had done nothing to change the assassin's opinion of him.

In spite of the way in which he had apparently been drinking when Beguinage had seen him during the evening, 'Rapido Clint's' inebriation had proved to be nothing more than a sham. Nor did the assassin's attempts at exculpation by telling himself he had never been close enough to notice the deception make him any the less appreciative of how well the other had conveyed the impression of imbibing whiskey after whiskey. It had been a masterly performance.

Measuring the ever decreasing distance between himself and his victim, Beguinage found he was almost wishing that the small Texan had proven sufficiently astute to detect and avoid the trap.

At which point, involuntarily, Dusty began to grant the assassin's wish!

Although the small Texan had heard nothing, his growing awareness of his danger demanded that he satisfy his curiosity. So he turned—

And discovered that the deductions were correct!

Seeing the way in which his proposed victim was behaving, a sensation of alarm bit through Beguinage. He was still well beyond reaching distance and realized that he must reach a range at which he could strike if he hoped to survive. With that thought uppermost, he changed his silent stalk into a savage charge.

Even as he was changing his pace, the assassin remembered the speed with which 'Rapido Clint' had reacted when caught between the three men on the darkened street. Thinking of the affair later, Beguinage was inclined to think he had been mistaken about the way in which the small Texan had coped with the first two assailants. *Nobody*, he had frequently declared when considering the matter, could produce a firearm from its holster in such a minute fraction of time, much less two almost simultaneously. While he could not imagine how it was done, he had convinced himself that some form of trickery was involved.

Beguinage was very soon to learn, but would never profit from the knowledge, just how great the misconception had been.

Startled by the discovery of how near his assailant had contrived to come undetected, Dusty did not let it impede his movements. Rather it gave an added urgency and produced an even great alacrity to the way he was already starting to react. Swinging around on the balls of his feet, his hands went to the butts of their respective weapons while he was still turning. By the time he was confronting the rapidly approaching assassin, the Colts were clear of leather and, with the barrels angling outwards, the hammers were at full-cock and the triggers depressed.

For all that, it was one of the closest brushes with death Dusty would ever have!

Detonated powder was expelling lead through the barrels as the *curare*-encrusted spear point of the knife lunged forward.

Once again forethought saved the small Texan's life!

On his way to the rendezvous, Dusty had taken the precaution of exchanging the 'town loads' in his Colt's cylinders for the far more potent fully charged variety he had had in the loops on the back of his gunbelt.

Under the impulsion of no less than thirty grains of prime du Pont black powder – two more than was considered the maximum load for the Winchester Model of 1866 *rifle* – the two hundred and fifty grain bullets packed considerable power. Hit in the centre of the chest by two of them, Beguinage was knocked backwards an instant before the blade of his knife reached Dusty's throat. Spinning from his grasp, it clattered to the floor and a moment later he was following it down.

'Whooee!' Dusty breathed. 'I don't ever want to be put *that* close into jeopardy again!'

Walking forward, with his recocked Colts ready for use if they should be needed, the small Texan only required a brief look to know they would not be.

'Beguinage is dead!' Dusty thought, studying the motionless figure. 'A lot of folk'll be able to sleep easier in their beds from now on.'

Yet, even as he was making the summation, the small Texan knew his work was not ended. There were others who wanted the Crown Prince Rudolph killed. However, still looking down, he told himself that – with Beguinage dead – the greatest threat had been brought to an end.

Details of how the Crown Prince of Bosgravnia fared against his enemies can be read in:
BEGUINAGE IS DEAD!

APPENDIX ONE

During the War Between The States, at seventeen years of age, Dustine Edward Marsden Fog had won promotion in the field and was put in command of the Texas Light Cavalry's hard-riding, harder-fighting Company 'C'.[1] Leading them in the Arkansas Campaign, he had earned the reputation for being an exceptionally capable military raider the equal of the South's other exponents, John Singleton Mosby and Turner Ashby.[2] In addition to preventing a pair of Union fanatics from starting an Indian uprising which would have decimated most of Texas,[3] he had supported Belle Boyd, the Rebel Spy,[4] on two of her most dangerous missions.[5]

When the War had finished, he had become the segundo of the great OD Connected ranch in Rio Hondo County, Texas. Its owner and his uncle, General Ole Devil Hardin, had been crippled in a riding accident[6] and it had thrown much of the work – including handling an important mission upon which the good relations between the United States and Mexico had hung in the balance[7] – upon him. After helping to gather horses to replenish the ranch's depleted remuda,[8] he had been sent to assist Colonel Charles Goodnight on the trail drive to Fort Sumner which had done much to help the Lone Star State to recover from the impoverished conditions left by the War.[9] With that achieved he had been equally successful in helping Goodnight to prove that it would be possible to take herds of cattle to the railroad in Kansas.[10]

Having proven himself to be a first class cowhand, Dusty went on to be acknowledged as a very capable trail boss,[11] round up captain,[12] and a town-taming lawman.[13] Competing at the Cochise County Fair he won the title of the Fastest Gun in the West, by beating many other exponents of the *pistolero* arts.[14]

In later years following his marriage to Lady Winifred Amelia Besgrove-Woodstole,[15] he became a diplomat.

Dusty Fog never found his lack of stature an impediment. In addition to being naturally strong, he had taught himself to be completely ambidextrous. Possessing fast reflexes, he could draw and fire either, or both, of his Colts with lightning speed and great accuracy. Ole Devil Hardin's valet, Tommy Okasi, was Japanese[16] and from him Dusty had learned *ju jitsu* and *karate*. Neither had received much publicity in the Western world, so the knowledge was very useful when he had to fight bare-handed against larger, heavier and stronger men.

1. Told in: YOU'RE IN COMMAND NOW, MR. FOG.

2. Told in: THE BIG GUN; UNDER THE STARS AND BARS; THE FASTEST GUN IN TEXAS and KILL DUSTY FOG!

3. Told in: THE DEVIL GUN.

4. Further details of Belle Boyd's career are given in: THE HOODED RIDERS; THE BAD BUNCH; TO ARMS, TO ARMS, IN DIXIE!; THE SOUTH WILL RISE AGAIN; THE REMITTANCE KID and THE WHIP AND THE WAR LANCE.

5. Told in: THE COLT AND THE SABRE and THE REBEL SPY.

6. Told in: 'The Paint' episode of: THE FASTEST GUN IN TEXAS.

7. Told in: THE YSABEL KID.

8. Told in: A HORSE CALLED MOGOLLON and ·44 CALIBRE MAN.

9. Told in: GOODNIGHT'S DREAM and FROM HIDE AND HORN.

10. Told in: SET TEXAS BACK ON HER FEET.

11. Told in: TRAIL BOSS.

12. Told in: THE MAN FROM TEXAS.

13. Told in: QUIET TOWN; THE MAKING OF A LAWMAN; THE TROUBLE BUSTERS; THE SMALL TEXAN and THE TOWN TAMERS.

14. Told in: GUN WIZARD.

15. The grandson, Alvin Dustine 'Cap' Fog became the finest combat pistol shot of his generation and the youngest man ever to become a captain in the Texas Rangers, see 'CAP' FOG, TEXAS RANGER, MEET MR. J. G. REEDER!

16. 'Tommy Okasi' is an Americanized corruption of the name he gave when picked up from a derelict vessel in the China Sea by a ship under the command of General Hardin's father. The author is unable to state how a trained *samurai* was compelled to flee from his homeland. The various members of the Hardin, Fog and Blaze clan with whom we discussed the matter in Fort Worth, Texas, in 1975 said that, because of the circumstances and the high social standing of the people involved – all of whom have descendants holding positions of importance and influence in Japan at the time of writing – it is inadvisable even at this late date to make the facts public. Details of how Tommy made use of his *samurai* training are given in the 'Ole Devil' series.

With his exceptional good looks and magnificent physical development, Mark Counter presented the kind of appearance which many people expected of Dusty Fog. It was a fact of which they would take advantage when the need arose.[1]

While serving as a lieutenant in General Bushrod Sheldon's cavalry regiment, Mark's merits as an efficient and courageous officer had been overshadowed by his taste in uniforms. Always a dandy, coming from a wealthy family had allowed him to indulge in his whims. His clothing, particularly a skirtless tunic, had been much copied by the other young bloods in the Confederate States' Army, despite considerable opposition and disapproval on the part of hidebound senior officers.

When peace had come, Mark followed Sheldon to fight for Emperor Maximilian in Mexico. There he had met Dusty Fog and the Ysabel Kid, helping with the former's mission. On returning to Texas, Mark had been invited to join the OD Connected's floating outfit.[2] Knowing that his elder brothers were sufficient to help his father, Big Rance Counter, run the R Over C ranch in the Big Bend country -- and suspecting that life would be more exciting with Dusty and the Kid -- he had accepted.

An expert cowhand, Mark was known as Dusty Fog's right bower,[3] and gained acclaim by virture of his enormous strength and ability in a rough-house brawl. However, due to being so much in the small Texan's company, his full potential as a gun-fighter received little attention. Men who were in a position to know stated that he was second only to the Rio Hondo gun wizard in speed and accuracy.

Many women found Mark's appearance irresistible, including Miss Martha Jane Canary,[4] who was better known as Calamity Jane.[5] Only one held his heart, the lady outlaw Belle Starr.[6] It was several years after her death that he courted and married Dawn Sutherland,[7] who he had met on the Goodnight trail drive to Fort Sumner.[8]

1. Told in: THE SOUTH WILL RISE AGAIN.

2. Floating outfit: a group of four to six cowhands employed on a large ranch to work the more distant sections of the property. Taking food in a chuck wagon, or 'greasy sack' on the back of a mule, they would be away from the ranch house for weeks at a time. Because of General Hardin's prominence in the affairs of Texas, the OD Connected's floating outfit were frequently sent to assist his friends who found themselves in trouble or danger.

3. Right bower; second highest trump card in the game of euchre.

4. Mark's main meetings with Calamity Jane are told in TROUBLED RANGE; THE WILDCATS and THE FORTUNE HUNTERS.

5. Books in which Calamity Jane takes a leading role are: COLD DECK, HOT LEAD; CALAMITY SPELLS TROUBLE; TROUBLE TRAIL; THE BULL WHIP BREED; THE COW THIEVES; WHITE STALLION, RED MARE (co-starring the Ysabel Kid); THE BIG HUNT (in which Mark makes a guest appearance); and THE WHIP AND THE WAR LANCE.

6. How Mark's romance with Belle Starr commenced, progressed and ended is told in the 'The Bounty On Belle Starr's Scalp' episode of TROUBLED RANGE; RANGELAND HERCULES; the 'The Lady Known As Belle' episode of THE HARD RIDERS and GUNS IN THE NIGHT. She also appears in HELL IN THE PALO DURO and GO BACK TO HELL, assisting Dusty Fog and the Ysabel Kid.

7. Two of Mark's great-grandchildren achieved considerable fame on their own behalf. Details of Deputy Sheriff Bradford Counter's career are given in the 'Rockabye County' series covering modern jet-age Texas law enforcement and James Allenvale Gunn, some of whose career is described in the 'Bunduki' series.

8. Told in: GOODNIGHT'S DREAM.

The only daughter of Long Walker, war leader of the Pehnane – Wasp, Quick Stinger or Raider – Comanche Dog Soldier lodge and his French Creole *pairaivo*[1] married an Irish Kentuckian adventurer called Sam Ysabel, but died giving birth to their first child. Given the name Loncey Dalton Ysabel, the boy was raised in the fashion of the *Nemenuh*.[2] With his father away much of the time on the family business of first mustanging, then smuggling, his education had been left to his maternal grandfather.[3] From Chief Long Walker, he had learned all those things a Comanche warrior must know; how to ride the wildest, freshly caught mustang, or when raiding – a polite name for the favourite *Nemenuh* sport of horse-stealing – to subjugate a domesticated mount to his will; to follow the faintest tracks and conceal traces of his own passing; to locate hidden enemies, yet remain concealed himself when the need arose; to move in silence through the thickest of cover, or on the darkest of nights; and to be highly proficient in the use of a variety of weapons. In all these subjects, the boy had proved an excellent pupil. He had inherited his father's rifle-shooting skill and, while not real fast on the draw – taking slightly over a second, where a tophand would come close to half of that time – he could perform adequately with his Colt Second Model Dragoon revolver. His excellent handling of one as a weapon had gained him the man-name *Cuchilo*, 'the Knife' among the Pehnane. It was claimed that he could equal the alleged designer of the knife,[4] Colonel James Bowie,[5] in wielding the massive and deadly blade.[6]

Joining his father on smuggling trips along the Rio Grande, he had become known to the Mexicans of the border country as *Cabrito*; which had come from hearing white men referring to him as the Ysabel Kid. Smuggling did not attract mild-mannered, gentle-natured pacifists, but even the toughest and roughest men on the bloody border had learned that it did not pay to tangle with Sam Ysabel's son. His education and upbringing had not been such that he was possessed by an over-inflated sense of the sanctity of

172

human life. When crossed, he dealt with the situation like a *Pehnane* Dog Soldier – to which lodge of savage, efficient warriors he belonged – swiftly and in a deadly effective manner.

During the War, the Kid and his father had commenced by riding as scouts for the Grey Ghost, John Singleton Mosby. Later, their specialized talents had been used by having them collect and deliver to the Confederate States' authorities in Texas supplies which had been run through the U.S. Navy's blockade into Matamoros, or purchased elsewhere in Mexico. It had been hard, dangerous work and never more so than on the two occasions when they had been involved in missions with Belle Boyd.[7]

Sam Ysabel had been murdered soon after the end of the War. While hunting for the killers the Kid had met Dusty Fog and, later, Mark Counter. Engaged on a mission of international importance, Dusty had been very grateful for the Kid's assistance. When it had been brought to a successful conclusion, learning that the Kid no longer wished to continue a career of smuggling, Dusty had offered him work at the OD Connected Ranch. When the Kid had stated that he knew little about being a cowhand, he had been told that it was his skill as a scout that would be required. His talents in that line had been most useful to the floating outfit.

In fact, the Kid's acceptance had been of great benefit all round. Dusty had gained a loyal friend, ready to stick by him through any danger. The ranch had obtained the services of an extremely capable and efficient man. For his part, the Kid had been turned from a life of petty crime – with the ever-present danger of having it develop into more serious law-breaking – and became a useful member of society. Peace officers and honest citizens might have been thankful for that as he would have made a terrible and murderous outlaw if he had been driven into such a life.

Obtaining his first repeating rifle while in Mexico with Dusty and Mark, the Kid became acknowledged as a master in its use. In fact, at the Cochise County Fair he won the first prize – one of the fabulous Winchester Model of 1873 'One Of A Thousand' rifles – against very stiff competition.[8] Also it was in great part through his efforts that the majority of the Comanche Indian bands agreed to go on to the Reservation.[9] Nor could Dusty Fog have cleaned out the outlaw town of Hell without the Kid's assistance.[10]

1. *Pairaivo:* first or favourite wife.
2. *Nemenuh:* 'The People', the Comanche Indians' name for their nation.
3. Told in: COMANCHE.
4. Some researchers claim that the actual designer of the knife was James Bowie's eldest brother, Rezin Pleasant.
5. What happened to James Bowie's knife after his death in the final assault on the Alamo Mission, San Antonio de Bexar, on March the 6th, 1836, is told in: GET URREA and THE QUEST FOR BOWIE'S BLADE.
6. As all of James Black's bowie knives were hand-made, there was a slight variation in their dimensions. That in the Kid's possession had a blade two and a half inches wide, eleven and a half inches long and a quarter of an inch thick. Bowie's knife weighed forty-three ounces, having its blade eleven inches long, two and a quarter inches wide and three-eights of an inch thick. One thing they all had in common was a clip point, where the last few inches of the back of the blade joins the main cutting edge in a concave arc and is sharpened to form an extension of it.
7. See Appendix One, Footnote 4. The two missions are described in: THE BLOODY BORDER and BACK TO THE BLOODY BORDER.
8. Told in: GUN WIZARD.
9. Told in: SIDEWINDER and how the dissenting tribe was persuaded to come in is told in BRING OUT THE KWEHAREHNUH.
10. Told in: HELL IN THE PALO DURO and GO BACK TO HELL.

APPENDIX FOUR

Left an orphan almost from birth by a Waco Indian raid, from whence had come the only name he knew, Waco had been raised as part of a North Texas rancher's large family.[1] Guns had always been a part of his life and his sixteenth birthday had seen him riding with Clay Allison's tough, hard bitten, 'wild onion' crew. The CA hands, like their employer, were notorious for their wild ways and frequently dangerous behaviour. Living in the company of such men, all older than himself, he had grown quick to take offence and eager to defend himself with his lightning fast draw and accurate shooting skill. It had seemed to be only a matter of time before one shoot out too many would have seen him branded as a killer and fleeing from the law with a price on his head.

Fortunately for Waco, that day did not come. From the moment that Dusty Fog, *q.v.*, saved his life – at considerable risk to his own – the youngster had started to change for the better.[2] Leaving Allison, with the Washita curly wolf's blessing, he had become a member of Ole Devil Hardin's floating outfit. From the other members of this élite brotherhood, who treated him as a favourite younger sibling, he had learned many useful lessons. The Ysabel Kid taught him to read tracks and act as a scout. Mark Counter, *q.v.*, gave him instruction in bare-handed self-defence. A gambler of their acquaintance, Frank Derringer, instructed him in the ways of crooked and honest gamblers.[3] From Dusty Fog, he learned much that would help him to gain fame as a peace officer of exceptional merit.[4] What was more, although he already knew *how* to shoot, he had learned when it was mandatory for him to do so.

From his education at his friends' hands, Waco was to become in later years a respected and extremely competent peace officer. He served with distinction in the Arizona Rangers,[5] as sheriff of Two Forks County, Utah[6] and finally as a U.S. Marshal.[7]

1. HOW Waco repaid his debt to his adoptive father is told in: WACO'S DEBT.

2. Told in: TRIGGER FAST.

3. Told in: THE MAKING OF A LAWMAN and THE TROUBLE BUSTERS.

4. Early examples of Waco's ability as a peace officer are given in the 'The Hired Butcher' episode of THE HARD RIDERS and the 'A Tolerable Straight Shooting Gun' episode of THE FLOATING OUTFIT (British title. The American Bantam Edition of GOODNIGHT'S DREAM was called THE FLOATING OUTFIT.)

5. Told in: SAGEBRUSH SLEUTH; ARIZONA RANGER and WACO RIDES IN.

6. Told in: THE DRIFTER and, by inference, in DOC LEROY, M.D.

7. Told in: HOUND DOG MAN.

THE END

If you have enjoyed reading this book and other works by the same author, why not join

THE J. T. EDSON APPRECIATION SOCIETY

You will receive a signed photograph of J. T. Edson, bi-monthly Newsletters giving details of all new books and re-prints of earlier titles.

Competitions with autographed prizes to be won in every issue of the Edson Newsletter.

A chance to meet J. T. Edson.

Send SAE for details and membership form to:

The Secretary,
J. T. Edson Appreciation Society,
P.O. Box 13,
MELTON MOWBRAY,
Leics.

COMING SOON . . .
watch out for
J. T.'s
HUNDREDTH . . .